Briar Rose

Kimberley J Brown

Published in 2006

by

Anna Luke Publications

© Copyright Kimberley J Brown, 2006

All rights reserved, no part of this publication
may be reproduced, stored in a retrieval system,
or transmitted, in any form or by any means,
without the prior permission in writing
of the author.

This book is sold subject to the condition
that it shall not, by way of trade or otherwise,
be lent, resold, hired out or otherwise circulated
without the author's prior consent in any form
other than that supplied by the author.

British Library Cataloguing in Publication Data
A catalogue record for this book is available from the British Library

ISBN 978-0-9551949-1-7

Produced by Bookchase, London
Printed and bound in the EU

What's in a name? That which we call a rose
by any other name would smell as sweet.

William Shakespeare – Romeo & Juliet

chapter one

"Yo' thievin' little skit, I'll knock yo'int' nex' week, see if I dunna."
Cheers from a nearby group of lads swiftly fell into silence as the voice of young Ben Lawson rang out.

"The master's comin' the master's comin' our Stan; we'll be locked up fur sure." Pushing forward with a very prominent limp Ben raised his voice once more. "The masters comin' our Stan."

Just for a fleeting moment the elder lad appeared to falter, his blue eyes flashed with anger as he stared at his younger brother, only to turn around once more to punch out at his victim.

Frantically Ben gazed around him for support from the other workhouse lads, but they had more sense, they were back to their benches, wood craft now their only concern.

"Stan." Ben hobbled towards his brother, but it was too late.
"ORDER, STAND ASIDE BOY."

Silence now filled the cold atmosphere of the workshop as the tall lean figure of the master appeared. A man whose heart was even blacker than his hair, whose piercing brown eyes scoured every pitiful face that stared blankly at him, their fear evident. For there clasped tightly in his hand was a rod which he frequently brought down upon the backs of the boys in his care. Ben hobbled to one side, the stick he held in his own hands steadying his slimly built frame, his dark brown eyes lowered to the floor as the master stared his way. Ben didn't mutter a sound, the two boys were still fighting ruthlessly on the ground and one of them was his own brother.

"ORDER." Once more the master bellowed, and then with a striking blow brought the rod sharply across the back of the elder lad.

"Lawson, get up." Not waiting for an answer the master took the lad by the scruff of his neck pulling him roughly to his feet. "Explain yourself before I beat the living daylights out of you boy." Not giving time for an answer he raised the rod in the air once more rending a violent blow across the lads back.

"please master…stop…I were only tryin' t' stop tha' little skit from stealin'."

"Go on." Holding onto the boy's scruff still firmly, he stared coldly into the furious blue eyes that searched him, a silent plea that he just might listen. "I haven't got all day boy."

Stan Lawson took a deep breath as he felt his master's grip release, then glowered at the young lad he had pounded as he struggled to get up, his nose bleeding heavily.

"Tha' little skit were in 'ere master behind the bench, bread in 'is hands an' our Ben's boots, guess he's new 'ere, 'anna seen 'im before. Stealin' I tell yo', stealin'." Stan Lawson pulled himself to his full height, the sudden feel of self importance all around him; he had made his master listen.

Before the master could answer, the lad in question tried hard to push past them, his only mission, the door, only to be grabbed by the master who looked more than ready to raise his rod once more.

"Is this true boy?"

Not a murmur did the boy make, his face half hidden by his black cap, only his eyes peered from beneath, holding onto those of Stan Lawson, not faltering for a second as the fifteen year old lad with the brightest of red hair glowered in contempt, his turned up freckled nose screwed up, his wide mouth contorted in an ugly sneer, his face bright red with fury. Slowly the younger lad stared towards the boy who had tried so very hard to break them up, a young crippled boy whose red hair was dull in comparison of his elder brother, whose dark brown eyes held fear caused by the scene in front of him, whose freckled nose also turned up, but whose mouth trembled with anticipation, and held no sneer.

Ben Lawson stared at the boy in question. Why hadn't he answered the master? He must know how much trouble he was in, for the rules were made more than plain to all those that entered the workhouse, either voluntary, or those that had been forced there.

"Silence, Order, and Decorum are to be upheld at all times." These were to be maintained at all times. No shouting or fighting, no talking whilst working, and never stealing. All these sins held serious punishment.

When the boy began to stare at Ben even more closely, his eyes roaming rudely over Ben's crippled leg, even Ben began to scowl.

"Answer me boy, have you no tongue?"

"Aye mister, I 'ave tha', I were only tekin' a lousy piece o' rotton bread, an' tha'…"

"SILENCE."

Gasps echoed around the workshop, as the other lads pushed themselves even harder, afraid the master might just look up, see their interest and call it slacking.

Another severe punishment, slacking.

Ben hobbled further backwards, his brown eyes even wider with anticipation for never had he known any boy talk back to the master like this boy had just dared.

Stan Lawson stepped towards his younger brother, a smirk brightening up his face, for now he would stand back and enjoy watching this lad be thrashed before his very eyes.

Only the sound of wood being sawn, and planed down could be heard as the master grabbed the younger lad by the front of his grey flannel shirts, his cap still half hiding his face. As the master bellowed out his words of cruel punishment he was ready to inflict upon the boy, the child raised his face to meet the cruel eyes of his master, eyes that held great menace. As the master glowered deep into the boys face – he blinked. Then, he began to frown even more deeply before lowering his rod and loosening his grip from the child's shirt. Yes, this child was new here, he had been here himself the day this dishevelled urchin had walked through his gates. A field child, a child of no parentage, who had no respect to any rules whatsoever, but a child whose sharp oddly coloured slate grey eyes had held him strangely captivated. Now here this child stood, those slate grey eyes staring straight back at him, holding him in challenge.

Not a movement did the child make as the cap was pulled from his head and flung to one side, but now each lad that had worked the benches was now staring their master's way, all eyes staring straight at the child whose grey eyes held an even firmer challenge.

"It's a bloody lass."

"ORDER." Turning his attention back to the Lawson boy the master struck out once more with his rod, ignoring his pleas for leniency. He had only one interest now, what had this child told him her name was?

"Name girl, give me your name."

Pouting the girl glowered at Stan once more then stared up to meet her master's gaze.

"Well, you do have a name I take it?"

"Aye mister, I do, mi names Briar."

"Briar?" His frown deepened

"Aye mister, Briar Rose, I were born under a hawthorn bush."

Muffled chuckles escaped the lips of the boys around them, much to the master's annoyance.

"Fetch the mistress Lawson, don't just stand there."

"Aye master, on the double." Grimacing from the last blow, Stan Lawson cast his eyes to the girl who was dressed as one of them once more. Never had he taken a thrashing for any girl before, but never had he fought with one, not a girl who could deliver a punch as this one had. His blue eyes roamed over the slender body and he half grinned. She had no figure to suggest she was a girl, she was no older than twelve though, and surely, he'd say the same age as Ben.

Stan almost smiled as he watched the girl shudder under his scrutinizing gaze, but his smile turned to a scowl as her slate grey eyes echoed a sudden fury, a fierceness that was ready to fight him once more.

"I'll ge' the mistress an' fas' master, canna le' this little alley cat loose now can we?"

Without another word Stan turned, making his way from the workshop's, down the long corridors, and out across the yard that would lead him away from the men's side of the workhouse, and over to the side of the workhouse that housed the many women.

Ben had watched his brother leave and now his gaze fell on the girl. She had a wild look about her face, her cheeks were flushed, her lips pouted heavily, her eyes flashed with contempt of them all. She was mad this girl, she had to be, no girl had ever sneaked into the men's side of the workhouse before. She'd stolen clothes to make herself look like a boy, and she had fought relentlessly.

As Briar glared back at the boy in front of her, a boy who held tightly onto a stick for support she pouted even harder, but she could see his own frown had slowly vanished. His look had changed to that of concern, his dark brown eyes held a depth of fear. Was it fear for her? Or fear for his brother?

Slowly she stared back at her master, a man who stood so very tall and firm, who dressed in the same thick corduroy trousers as the boys, the same grey flannel shirt, only the master wore a black jacket and had high boots on.

What Briar saw was a window in her master's eyes, the same window that had displayed male interest towards her once before, she swore she saw it also in the eyes of the boy no older than herself.

What the master and young Ben Lawson could both see was a girl whose slender body had not yet matured, whose slate grey eyes sparked with life and defiance. Whose immature heart shaped face already warned that she would not be used. Whose glaring almost fierce eyes told them that she already knew what pleasure could be asked of her, but dared anybody to even try. Standing there dressed as a boy, her eyes wildly staring from one to the other, and her waist length silver blonde hair hanging loosely over her shoulders only added to her strange young qualities.

Once more Briar Rose shuddered.

chapter two

"What do we imply girl?"

The shrill high pitched tone of the mistress had long since been buried under the cold damp mould that penetrated these cold walls. All that was left was the echo of the cruel voice as it played deeply in the mind of Briar Rose the young girl who had managed to offend everybody who came into contact with her.

"Order, Silence and Decorum...Ma'am." The gentle voice of the child spoke to the cell walls, but no answer was given, for nobody was there. Folding her arms tightly around herself in an effort to keep warm, her slate grey eyes squinted in the darkness.

"Usefulness, Industry and Virtue...Ma'am." Pouting heavily she kicked out in virtual blindness, an air of defiance heavily cloaking the gangly childlike figure as her bony fingers now clung tightly to the rusty bars that separated her from the outside world. The door behind her securely locked, keeping her troublesome nature away from those that knew the rules only too well. Now, left alone for another long night, Briar Rose had time to reflect on her own life, but right now all she could see was a cell that had become her night time prison. She had no conception of an industrious work life, or just what entering this workhouse would really mean to her. "Usefulness, industry and virtue...aye...I'll learn yore ways bu' fur me Ma'am an' when I do, I'll spit in yore face, aye I will."

"In fur a rough time 'ere lass yo' keepin' on liken tha', bloody deserve it an' all yo' thievin' young skit...dunna thinken I furgo' the trouble yo' caused me."

Peering through the bars of her incarceration Briar Rose stared into the darkness ahead of her, her slate grey eyes searching frantically for the face she remembered. The lad she had fought with for the stale bread she had tried to hide in her trouser pockets almost two weeks ago. Stan Lawson.

"Aye well I furgo' yo' excep' fur yore squealin' liken a babby pig… squealin' fur yore mammy." Pausing momentarily she wiped her nose on her sleeve then pushed her face tightly against the bars. She could now very clearly see the boys face, his bright blue eyes sparking with the fury she'd witnessed the day she had fought him. "Nobody 'ere will break me, yore daf' rules, wantin' t' feed folk nowt bu' stale bread, forcin' them int' hard labour. I've worked since I could walk, in places yo' wouldna las' in, so dunna thinken I'm scared o' yo' lo', cause I inna."

Stan Lawson glared down at the gangly youngster just inches from him, only the rusty bars stopping him from grabbing her and throttling the life out of her. "Well yo' bes' listen lass, or yo'll ge' thrashed the 'ell owt o' 'ere, an' yo'll spend yore life down theer wi' the rats." Stan clearly saw the girl startle, her eyes widened with a sudden anticipation, and he began to slowly grin, the anger subsiding from his face as pure mischief made his blue eyes sparkle. "So nod as tough as I firs' though', jus' liken any other lass, daf' and bloody squeamish."

"Go t' 'ell, see wha' I care anyway." Folding her arms Briar pouted heavily, her eyes not leaving the red headed boy that now scowled at her.

Stan stood in complete silence, even though his main desire was to grab this field urchin and half strangle her, there was something about this girl that had sparked a strange interest deep within him. She could hardly be more than twelve years old, three years his junior, but she had an air about her, a wildness that knew about life. There was something else as well, he'd heard things being said, and now he could make out the sash that draped over her shoulders, and down her shift, a yellow sash that marked her out to be different from most of the rest. "I wouldna mek an enemy owt o' me lass. Goin' by wha' I hear, yo' 'ave no friends, or folk."

Glowering back at the boy Briar Rose bit hard into her lower lip, before screwing her nose up into an ugly sneer. "Ne'er 'ad no friends or folk, ne'er needed none, ne'er will." She waited, her body tense, the cold really beginning to take its hold, but she meant every word she had said. Her words had been spoken truthfully, but with a conviction of regretful knowledge.

Just for a short while Stan watched the girl as she stood so very firm, nothing about this girl gave any impression of friendliness, maybe she just didn't know how to be friendly. Reaching deep into his pocket he sighed. "Well, tek this anyway, though' yo' migh' 'ave been more civil like. I wunna waste me time on yo' again." Standing back Stan watched as the girl hungrily pushed the stale piece of cake in her mouth, choking herself on it's dryness as she did. "Dunna need friends eh? Yo' better change yore ways lass, yo' wunna las' 'ere else, nod the way yo' are. Yo' wearin' tha' sash tells any decent folk t' keep away." Stan also spoke truthfully, for a girl wearing that colour would never come of any good. "Yo'll only end up in one place if yo' dunna, back in the fields on yore back wi' yore skirts over yore 'ead." Again the mischievous grin brought sparkle to his eyes, for all knew about the field girls the ones that belonged to the gang masters. They were all ready and willing for the taking.

"Go t' hell yo' 'ear me? Go t' hell." Screaming her last words Briar Rose pulled at the rusty bars of her prison wildly, and when she couldn't reach the chuckling boy she brought her head back and spat, her venom hurting her victim more than any punch could muster.

"Yo' dirty little trollop…" Wiping away the remnants of chewed spat cake from his face Stan now reached through the bars to take hold of the girl, but she was too quick, she had already stepped back and now happily hurled obscenities that even he hadn't heard the likes off.

"Stan, our Stan, the master's lookin' fur yo' our Stan, come on. We're both be in fur it else." The uneven hobbled steps of a younger boy brought a sudden silence, as the glow from the lantern he held tightly in his hands flickered upon the face of his older brother Stan.

"Ne'er told yo' t' follow me Ben. Come on, I wasted mi time 'ere, she really is a skit, a foul mouthed dirty little trollop." As Stan placed his arm upon the shoulder of his brother, the pair turned to make back towards the men's side of the workhouse, their pace much slower as Ben hobbled as fast as he could.

"Go on yo', clear off yo' dull bastards, bu' I'll tell yo' this. I inna no trollop, ne'er were, ne'er will be. Tha' bitch o' a mistress placed this on me t' mark me."

It was Ben that stopped first and turned, the lantern light clearly displaying his features. His face so resembled that of his older brother, only his eyes were soft brown, and his hair was not such a fiery red. Briar Rose squinted towards the lantern light. Once more, just as she had on the day she fought with Stan, she saw a deep look etching the face of the younger brother. Was it concern? But why? She didn't know him, and going by the way he limped so badly, he should save his concern for himself. Ben watched as the distressed yet angry girl ripped the yellow sash from her shift and threw it through the bars, only then did he begin to hobble back towards her, his brother close by.

Briar grasped the bars once more, her words now aimed at Ben. "I work 'ere the same as everyone else, bu' they wunna gi' me a chance. The master an' the mistress see me as nowt bu' a field tramp an' I inna, bu' I'll tell yo' this…" Taking a deep breath, Briar pushed her face as close to the bars as she could, her fury shaking her young body. "They can bea' me until I canna stand an' leave me down 'ere, an' feed me stale cake. But I'll learn their daf' lessons, I'll learn when t' keep silen', their order and decorum, which the mistress screams at me. I'll learn usefulness, industry an' virtue, an' then I'm owt o' 'ere, I'll spit in the eye o' all o' yo'. I may be 'ere now, bu' I wunna die 'ere."

Complete silence. Not even the distant hoot of an owl dared break this silence. Both brothers stood united, their gaze on the girl with the slate grey eyes. Stan stared deeply into the wild glaring eyes that challenged him, his gaze roaming over her silvery blond hair that hung loosely over her shoulders. In the twinkle of the lantern glow he began to grin, she looked almost angelic, and he would have laughed aloud only the look in Briar Rose's eyes stopped him. She was waiting, for that chance to fly at him again, how she had the first day their paths had crossed, and though he would never admit it openly, she had done a pretty good job that day of trying to beat the living daylights out of him.

In that split instance, as the three of them stood, their eyes searching the other, only the night stars witness to their confrontation Stan believed wholly that this girl would in fact one day walk out of this place with her head held high. She had spirit, like none he had ever seen before; this girl would surely make a stand for herself – that was if nobody lynched her first. As he had on that very first day, Stan felt a deep stirring within him, an urge to reach out and hold this girl, to hold her so tightly he'd have her gasping for breath. But not yet, he would wait, when this girl was older, he'd have some fun with her, but when he did, and he would, he would make sure that she would want him too. For some strange reason he wanted to win this girls affections, just why he did not know, for she clearly was a mere alley cat. Ben stood silently, his body relying on the walking stick that held him as straight as it possibly could. He too found this girl unusually fascinating. His mind also went back to the first day he had seen her, when she had so daringly glared their master out. He had wondered then, and now he was sure that this girl was mad, disturbed in the mind, for no girl he had ever known acted quite like this one. But the feeling Ben felt for her was just as strong as his brothers, only Ben's was full of concern that this girl would get hurt here. Why he should feel concern for such a girl he did not understand. But he did understand even at his age that this wild creature whose temper knew no restraint, whose slate grey eyes could pierce with vengeance, but whose heart shaped face held such a rare quality, would only mean trouble for her. For this girl would always unwillingly attract men towards her, and not men that would do her any good. "Mi brother mean' yo' no 'arm miss, bu' we'll be off now before yo' land us all int' trouble." Bending down Ben picked up her discarded sash, holding his lantern up to face her more clearly. "Yo' wunna be needin' this will yo' miss? I'll tek it an' burn it."

Briar Rose glared as she watched the younger lad pushed her sash deep into his pocket, and then she closed her eyes tightly as the brothers turned and slowly walked away, the sound of Ben's footsteps uneven as they ventured further into the darkness. With no one left to see her Briar Rose peered through the bars of her prison, her eyes searching the night sky, her anger now diminished, just a feeling of utter loneliness haunting her miserable life. What choice had life really given her? Before she had come here, her whole twelve years of life had been spent as part of a field gang. A group of lowly women who roamed the countryside searching for work, and stopping wherever there was any, with just one man to protect them, to find them work, and then cut a deal with the land owners, who made sure they had some type of shelter for sleep. The gang master. A man of the most cruel unscrupulous nature, who sat by while the women worked their fingers to the bone, taking their wages and giving them handouts for the liquor they cheerfully drank, the gang master their protector. A man who kept these women out of the workhouse, or worse yet the whorehouses that would have happily taken on even the youngest of girls, but he stopped all of that. He kept them sheltered from the many men that would have gladly taken them, and he kept them for himself. The field gangs were used for their cheap labour, but were often classed as far worse than any gypsy traveller, for gypsies had a strong loyalty unto their own but the field gangs had only a loyalty unto themselves, and if anybody stumbled or died along the way; well, they were better off without them.

    From the time she could toddle Briar Rose had began to pick up many an apple from the orchard, or gather up wood for the farmer's wife. Later she had known what it was like to feel her tiny back break as she helped rid a section of field from stones, ready for the farmer to plough. She had watched as a small child how the women in the gang had eagerly held out their grubby chapped hands on a Friday night for their meagre share of the earnings. She had witnessed them searching for the cheapest of liquor to help rid themselves of their own miserable life. Then later, she had tried to cover her ears in disgust when several of them had brought back a willing man, who would give them a farthing for services rendered. Over the years Briar Rose had watched as those women bore children, many of them fathered by the gang master himself. She had seen how delighted he had been when a girl child was born, for later that girl child would work for him, and undoubtedly eventually be used for his own sadistic pleasures, and she had wept openly when they had left newborn boy children on the doorstep of some unsuspecting land owner. She shuddered as she remembered the many beatings she herself had received by his hands, beatings for her upfront manner, and the spirit she wildly displayed from time to time. When she had repeatedly tried to escape the field gang and make her own way in life, the gang master had been hot on her heels, for despite her will, Briar had proved herself to be a hard worker, not a girl he would want to lose. But when she had tired to find herself employment at the Shrewsbury Town Hiring, he had been so incensed by her difficult nature, he had dragged her screaming from the town centre back to her true fold, his fold. But before he had handed her back to the women the cruel gang master had forced the youngster to promise she would never try to leave him again, and to swear that he would always be her master. When she had repeatedly refused, and had actually spat at him, he had callously beaten her in the loneliness of a field, his clenched fists bruising her body, not showing any mercy towards her as she choked helplessly to breathe. Then, he had laughed, his rotten teeth leering into her face, his breath stale from liquor as he pushed her to the ground, his hands eager to rip her clothes from her young body, his sheer pleasure at her terror as he brutally raped her, ripping into her child body until her screams of agony and promises of submission escaped her sobbing soul. As the flicker of Ben Lawson's lantern turned into a memory she stared blankly into the darkness now facing her, and only then when she knew she was away from prying eyes did her tears begin to fall. Her heart rending sobs pitiful. Her arms tightly wrapped around herself for comfort, a comfort that she would never find anywhere on this earth, and certainly not here. All these walls offered her was a cruelty of another kind, and the stone arch of the Crosshouses Workhouse that had led her through the front doors, had only proved to be an archway of tears. She was marked, scarred for life by her master's vicious brutality, and now everybody must be able to see what he had done to her, that had given her new mistress the delight of making her wear the yellow sash that declared her a loose woman, that had made the likes of Stan Lawson call her a trollop. Because of this, Briar Rose knew she would never belong anywhere, and that men would indeed see her for what the gang master had turned her into. A dirty easy trollop.

chapter three

Rolling up her sleeves, Briar Rose took a deep breath, wiped her brow then rubbed the pit of her back firmly, her chapped hands only causing her more pain as she did so.

"Get on with it girl, there's no time for slacking here. When you're done there, you can take the pails for more water, so hurry up."

"Aye mistress...sorry mistress." Slowly dragging out her words deliberately, Briar held perfect eye contact, a slight smirk turning up the corner of her mouth as she saw the mistress of the Workhouse shudder at the very sight of her. In the two years that had passed, Briar Rose had learnt many lessons, most of them harsh. But never in all this time had she allowed those around her to see how bothered she was by their continued treatment towards her. To have let them see how desperately lonely she felt would have meant defeat, and Briar would have rather gone back to the field gangs than let anybody here see that. But still, as she slogged over her tedious work, and laid awake way into the coldest of nights, she clung fast to one simple dream. One day she would use her basic education she had been forced to learn here, she would use her sewing skills, her laundry skills, even her knowledge of work in the fields and she would leave here. When the time was right, she would leave this life of continual labour, and she would walk back through that archway that housed an ocean of tears and she would flee to pastures new. If she was just given the chance she could prove herself in any man's household to be a valuable asset, she would make the best chambermaid, or nursemaid anybody could wish for. The hirings in Shrewsbury Town Square could be her solution. The mistress glowered at the girl before her, her stern unkindly face ashen with anger. This girl was being impudent towards her she could sense that, but this girl had proved time and time again just how cunning she could be. For this girl had also learnt to fear punishment, and she knew that it would be dealt her at the first given opportunity, so she minded her manners. But the mistress wasn't fooled, she could see the look behind those slate grey eyes of hers, and that look held a story of sheer defiance. As Briar Rose picked up her pail and simply bowed her head, slowly making her way across the laundry, the mistress shuddered. She had no liking for this girl at all, she considered her to be an odd looking creature. Those slate grey eyes of hers were bad enough, always holding those around her in contempt. Her silvery blond hair was always tied neatly back out of place, and the girl never failed to be without her bonnet, stray strands often escaped that shone against the girl's pale skin with glory. But her heart shaped face, the mistress hated most of all, for the girl was a common little slut she had no doubt about that, but the look of childlike innocence that betrayed the onlooker would win this girl her ticket to a better life. That the mistress was sure of, a life where the girl would be looked after, looked up to even, that would gain her a place in some rich mans house, to luxuries she did not deserve. The girl was slightly tall for her age, but her slender body, her long legs and capability to work harder than she had seen many do would all add in the her favour. Briar Rose muttered wildly to herself once she was out of hearing distance. She left her dolly tub and soiled linen behind and made towards the door that would lead her up the stone steps and towards the ground floor. Here she would pass though the first door on her right and onto the cobbled courtyard, that housed the nearest water pump, the one all the laundry women used. For a long moment Briar closed her eyes and took a deep breath, the gentle kiss of the May sun promising her of better things to come. The soft teasing breeze of the light warm air swiftly drying the sweat from her brow, the odour of the soiled sheets lost in the simple delight of nature's freshness. A brief smile escaped her lips as a playful sparrow flew past her, for that small moment in time her worries and sad memories of days gone by were lost.

"Dunna thinken we're carryin' yore load miss, inna no time 'ere fur stickin' yore 'ead in the clouds and daydreamin'."

Defiantly Briar glowered at the two older women, each in the same drab shift as her own, their grubby pinnies soiled from the filth they also worked with, their hair tied tightly back, mop caps covering most of it. A scowl covered her face. "I do me own work, an' it'll be done as always." She watched intently as the two women tutted to each other then made their way back towards the laundry, each one struggling under the weight of their pails. With the task foremost in her mind Briar began to pump the water into her own pails. One thing she did know, she would not be here when she reached the age of those other women. If she was, she vowed there and then she'd take one of the freshly laundered sheets, tie it into a noose, and with it she would hang herself. Each day held the same boring routine. A bell woke the long wards of the women, every one moving, still aching from the work the day before, but knowing they had to move fast, they had to fold their one blanket and stack the wooden crate like beds against the far wall before they could think of washing down. If they did not move fast enough they would miss out of the bowl of hot watery unappetising porridge, and a mug of black mushed tea. Work started at seven sharp, each woman making her way to her place of work. For two years Briar had been given just one task, downstairs under the ground, in the laundry room, as far out of sight as the mistress could place her. A basement cellar that stunk from human excrement and dried urine, the lingering stench of the infirm. The sweat room, the women called it, for there was no window to relief them from the stink, their own sweat mingling against the already putrid smell of decay. Briar called it 'Hell' and had been punished more than once for saying it aloud. For Briar to miss out on her midday meal of broth and often stale bread, or to have her meat ration of no distinguished taste stopped was a regular habit. But there was one reprieve, for after lunch Briar attended the workhouse school, being fourteen still classed her to be young enough to receive this one luxury. So the mistress had said. "Virtue, Usefulness and Industry, are all you need to know. To write your name is a great asset." That was where the education ended. Briar could now write her name backwards much to her own amusement; she knew what her education meant to the mistress. One day she would be expected to be a good loyal wife, and lay down with a man when he demanded her too. She knew to be useful meant how to darn a pair of worn out socks properly, or make woven mats, or cook a meal out of sheer scraps. But what about industry? That never came into it; she guessed that alone belonged to the other side of the workhouse the men's side. When lessons were finished she would return to the laundry, and eventually make her way back towards the dining hall where long rows of tables and wooden benches were placed neatly, all facing one way. Rows of women would quietly sit here and eat their last meal of the day, a meal of hot potatoes, and mashed vegetables, something they were frequently reminded to be thankful for. Every meal time was the same, spent in silence; for talking at the table was also forbidden. Lastly the women would clean the dining room, and make their way back to the sleeping wards, many of them asleep by the time the clock struck nine. For many women workhouse life was the only way for them, a way to keep themselves and small children off the streets. To Briar Rose though, it had been she who had walked through those dreaded gates, and under that archway of tears and into another type of imprisonment forced upon her by those in charge. Here nothing was her own; she had no rights, no opinion, not even her own rags. She, alongside the others was just another no hoper, and as with the others it was expected of her to be eternally grateful to the mistress and the master for allowing her the bed space. Briar Rose had come to hate her work, her envy was with the women that worked the gardens, an abundance of vegetable gardens that not just fed them, but supplied the community around them. Briar knew she could work alongside those women with great capability. But she also envied the men, they had decent jobs, they never had to launder, all their clothes were sent down to her. They learnt how to harvest and value the women's grown produce, they knew how to shod a horses hooves, how to make cart wheels, and she had often heard the sound of the hammers and sawing coming from the nearby mill, and it's workshop. She had seen chairs and tables appearing through the workshop doors. She had witnessed outsiders passing through these very gates to buy the wares made on these grounds. All of this, while all she ever did was launder the stinking linen. How often she had felt the urge to cross the line, to make her way to the fence that split the workhouse in two, just to take a better look at what went on. She'd crossed the fence on her first few days here, but the mistress had severely beaten her, and she'd spent nights down in the cells for punishment. But if only she could take just one piece of wood and a few tools, she was sure that she could prove herself to be useful, and if the mistress did turn to the master over her behaviour again, maybe he would notice that she too could be industrious. Briar had worked the fields sometimes better than any man in her past years, well now; she could work alongside the boys and men, if only she was given the chance. Temptation became too much, and when sleep succumbed the weariness from the souls of the many women that shared the one room, Briar pushed her blanket to one side, swiftly dressed into her shift, her boots in her hand so she could tiptoe quietly, and then she ran down the long corridor stopping only to light herself a candle. Once outside the back door, she quickly placed her boots on, then as fast as she could she ran across the yard without looking back, her hand shielding her candle, fearful that the night air would steal it from her, her one small ray of light. Alongside the fence she paused and took a deep breath, then kneeling down on the sodden grass she gently placed the candle through the fence, placing it safely as she did so. "Please dunna go owt, it'll be no good if yo' do."

Without further ado Briar expertly climbed the fence, dropping herself to the ground as quietly as she could do so. She had made it; she was now on the other side of the workhouse. Looking wildly around her, her eyes searching the darkness, she sighed with relief, nobody was about. Taking her candle once more, she ran towards the building she knew to be the workshop, the mill where many of the men worked, her heart pounding wildly as she gasped for breath. "Damn." Pushing hard she kicked the bottom of the door, but to no avail she'd have to walk around, go through the main doors and hopefully make her way around. "Damn it." Screwing her face up in frustration she flitted through the darkness and sure enough the front door had been left unlocked. Only now did Briar begin to wonder if this had been a good idea, as she gently pushed the door open. If she was caught now, she feared to think what punishment she would be faced with. For how on earth could she explain what she was doing late at night sneaking into the men's side of the workhouse? Nobody would believe her. They may even make her wear another yellow sash over her shift, how they had when she had first arrived here. Breathing heavily she tiptoed down the corridor, her eyes wide in anticipation, the flicker from her candle sending eerie images against the cold white washed walls. She would have to move fast, somebody would notice surely? Where on earth were the men's dormitory?

"God 'elp me owt if I run into them by mistake, the mistress will skin me alive."

Pausing momentarily Briar bit down hard on her lip, "Righ'...no lef', got t' be lef', tha' will brin' me opposite the fence an' the laundry, aye, lef'." Twice Briar Rose opened the wrong door, once into what had to be the men's washroom, as the smell of slop pails made her cringe, and then she accidentally found what she didn't want, the men's dormitory. She hadn't needed to hold her candle up high in this room, she could smell the stench of human flesh, and hear the laboured breathing, it was enough to make her heart skip a beat and quickly close the door. Leaning against it for support, she struggled to compose herself, as her own heavy breathing threatened to strangle her. But then when she was about to give up, she found it, the workshop, 'the mill'. Holding her candle further in front of her she could faintly make out the rows of wooden benches, she could clearly smell the freshly sawn timber as its odour danced towards her fermenting the air with a promise of newness. She could almost see the evergreen trees, and the forests before her. Briar Rose sighed, how mundane her own work was compared to this, no smell of human waste and ground in filth hung like a thunder cloud in this room. She could cope with this; she could work in this room – if only. Moving around almost frantically now she began her search for small pieces of wood, tools, anything that she may use to make something, anything that could be presented to the master with the arguement that she too could be useful in the outside world of industry. But make what exactly? Briar shook her head sadly, she had no idea, but never-the-less that would come later, and right now she just needed as much as she could carry in her pinny. With just the lowly flicker of her candle Briar Rose floundered around in the near darkness, her heart set on just one thing. The means to learn something that would buy her ticket out of this place and set her up in the outside world. Just outside the workshop doorway stood another, a lad no taller than Briar Rose, a lad who now quietly hobbled inside, a stick helping to support his lean frame. His only light, that from the lowly candle glow that Briar held so tightly. Ben Lawson had been awake when she had stood just inside the men's dormitory, he'd blinked fiercely to convince himself he was awake and that the vision not too far from him had in fact been real, and not some dream. He had pulled on his trousers, and working shirt as quickly as possible, and had then followed the figure of the flitting girl silently from door to door. Only now as he watched her closely, the curious look he wore turned to a frown, his brown eyes narrowing into slits, and his mouth tightening as if in a grimace. He had watched the girl use her pinny to bundle oddments of wood and chisels into it, tying them securely in place, but what would she want them for? She wouldn't know what to do with them. Now here she stood a small wooden figure in her hands, a tiny wooden duck that he himself had worked on long into the night, until his fingers expertly knew every smooth contour that he himself had created. Briar Rose had found the answer, the tiny wooden duck she held in her hands would be her place in the world of industry. Oblivious that anybody else was in the room she pushed the tiny duck inside her pocket, and now began to gather up the wooden bowls, decorative bowls that would serve an infant child, their touch so smooth to her fingertips, the smell of the freshly sanded surface telling her that they had recently been finished. Placing them too inside her pinny Briar Rose smiled to herself. Yes, she would copy them and present her own work to the master. Maybe then the stench of the sweat room would be a distant memory.

"Yo' wunna mek it owt this room until yo' put tha' back miss."

A startled cry escaped the girls lips, but Briar was quick to conform herself. She had come this far, and no crippled lad was going to stop her.

"I mean it miss, yo' bes' pu' tha' back."

Briar glowered at the lad in front of her, as he had spoken to her, his voice so low, quiet even, but it held a note of deep conviction, and it stopped Briar from attempting to push rudely past him.

"Aye, yo' thievin' little skit, yo' bes' do wha' our Ben tells yo'."

Only now did Briar Rose falter, what could she do? Push past both of them?

No, she knew that for now she was beat, but she would compromise. Without a word she lay down her pinny, placing down her wood and tools, and neatly laying out the wooden bowls exactly as she had found them, peering up every so often and glaring at the elder brother, her slate grey eyes telling Stan Lawson she was only beat for now. She'd seen these brothers every day of her life across the courtyard, but standing here so very close to them she could see how much they had changed. Ben's eyes were now level to her own, he could be classed as rather short for his age, but then some had said she was tall. She could see how much he still needed the aid of a walking stick, but instead of hunching his back, he held himself as straight as he possibly could. Slowly Briar glared over at Stan and looked him up and down. He was much taller than his brother, with the same lean frame but he still held a look of fury in his bright blue eyes, a look he held whenever he had faced her. Staring down into her pinny, Briar Rose picked up the last piece she had taken, the wooden duck. Clutching it tightly to her she turned her attention to Ben. "Nod this, I need this, yo' can tek the res' back, bu' nod this."

"Tha' miss yo' inna tekin'." Ben spoke low, but still with conviction, for he had a dream too, and he also needed that small wooden figure. "It inna no use t' yo' miss, an' yo' know as well as I do they wunna le' yo' keep it."

Briar Rose tutted loudly, oh she knew that only too well, did he think she was stupid? But how could she possibly try and make a toy like this without this one to copy? Come to think of it, how could she anyway? She had handed her wood and tools back over. It was impossible. But was it? She had but one chance left, she knew it would probably make her a laughing stock, but as she had once before she noticed one thing. In the flicker of the candle light she saw the look behind Ben Lawson's eyes; softness lay behind them, something that his elder brother's bright blue eyes lacked. Taking a deep breath she closed her eyes. To hear them laugh would be one thing, but to see them laugh at her would be unbearable. "I came 'ere t' prove mi worth, I can work as 'ard as any man, I 'ave done it before. I wanna mek thin's liken this." Pausing only to look down at the wooden duck she carried on, "I inna stayin' 'ere, one day I'm off, an' when I do I wan' t' be able t' do somethin' nod many other women can. I wan' t' mek toys liken this, darnin' rotten socks an' spendin' all day over a dolly tub inna fur me…"

"Is that so?"

Immediately Briar Rose tensed, opening her eyes wide as she stepped back quickly. A lantern had borrowed the workshop a generous glow, and there standing in the doorway was the silhouette of the master. His tall lean figure shadowy against the lantern light, but Briar Rose could see him, and it made her shudder violently, until she gasped with sudden recognition of just how frightened she had been of this happening. What this would mean to her now made her heart race. Silence overcame the two brothers, and filled the workshop air with a thick mist that nobody would dare try to walk through, or even utter a sound. The master entered the room, his arms folded tightly, slowly circling the three of them as he did so, the hunter and the hunted. Glaring at the Lawson brothers and then the girl, he half smirked. This was no arranged meeting that was plain to see, the anger was still there in Stan's eyes, his jaw still tense from clenching his teeth together. He could also sense certain anger in Ben, which was seldom seen, no, these two boys were two of the best workers he had; they were not stupid enough to risk a beating for this girl. The culprit had to be the girl, not a day went by when the mistress didn't complain about this wretched creature, and up to now he had kept his distance. Delivering punishment of any kind on his female workers brought him no pleasure at all. Looking the girl over he stared down at her crumpled pinny that was laid down on the bench, a variety of tools and wood discarded around them, and then he raised his eyebrows with interest. When he saw the tiny wooden duck still clutched tightly in her hands he began to frown deeply. So she had come to steal from here once more, only this time to put him out of pocket. "Put that down now girl."

Briar Rose glowered at the master and pouted heavily in defiance, her slate grey eyes dared to flash wildly with her annoyance. But once more she knew there was nothing she could do. For without any wood or tools, she would never be able to argue her case. Reaching out slowly she handed the wooden duck over, but not to the master, she gave it back to Ben. For what seemed an age the master glared down at the girl in front of him, a girl with the most extraordinary looks that gave her an almost ghostly appearance. Her heart shaped face was almost too small for the slate grey eyes that penetrated wildly from it giving her an almost angelic appearance. She was certainly a strange girl, very ghostly and a scavenging thief.

"Lawson go fetch the mistress. Ring the bell at the front door and have her sent for."

Stan also stared hard at the girl, why she should have this affect on him he had no idea. He felt burnt up with fury at the very sight of her, and would welcome any punishment that was bestowed upon her, but even still that did not explain why he had the hidden desire to reach out and grab her, to force his lips hard against hers. Given the chance and enough time, he knew he would. "Immediately."

"Aye master, sorry master."

Briar Rose stood rigid to the spot, her heart pounding so fiercely she felt it would choke her. She had never felt so hot, so very dry that she felt she would choke to death. How she wished the ground would just open up and swallow her, come to that, she would gladly crawl away never to be seen again. But before she was humiliated, beaten and probably locked away she had nothing else left to lose. She would speak up to her master and hope for the best. It would probably do no good, but she had just this one last chance. Taking a deep breath she faced him squarely, and held her shoulders well back. She would have considered herself brave, only the mad racing of her heart told her otherwise. "I wunna stealin' mister, nod really, borrowin' I were, aye borrowin'." Nervously Briar Rose shuffled from foot to foot. The master was glaring fiercely at her, but uttered not a single word. "Yo' see mister, Usefulness, Virtue an' Industry', tha's wha' yo' an' the mistress tell us, bu' I inna go' no teachin' on industry ye' so theer it is, I come over 'ere an' risked mi neck t' borrow a few bits. I too can be useful as well as any lad, aye I can." Briar Rose stepped another pace backwards, she had said it, and now she awaited her fate.

Ben also waited his throat dry, the palms of his hands sweaty. What would be done with this girl? Once more he had to wonder if she was crazy. Surely she must know by now she would not be dealt with leniently. But even still, as her slate grey eyes peered his way, he felt a strange rush come over him, a wave that flooded his veins and filled him with a silent hope that she would be able to cope with what would lay ahead of her. She certainly had guts, like he'd never witnessed in any lass before, and the desire to better herself. 'Borrowing' she had said, to try and copy his work no doubt. The grin that crept over Ben Lawson's face momentarily lit up his brown eyes, but only for a moment, for his brother had now returned with the Mistress beside him, and the look on her face made even him quiver. The scene that unfolded before Briar Rose and the Lawson brothers would not easily be forgotten, and the punishment forced upon Briar Rose would leave both brothers knowing exactly how they both felt about her, emotions that in turn would turn their three life's upside down, enter them into a world of bitterness, betrayal, and deceit, bringing them all great despair along the way. The master had been furious with the mistress for not being able to control the girl in her care.

"May I remind you this is a workhouse, we are not here to offer girls like this a better choice in life, their way in life has been chosen, hers by her own hands."

The mistress pulled herself to her full height as she faced her husband, her eyes just as cold as his. "I know, but as I have said before this girl has been an impossibility from the start, she is completely untrustworthy, a menace to all the other women." Briar Rose shivered visibly as she coldly looked her over. "She is a thief, a field girl, the worst of her kind. She had learnt nothing under my guidance, nothing, she is incapable."

As the mistress ended her last words on a shrill note that nearly ended the flicker from Briar's lowly candle, the master pulled his shoulders well back and glared down at the girl in question.

"You have been warned many times have you not girl?"

Briar cleared her throat, how hot she suddenly felt. How she wished she had never come sneaking over here. But they would expect her to plead with them, and deep down Briar still knew that given the chance she could prove her worth. "Aye mister I've been warned as yo' pu' it wi' a cane across mi legs, an' fed stale cake, till I threw it back up t' the rats in the cellar. Bu' yo' 'anna taugh' me nowt abou' industry, an' jus' because I'm a girl dunna mean I 'ave t' darn stinkin' socks fur the res' o' me days." Briar glared at all of them, she was fearful, but angry and it was that very same anger that had caused her so many problems in the past that now over rode her fear. "I can work as 'ard as any lad, I inna scared o' it, aye any o' it."

Silence. The mistress's eyes were wide with anticipation as her hand reached for her mouth in shock. Was this girl insane? Industry? No girl ever learnt a mans work, what need could she possibly have for it? There was no place in the working mans life for women, didn't this girl realise that? Indeed she did not, well then she herself would have her flogged by first light, and incarcerated in the cells until she did develop understanding. The master stood so very still, only the tightening of his jaw and the narrowing of his sharp brown eyes gave them warning. As the colour rose up his neck flushing his cheeks to a shade of scarlet did he begin to have trouble controlling the welled up anger inside of him. Never had any man or boy dared to raise their voices to him or query him this way. Never had any woman tried to stand her ground, even his wife, for she knew when to back down, but here he was faced with this strange youngster whose heart shaped face held such soft contours. Whose skin was so very pale yet clean, and whose silvery blond waist length hair shone with her youth. But those eyes, those slate grey eyes pierced straight through him as if daring him to hold her in contempt.

He had seen enough, and he had certainly heard more than enough, the mistress was obviously right all along about this girl. She was a common field girl, a thief, but he would see to it himself that she was not incapable of learning. "So you dare to ask about your place here, to query it even? If it was not for your mistress girl you would undoubtedly be in the nearest whorehouse, riddled with disease, without a hope in hell." Pausing, he waited, he expected to see some sign of remorse, but none came, the girl now pouted heavily, her arms folded tightly in front of her in complete protest. "So you say you want to learn industry, then, lets see shall we, let's see how long you last this side of the fence." Gasps escaped the lips of the mistress once more, causing Briar Rose to actually startle. "You want to work with my lads, then I'll treat you like one." Turning to his wife, he now spoke. "Bring the wench to my study, and then you can be relieved from the monstrosity. Dismissed Lawson, on your way."

As simply as that the Lawson brothers were dismissed, but not before they witnessed the cruel hand of their master grab the girl roughly by the scruff, the mistress close behind.

Left in the dark except for the dying embers of one mean candle Ben Lawson stared down at the wooden duck Briar had tried so hard to hold onto. So she had a dream, and was desperate to leave this place with the knowledge of a craft. He had been blessed himself with a gift. His arms were strong, and his fingers nimble, there was nothing he could not do with wood even though he was of such tender years. But when he held wood and tool in his hands, his imagination left the workshop behind and took him to greater places, and in his peace he had crafted some of the most skilful pieces of small furniture and toys the master had ever witnessed. Ben Lawson was already taking orders for stools, tables, cart wheels and toys for children of the gentry. Sadly Ben shook his head, he didn't begrudge the girl her dreams, not he, in fact it would have been fun trying to teach her how to do simple woodwork, and he would have liked that. But now...he closed his eyes, they'd half kill the girl here, that's if the master didn't do it first.

"Come on our Ben, theer's nowt we can t' 'elp the lass now." Placing his arm around his younger brothers shoulder, Stan held his candle in front of him as Ben hobbled as fast as possible, the wooden duck tightly in his grasp. Stan was known for his sharpness with the lads and at seventeen he had been honoured when the master had declared him charge hand of all the boys under sixteen. There was a great possibility that the girl would be placed right here, with him to answer too, and that would give him the greatest of pleasure. But would it? Stan sighed heavily, he thought he would welcome the little skit landing herself into this much trouble, but surprisingly he didn't. As she'd been led away a stirring deep within him had made him want to speak out on her behalf, ask for a little leniency. For at the end of the day, she was but a lass, and no lass would cope with the thrashing the master would surely deal her with. That he was certain off. But Stan grinned to himself, other girls would not cope, but this one would, and would probably stand there facing him in the morning with those slate grey eyes of hers. It would indeed bring him great pleasure having her at such closeness.

chapter four

"Yo' di' well our Ben, one day we'll walk from 'ere me and yo', aye we will."

With a gentle cuff around the side of the head Stan chuckled, his bright blue eyes shone with laughter, but held a true depth of the pride he felt towards his younger brother. Stan had watched his whole life as Ben had lived through one cruel struggle after another. He had wept his own nights away as Ben had screamed in agony as a small toddler when childhood polio brutally crippled his left leg. But then as the youngster grew, he had watched with a silent pride as Ben worked at turning his misfortunes into a craft. A gift some would call it, but he knew just how hard Ben had worked, how he had sat there until the early hours of the morning, often with just the flicker of a single candle for light. And now, Ben was fast becoming known as an unusual craftsman, at the ripe age of hardly fifteen. Ben returned his brothers smile, and nodded knowingly. How in the past he had wished he was more like Stan, his older brother. Stan was tall, where his own height had been stumped short by his diseased leg. Stan had the brightest of red hair, where his hair was dull in comparison, and Stan had confidence, for he was proving himself fast in becoming a leader. He had the ability to gain respect of the boys under him, and was managing the responsibility well. When the master wasn't around Stan took charge of the younger boys. He was known as the main mill hand. But as for himself, well, he had long since settled for a quiet back seat, his wood work, and with the bench full of sharpened tools, and the natural beauty of unspoilt wood in his hands Ben had found the perfect escape from his sharp reality. Until now. Ben leant forward, staring past his brother and towards the figure of what looked like any other lad. The over large black corduroy trousers, and the grey flannel shirt gave the opinion of a first class set of hand me downs. The black cap hid all but a hint of hair from view. Only one thing could not be hidden, the slate grey eyes that glared from the gaunt withdrawn face. Neither could the wild spirit be hidden that echoed from their very depths, searching the souls of those that noticed. Briar Rose. Slowly Briar Rose raised her eyes to meet those of the Lawson brothers. She watched the mischievous grin creep over Stan's face, his bright blue eyes sparkling as it did so, his tall lean frame shaking with laughter as she pouted heavily at him. She had expected a hard time with him; she had been so sure that he would have taken great delight in getting her into even more trouble with their master. But what had surprised her somewhat was he had not used his role as mill hand to intimidate her. He had not yet threatened her with the master, although he had made it plain she had best do as he had bid, or face the consequences. Briar Rose had done just that, she had followed his orders, swept the floors, ran around the workshop at every beck and call, fetching whatever was asked of her, until she very soon knew the name of every tool used. She had then followed the master's instructions, and when he had given her work in the hope of breaking her she had pouted heavily before knuckling down to the task given. Briar Rose quickly learnt the art of how to hold a saw properly, she had gone through lengths of timber sawing them down to the appropriate length until her own blisters cut her hands, and her back burnt with fury.

"Yo' watch yore step lass, or is it laddie? Yo' break tha' chair by slippin' jus' because yo' canna tek yore eyes off me I'll skin yo' alive mesel'." Stan frowned mockingly, the grin wide on his face, though his voice held a firmness as it did with all the lads in his charge.

Without a word Briar turned and stared at Ben. No grin was evident on his face; he just stood quietly watching her intently.

Again Briar pouted, Ben seemed even shorter than he was with his brother standing so close always shadowing Ben with his arrogant appearance. But then Ben relied heavily on his stick, his stick keeping his as straight as it possibly could. Pouting all the more Briar held her head high, she'd had just about enough of these brothers, flicking her black cap to one side, the same black cap as the lads wore she began to stomp away from the brothers, she had to load this chair onto the cart and then get another. When she did stumble over her own feet, only to gasp aloud as she only just managed to save the chair she had been carrying, Ben did smile with sheer amusement, his brown eyes lighting up as he did so only for the light to quickly vanish.

"Watch yore step yo' daf' bloody lass, God above yo' thinken yo' can do a lads work eh? Born in a bloody field yo' were lass. Once a field urchin, always a field urchin, no brain at all."

Chuckles escaped the lips of nearby workhouse lads, suppressed laughter that quickly fell silent, for not far behind Briar Rose the master had now appeared, his face thunderous at hearing Stan's colourful outburst. His whole intentions to punish this lad and make a spectacle out of him, but his attentions were very quickly turned to another. Briar Rose had never been able to take an insult and remain silent, and now this, other workhouse lads laughing at her, she was going to make no exception this time.

"Aye born in a field I were an' proud o' it." Placing the chair safely to the side of her she slowly strode over towards the Lawson brothers, her eyes transfixed on those of Stan. "Bu' I'll tell yo' this, better than bein' liken yo', born up an ugly tree before fallin' owt yore nest an' hittin' every branch on yore way down." Briar smiled cunningly at her own wit, especially seeing the flash of anger rising swiftly over Stan's face. Folding her arms she held her head high, her slate grey eyes sparked with defiance as she carried on "Wha's the matter ugly bird, canna find nowt lef' t' say owt tha' big beak o' yore's?" Folding her arms even tighter she laughed aloud. Her outburst was highly childish she knew that but even still it made her feel so much better.

"Yo' little skit, ge' back t' work an' fas' bu' before yo' do, I'll thinken I'll jus' tek the hide o' yo' mesel'." Stan's voice held clear authority, for he had seen the master approaching fast, and he needed to impress before he found himself at the end of a rod.

Briar Rose stood very still, her arms unfolded, her fists clenched tightly, her slate grey eyes now narrowed into slits at the sudden threat she felt bestowed on her by Stan. Kicking the chair onto one side she approached Stan herself, her slate grey eyes piercing through him. It didn't matter to Briar that Stan was three years her senior or that he towered over her. What did matter was her pride, and between the lot of them they had done a good job of trying to destroy it. She had thought she was going to work alongside them, but all she had been was a run around; she had learnt nothing at all.

"Yo' thinken yo' go' me beat? Well thinken again, I've done nowt bu' run yore errands since I go' 'ere, I've done nowt else and I've learnt even less." Clenching her fists even tighter she waited, for surely now he would go for her as she'd seen him do with the younger lads, and then when he did, she'd raise those fists of hers as she'd done before. But nothing. Taking a deep breath she cast her eyes towards Ben who seemed to look past her, then straight at her frowning as he did so, but not moving an inch.

"If I were yo' lass, I'd pick tha' chair up, ge' back t' work before I ge' heavy handed." Stan glared at the girl in front of him, his jaw tightening, his bright blue eyes fleeting past her. Still he could not get through to her, to warn her that the master was now standing right behind her, in fact every move he made she was taking as a challenge.

"Carry the bloody chair yoresel', I'm goin' in the workshop, an' I'm goin' t' do wha' I came t' do." In sheer defiance Briar snarled at both the Lawson brothers, unaware that now all eyes were on her. Every lad that worked in the mill, that had been carrying now stopped and stared in deathly silence, not even the playful song from the cheery sparrow dared make itself known. Briar hardly recognised the roar that escaped the master's lips, all she was aware of was that Stan had made to grab her, and she did exactly as she would have done out in the fields she dug her teeth deep into the nearest arm only releasing when the grasp was gone from her. In the confusion of voices, of bellows and gasps around her Briar Rose used her next defence her fists and lashed out in all fury spitting at her victims as she did so. Ben Lawson stood alone, his stick his only support, the pounding of his heart heavy inside his chest. He watched in pitiful silence as his brother Stan and the master, one on either side dragged the girl away, still kicking and screaming abuse, ready to fight the whole world. It would be the finish of this girl Ben was sure. The punishment she could receive for this even he feared to contemplate. If only he had had the chance, he was certain he would have been able to teach her anything that would have kept her mind occupied and away from trouble. But he hadn't been given the chance; every lad in the workshop had only been too pleased to load her with errands to make their own work load easier. Stan briefly stared over his shoulder at his brother sadly shaking his head, before taking an even firmer grip of the girl. There was nothing he could do to help her now, she had been her own worse enemy, and by the look in his master's eyes he himself made a silent pact. If this girl was cast back to them, he himself would promise he would make sure she was so occupied with learning the basic woodcraft skills, that she would undoubtedly calm down somewhat. Taking a deep breath to help himself calm down, he pushed the girl as gently as he could towards the steps that would lead her down the long corridor and to the master's study. As her slate grey eyes furiously glared up at him Stan frowned, showing as little emotion as he could. But how did he feel? Part of him wanted to skin her alive, while the urge was even stronger than ever to grab her and taste those pouting lips of hers. Did he really want to calm her down? In all honesty, no, he found her wild streak strangely fascinating, though he hoped she would have the sense to plead with the master herself to spare her. As if. All in all Stan felt as confused and frustrated about his feelings as this girl did about being industrious. Never had he felt this way before and to think that a mere field urchin that had belonged to the gang masters could actually make his blood boil one minute then make him want to grab her the next was enough to make his head spin. Right now Stan felt he could slap her himself.

"Fetch the mistress Lawson."

"Aye master."

Briar Rose stopped struggling as she watched Stan turn and leave her, in search of the mistress. She winched when the cruel fingers of her master dug deep into her upper arm, as he tightened his grip. The master glared down at the silvery blond haired girl. The girl dressed in thick corduroy trousers, woven shirt and patched black jacket, heavy working boots on her blistered feet. He didn't need to call for the mistress; he had taken this girl to his side of the workhouse to teach her a lesson, to work her hard enough to make her beg to be returned to the women's side. But this girl he firmly gripped hold of, had done none of this. He could punish her himself and make sure she did not step out of line again, but still he waited. Why? The reason was clear enough; he did not trust his judgement with this strange young girl. Her eyes so wild and the oddest of slate grey, but sharp eyes that dared to glare straight at him in defiance. She had a heart shaped face that could one day be pretty, and her pale skin that even in hard work looked silky and soft, her slender youth that radiated sheer promise and satisfaction. Never had he felt tempted to take before, he had never used his position to ensnare any girl, but this girl with her rare gift to challenge, and her promise of youth itself were becoming just too tempting. How easily it would be for him to take that wild streak and break it, so slowly and firmly, she'd never look at him the way she dared do now, ever again. Slowly as if in pain the master took a deep breath, his hand reaching to undo his top button, he needed to breathe a little more easily. As he turned the girl towards his study door and reached for the handle, he waited. Staring down deep into the slate grey eyes that glared deep into his, he waited for her to say something, beg for mercy, but nothing. "Stop girl, wait here for your mistress." As if his sudden decision not to take the girl into his study gave him the right to breath, he slightly relaxed his grip. He would not allow himself to be left alone with this particular girl. When he had decided her appropriate punishment with the mistress, he would make sure he worked her harder than he ever did his lads. But never would she beat him with those eyes of hers and never would he succumb to the brutish desire that had almost just taken his breath, or the ache deep within him, that certain wanting had threatened to destroy his judgement. He was a cruel hard master, he knew that, but he had never taken any girl against her will, and he hoped he never would.

Briar Rose glared up at her master, she saw him undo his top button, and could almost hear the turmoil he was fighting inside. His chest had heaved visibly from some unseen exertion, and as he ran his tongue over his top lip, his cold brown eyes had not left her for a single second. She had lowered her eyes suddenly to the floor and shuddered, when she had felt his grip on her arm ease, his fingers almost gently running down her arm only to grip hold of her wrist.

"I'm sorry master, it wunna 'appen again." Briar spoke, her words shaky as they spluttered from her lips. How angry she felt with herself, she had never pleaded in her life or begged for mercy. Closing her eyes tightly she shuddered violently as she remembered. Oh yes she had once begged and pleaded the day the gang master had brutally taken her childhood from her. As she stared up at her master once more she could feel the same danger with this master, his breathing was heavy, he had wiped the sudden sweat from his brow, and she had noticed his hardness when she had lowered her eyes. As the mistress stormed down the corridor, a thick cane in her hand Briar Rose's relief was evident, the smirk on her pretty heart shaped

face surprised both her master and mistress, but anger quickly found its place when Briar Rose closed her eyes, her hands clenched together as she loudly declared.
"Thank God fur the old bat."

chapter five

Heaving until her stomach ached; Briar Rose picked up the last of the chamber pots and crossed the yard making her way towards the old log sheds, emptying the nightly contents into the squalid stinking cesspits. But nothing could stop her from retching up the acid from the pits of her stomach leaving its acrid taste in her mouth as she struggled to stop heaving once more. Dawn had hardly broken, but here she was her first job of the day, not just to empty the men's chamber pots but to clear out the earth closets. Large boxes of dry soil that were used by the more able bodied men, toilets of human waste left to eventually be used as fertiliser, natural elements that had to be spread over the vegetable gardens that the women attended. Briar stopped just for a moment and took a deep breath, wiping her weary brow on her sleeve. At least she was spared from facing the women, for seeing her dressed as a boy, her heavy boots too large for her feet, her silvery blond hair hidden by her cap, and her arms covered in human filth, would indeed make her a complete laughing stock. To have watched her struggle with the stinking boxes and have to spread the contents would have filled the garden with a fountain of riotous laughter, something Briar Rose could not even contemplate. "Dear God." Briar gasped to herself, when she did get sent back to the women's side her life would become even more unbearable, for she had witnessed even at a distance the sheer look of horror when one of the women had seen her dressed as if she was a boy. With the earth closets done, Briar swiftly made her way back across the yard and towards the side door that would lead her down the long whitewashed corridor and towards the narrow latched door that took her down the grey cold steps and into the main of the cellar, and her 'confinement'. It wasn't a confinement as such for the door was never bolted on her, and she had the freedom of the whole cellar. Often she would talk to the young lads that had been locked down there, she would peer through the cracks of their bolted cellar doors and learn why and who had been sent down there for punishment. But for Briar, the cellar was the only part of the workhouse that the master could place her safely, especially at night time, for it kept her away from the lads. There was no chance of any prying eyes resting upon her down here; she was out of reach of any temptation.

Reaching for her clean undergarments, Briar sighed with relief. At last she was washed and clean after the morning muck out, and now she could quietly relish one simple comfort, her plain cotton undergarments so soft and clean against her skin. So carefully she did up the three tiny bows of her camisole to subtly cover her small breasts, but revealing her femininity so beautifully. Next Briar reached for her grey flannel shirt and shuddered, how the material made her skin itch, rolling up her sleeves so she could see her hands she swiftly did up each dark button. Grabbing the black corduroy trousers that lay on her make shift bed and the black thick patched socks she dressed as fast as possible, nothing pleased her as her delicate skin was slowly being hidden from view, and lastly, the one thing she hated most of all…her footwear. Hobnailed boots at least two sizes too big that never failed to make her look completely clumsy and large footed. Never would she ever complain again about wearing worsted stockings or woven slippers. Lastly she took her black cap, pulled her hair up and hid it from sight as she tipped the cap slightly from one side of her head. Nobody who didn't know about her punishment here would have even noticed she was a girl. She looked the same as all the other lads, the size of her shirt and her trousers being too baggy made a good job of hiding her youthful figure from view.

"Wondered where yo' were lass, theer's a pile o' wood over theer. Every length needs sawin' in half, then sandin' down…"

"Aye I know so smooth tha' when the master comes an' runs his finger over it theer's nod a splinter in sigh'." Briar paused as Stan Lawson's bright blue eyes locked tightly with hers. "Ask me, the master deserves more than a splinter."

"Aye well I wunna askin' yo' nowt lass. Now yo' do as I ask. If the master ge's any splinters from any piece yo' do I'll skin yo' alive wi' it."

Briar Rose held her head high in defiance, a pout heavy on her lips, the spark of unspoken anger immediate to reflect in her slate grey eyes. But she very simply answered. "Aye Mister Lawson…sir…I'll mek sure it's so smooth 'e can wipe 'is bloody arse on it."

Chuckles from nearby lads soon ceased when Stan glanced their way. But he didn't blame them, for he too had to quickly clear his throat. "Work lass."

Just for a fleeting moment Briar Rose looked like she may even smile at him, her eyes softened towards him, their fury gone. As she stared up at him, his bright shock of red hair even more startling against his black clothes, she also noticed that his bright blue eyes that always appeared so angry with her, sparked with a sudden mischief, that of a friendly kind. She noticed how his freckles covered his slightly turned up nose, and now by the way she was probably staring at him his wide shaped mouth held a broad grin.

"I'll nod ask again lass."

"Hhmph." With a quick turn of her head Briar twisted around and made her way over to the far corner, and the pile of wood she would have to contend with. She knew better than to keep arguing with Stan that was if she wanted any supper at all. "No splinters, hhmph." Muttering under her breath Briar took the first piece of wood and set to work. She knew exactly what she would like to do with it, but she also knew that if this wood was not sanded down properly the master would come down on Stan Lawson like a ton of bricks and then her. The thought made her shudder the last episode had been enough, even she knew in her wildest of moments not to step on his feet again. Stan looked on in keen interest. This girl was a worker no doubt about that and one with spirit. After he had helped drag her that day and then left her to the mercy of their master and mistress he had not expected to see her in these workshops again, or hear her voice her opinion quite so openly as she still did. But here she was, attacking the task in front of her with a vengeance, and she'd already done more than her fair share. Stan nodded in silent agreement. He too had plans to leave here, quite what too he did not yet know but the skill he was learning here, and being foreman would surely account for something? When he found what it was he was looking for he would ask Briar Rose if she wanted to go with him. Her attitude towards work would be an asset, but for now, he'd keep his promise to himself and keep her as busy as possible, and hopefully out of trouble.

Ben Lawson also watched closely with interest, he noticed how quick she accomplished any task, and how she only had to be shown once before she knuckled down and got on with it. He half smirked as he watched her struggle to keep the wood straight, before having to get up onto the work bench and actually kneeling on it to hold it there, her hobnailed boots clumsily knocking her tools onto the floor as she did so. Even in those drab boys clothes, with the black cap covering her silvery blond hair from view, Ben knew her every facial contour, her soft angel like features as they blossomed in her heart shaped face. He knew her mood by the look in those slate grey eyes of hers, how she pouted those lips when agitated, and how her face threatened to burst into laughter when mischief did find its way into the workshop. Her over large black flannel shirt hid her figure from sight, but Ben could tell just how exquisite this girl would one day become. He'd never seen her qualities in any boys face, and he'd never seen the likes of them in any lass. To him she was as pretty as the early morning sunrise, and if there was anything he could do to keep her out of harms reach he would do so. In fact he'd ask her himself to help him with various tasks, maybe then that would keep her curious mind out of trouble. Ben shuddered…trouble…to hear the sounds of what had gone on in the masters study the last time, well it was something he didn't want to hear the likes of again. "When yore through theer miss, would yo' liken t' 'elp smooth down the edges o' this? Needs a gentle hand mind."

As Briar looked up from her work, a spark of interest lighting up her slate grey eyes, Ben grinned. "Aye I would."

"And can yo' keep a gentle steady hand?"

Briar watched as Ben proudly pointed to his work, his brown eyes warm with laughter, so unlike his brothers bright blue eyes that never missed a trick. Briar liked Ben's face, his nose was slightly up turned and not covered with freckles like Stan's, there was also a far softer edge to Ben. What Briar Rose liked even more was the fact Ben's hair was not quite the vibrant red of his brothers. She took a deep breath then smiled in response; her slate grey eyes alight with life. She had watched Ben on the sly as he had skilfully drawn, then had turned what looked like a tedious sketch into a child's dolls house, an extravagant toy made for some child that belonged to the gentry, for no poor family would be able to afford this. Briar had secretly peeped up from her own work and had watched in awe as each tiny room had been made, with fragile opening doors and then finally a roof that Ben had engraved a pattern on. Of course she would help sand down the delicate pieces of furniture that would be placed in each room; she couldn't wait to take a closer look. Ever since she had held that tiny wooden duck in her hands, she had known from that moment on that she could learn something from Ben Lawson. Oh he wasn't very old, hardly a year older than herself, but with an extraordinary talent.

"I'd love t' 'elp an' I'll keep a steady 'and, I promise."

Ben nodded his smile widening. God she was pretty when she smiled.

"Back t' work lass." Stan's firm command stopped the spark of interest that had warmly shone between the two young workers. Stan watched her a moment longer then turned around to make sure everybody else was working to their full ability. He had agreed with Ben when they'd talked together late at night and had discussed in length how to keep Briar occupied. But, he had not quite been ready for her appreciative response, or the smile that she had willingly just given to his younger brother. A smile she had never even hinted towards him. Looking back towards his brother Stan frowned, Ben had enormous obstacles to face, even with his unusual talent, for who would employ a cripple at the end of the day, and that was exactly what Ben was, a cripple, and in future years nobody could guarantee his health. Stan was so much taller than Ben, which was only down to Ben's childhood polio, but Ben had strength in his arms, maybe even more so than other lads of his own age, and Ben also had the determination that would somehow make sure he succeeded in his own small corner of the world. One day Stan sincerely hoped that Ben would find his own place in life, one that would not see his crippled leg as a big issue. Stan was pleased that his brother did have the sheer guts, and the determination to make the very best of what he could, but it didn't stop the flutter that was turning his stomach into knots. For the first time in his life Stan knew what it was like to feel the bitter sharp pang of jealousy towards his younger brother, for he could clearly see the deep infatuation Ben had for this girl, and now with the radiant smile she had just given him it had only added fuel to the burning fire. Biting down hard on his bottom lip, Stan stood tall, his lean frame tense. He still had the urge to take hold of the girl and press his lips down hard onto her pouting ones, and just hold her close to him for a while, she was a strange interesting creature, but however hard he tried to be pleasant to her, she somehow made him want to suddenly strike her. Stan took a deep breath, hold her…kiss her…strike her. He hadn't felt so mixed up in his whole life. Day after day Briar Rose worked until she felt her world would crumble before her. Every day she saw to the earth closets, the chamber pots, she set the tables, washed up the dishes, then cut wood, sanded it down and swept the floors. She sharpened chisels, carried out finished work to waiting carts and did any tedious duty asked of her. She ran every errand until she could hardly stand up, or remember what day it was, or even if she had washed her hands before her evening meal. At the best of times she could hardly be bothered to say grace as she sat alone at a small table up the far corner of the dining hall, or even to pick up her spoon and feed herself the offerings of barley soup and potato hash. What she did enjoy was the small luxury of a tin mug of hot mushed tea, black tea helped to ease her aching bones, and lull her senses into a gentle rhythm that promised sleep was just around the corner. It was at these times that she closed her eyes at the table only to find herself very rudely brought back to reality as the master's rod found her knuckles. As time wore on the master could see that the girl would not be broken, she had a spirit like he had never witnessed before, a spirit that grinded him, for any other natural lass would have keeled over in the first couple of days and crumpled into a heap. But not this girl. So determined he was to see her on her knees and plead with him to allow her to go back to the women's side of the workhouse, that he placed even more work upon her weary shoulders. He made frequent visits to the workshop, and complained loudly that the girl was not working fast enough, or well enough, causing a major strain on all who worked there. Each lad had his own work to finish, and if the girl was lagging in some way it would hold all of them back, and then the punishment would be hard. Tempers began to flair among the lads until Briar pushed herself even harder, making herself nauseous under the strain, and then finally making silly mistakes because of her tiredness.

"Dunna panic lass, yore workin' 'as 'ard as anyone in 'ere." Stan had kindly taken Briar to one side, for he had seen the sheer panic welling up inside the girl, and the master was looking for her to fail.

Briar Rose had simply nodded, but when the master put even more work on her at the end of that week, she knew she was beat; she just could not finish it. Every lad in the workshop knew that Briar had not finished her tasks, and though Stan had tried to ease the load himself, he too had to stop quickly when the bellow of the master down the corridor told them all that he was on his way for inspection. Every lad was worried that his own work would not make the grade that they soon forgot about the girl, each one in a hurry to make sure his part of the bench was clear, and no tools were left hanging around. For the first time since her last beating Briar stood alongside the rest of the lads and waited, each one of them forming a pitiful row of expectancy, each one keeping their head bowed scared that the master would hold up their piece of work and bellow for the offender to step forward. Pacing up and down the work benches the master took great delight in poking and prodding the work produced, his fingers running along every edge waiting for a splinter to dare show itself. With a smirk of satisfaction he watched each lad squirm as he scrutinised his work for mistakes, and if there was any, well that offender would quickly come to know that mistakes in his workhouse were inexcusable, they meant a loss of money. There were many men this side of the workhouse; the master prided himself on the skill of his blacksmiths, his whitewashers, and young tailors. But every man or boy that worked there was counted; each piece of work was scored on his card, and work not done properly meant wasted time, materials and money. "Edwards, this rung is shorter than the rest." Standing still the master faced the lad in question, a gleam of satisfaction lighting up his sharp brown eyes when the boy flustered. Slowly and deliberately to frighten the boy more the master took hold of a wooden rule and measured the wooden rung in question. Sure enough it proved to be a fraction too short. "Hands Boy." Every lad in the room gasped, their bodies tense as the master took great delight in punishing his trembling victim, before slowly walking onto the next lad's piece of work. For an age the master eyed over Ben

Lawson's dolls house, his scrutinising eyes searching every corner for a mistake, his fingers running over the tiny pieces of furniture hoping that maybe there would be a chance here to punish this lad also. But he had never been given that pleasure, for this lad's workmanship was exquisite and never had he found a fault. Ben gulped slouching hard onto his stick for support. He had never worried about his work, but he knew that he had given certain pieces to Briar to sand down, and he just hoped that she had done a thorough job. He was certain that she had for he had quickly checked himself, but even still it wasn't enough to stop the butterflies that were turning his stomach upside down.

The master gently placed the pieces of dolls furniture down, his eyes resting on the dolls house once more. Never had a boy or man in the whole time he had been master in this dratted workhouse shown such great talent as young Ben Lawson. His work was excellent, and what was more he had taken orders for more. This lad would make him a fair profit. Turning to face Ben the master simply nodded his approval and moved on.

"Whose work is this?" Poking the sanded timber lengths with the cane he held so tightly he turned and spoke sharply to Stan.

"The lasses master."

"So I see." Slowly and deliberately he turned each piece before running his fingers along the edges. No splinters. Interesting. Picking up each piece he cast his eyes down the lengths and to the ends. "They are not rounded off properly, none of them are." Frowning he placed them back down. "Have I not made it plain that each end is to be slightly rounded so as not to leave a raw corner, I can plainly see a raw corner on every single piece!"

"Aye master."

Stan answered confidently.

"Did you not then tell the girl?"

Waiting for a moment Stan sighed then answered quietly, "Aye master."

Silence. First the master cast his eyes over the girl, there she stood along side the other lads, she was dressed as one of them and with her hair hidden from his view she looked like one of them. He had insisted she dressed as a lad whilst in his care, for it made it far easier for him to deal with her, and he had told her he would make no exceptions on her behalf. Stan slowly shook his head as he too glanced the girl's way. He knew she had worked harder than most of the lads there, but the master was obviously looking for somebody to come down hard upon, and that somebody was the girl. Ben gave her a quick glance but turned away. He could see the light had gone from those slate grey eyes of hers. The fierce streak was there once more, the fiery glow that was threatening all to keep away from her, daring those in question not to get too close.

The master also sensed this, for he had pulled himself even taller, his shoulders right back, and the stance he held meant business. "Come here girl and take a closer look at your slovenly work. Briar Rose stood perfectly still, her lips already turning into a heavy pout. "I said step forward." The masters voice rose, but still the girl stood, her slate grey eyes piercing to look at. Had this girl no fear at all? Briar Rose could hear his orders, she could see Stan behind the masters back quietly urging her to step forward, and she felt Ben's hand reach out gently pushing her in the pit of her back. Both the Lawson brothers and every other lad in the workshop knew that it was best if the girl did as she was bid. Only Briar could not move, her knees felt as if they had locked in place, and her feet were firmly fixed to the floor. Her hands fidgeted wildly, they were so clammy, that her own fingers felt as if they were somebody else's, not hers. When she tried to swallow, she felt she would choke, how dry her throat was, how she needed a ladle of water, if only she could get out into the yard, but then the master's voice bellowed, slicing her heart in two. Every lad in the workshop held his breath, a certain fear filling them with dread, even though they knew it was not them in question. "Are you completely stupid girl? Can you not understand anything anybody tells you?" Still the girl stood, so very rigid, the pout heavy on her lips. So tightly the master gripped the cane in his hand that his knuckles gleamed a stony whiteness. Not taking his eyes of the slate grey eyes that pierced straight through him he slowly reached up and undid his top shirt button. His chest was heaving with built up frustration, he could feel the prickly rash creep up his neck towards his face, turning him crimson, and his temper was ready to explode. As his powerful voice visibly shook every lad in the workshop, his voice bounced from the walls and echoed way down the long whitewashed corridors. Briar Rose tried but found she had also lost her voice, she could not even mutter, but with every choked sob that filled her throat as she tried, she struggled relentlessly against the tightening that gripped her chest, and the pounding that hurt deep inside her head making her so very hot and dizzy. With each ferocious strike that landed across her hands bruising her flesh even further she only heard her master's cruel words against her. His never ending barrage of questions.

Why hadn't she gone to the workhouse chapel with the others?

Why did she not listen or understand simple instruction? Did she not understand why she was punished so often? On and on he went. Briar still could not answer, how could she? She'd been forced to work hours when everyone else did go to chapel, she had done her best to prove her worth, and so no, the answer had to be no. She did not understand her punishment. She had missed so many meals, her milk and meat allowance had been stopped regularly, and her whole body had ached with constant tiredness, and now pain.

"Usefulness, Virtue and Industry, repeat it girl until you understand what you are here for…did you hear me?" Still no response except stifled chokes and sobs that only incensed him further. Throwing his cane to one side he grabbed the girl by the shoulders shaking her roughly, his fingers digging deep into her flesh until she could clearly be heard gasping for breathe. As her black cap fell from her head allowing her waist length silvery blond hair to drape over her shoulders and down her back the master released his grip and stepped backwards. "Get out of my sight."

Nobody moved, not even Briar as she struggled to stop the uneasy feeling that was cheerfully turning her world into a spinning turmoil. She felt so very sick, she so badly needed that water, and the air, and she just had to get out of this workshop and away from the smell of freshly cut wood and drifting sawdust.

"Lawson don't just stand there, get that girl out of my sight."

Both brothers moved instantly, but it was Ben who was first to touch Briar's hand, his voice soft as he spoke. "Hold on miss, I'll 'elp yo', hold ont' me now."

Briar tearfully turned her face to the voice she knew so well, an ocean of understanding in Ben's warm brown eyes, a look that held deep concern.

"Come on miss." On and on Ben tried to coax the girl to walk with him, but he did not know that Briar's whole world was spinning, he could only see what looked to be a terrified girl, who had been struck dumb by the cruel treatment inflicted upon her.

As Briar took her first step away from the master, she felt her whole life collapse around her, leaving her completely helpless, as darkness clouded her vision and voices turned to long distance echoes, Briar lay lifeless among the drifting sawdust her long silvery blond hair hiding her pale face from view. It was Stan that was quick to spring into action, pushing Ben almost roughly to one side. "Yo' canna manage now lad, leave 'er t' me." Not waiting, Stan bent down and with no trouble picked up the still limp form of Briar Rose. So still she lay in his arms completely unaware of the bright blue eyes that now slowly gazed over her sleeping slender figure. Turning back Stan gave one order much to the delight of his master. "Back t' work lads, theer's thin's t' be pu' righ' before anybodys fed t' nigh'."

Not a murmur escaped their lips, for to do so would bring them the same harsh punishment that had caused the girl to faint. Ben locked eyes with his elder brother, there was no need for him to speak for his eyes spoke for him. Ben could have managed the girl given the chance. His arms were strong, and his back knew only too well how to carry enormous strain, and the girl would have been no strain to him. But his brother had found fit to push him aside, and why? Because he had his eye on the girl himself or because he simply considered him unable? Ben glared down at his crippled leg, why should it have been him struck down with childhood polio? It had left his one leg noticeably shorter than the other one, but he had tried so very hard to rectify it. Ben had spent hours by candle light way into the night building up the bottom of his boot with a wooden sole he had carved himself. It had made a difference; at least to him it had made a difference, for though he still relied on his stick, his hobble was now more of a bad limp. Again Ben glared at his bother, his feelings deeply hurt, for all Stan saw was what so many other lads and men saw, and that was the damn walking stick. For the first time in his life Ben felt a deep sense of resentment for his brother an emotion he would have argued was impossible, but for Stan to have stepped in with the girl and pushed him aside had near enough shouted out to Ben that Stan also saw him as the cripple he had become so used to being. As Stan turned and left the workshop with the girl in his arms, he felt no sense of elation, he felt a stone had settled deep in his heart and would not move. He had seen the hurt in Ben's eyes and that was something he had never meant to do. He was as proud of Ben as a father would have been, but where his work and fight to be independent was concerned. When the girl came into it Stan felt something towards Ben he would have also thought was impossible, a feeling that tightened his chest and took his reason away, and a feeling that troubled him greatly. Jealousy. Hastening his step Stan followed the long corridor, and then took a sharp right turn. Here he opened the door and carefully walked down the grey stone steps that would lead him to the confinement cells, and to the small room that Briar had been given. So gently he lay the girl down on the makeshift bed, then stood and watched her sleep. She had stirred in his arms, but he had spoken softly telling her to rest now, her work was over for the day. It had worked, and Briar Rose, so very fatigued had given up the fight to wake, her tired aching body welcoming sleep. How peaceful she looked, how very angelic. Stan gazed down at her slim frame, her long silvery blond hair as it lay over her shoulders, resting on her arms. How very sweet her heart shaped face appeared, so very innocent. He hadn't noticed the perfect bone structure before, but now he could see how high her cheekbones were, her nose small and just slightly turned up, and to think that she had remarked about his nose. Stan grinned as he remembered some of her wild remarks, and how those lips of hers pouted so often, but lips that could smile as radiantly as they had at Ben. How he'd longed to taste them, to force his mouth onto hers and make her want him back. And here she was just inches from him, he could have her if he wanted, but the strong urge he'd felt so many times before had gone as he looked down at her, she was like a sleeping angel. Again he grinned. Sleeping wild cat more like. Peering over his shoulder he listened, not a sound, just the gentle breathing of the girl who had fainted, but who now lay sleeping oblivious to where she was or how she had got there. Once more Stan's eyes roamed over her slender frame. She hardly looked attractive in the clothes she had on, but that hair of hers, so very clean and long. Gently Stan reached out and touched, allowing the strands of silvery blond hair to slip through his fingers, and then he touched her face, her heart shaped face. Her skin was as smooth as he had imagined, as soft as a rose petal, as new and innocent as the morning bird song. Pulling his hand away suddenly, Stan stood up and turned to leave, he felt uncomfortable and very uneasy. Not with the girl, but with himself. The feel of her delicate skin had just as good as stung him for he was burning inside, his chest pounding and ready to burst wide open. His lips were dry with sudden want, and the fearful ache in his groin warned him to clear off, to get out before it was too late. Reaching for the door handle Stan was ready to leave, but he turned just once more to look, he wanted just one more time to see her so very peaceful looking, like a serene angel. "Poor lass, yo' looken worn owt, an' righ' now a real sweet heart." Stan whispered, he must leave, go right now and get back to the workshop. But instead he very slowly walked back towards the bed. For a long moment that seemed frozen in time Stan sat and stared, his fingers softly running over the contours of her face until they rested on her lips that expressed an immediate pout even in sleep. Stan grinned, and then knelt down very gently kissing the lips that had teased him since the day she had come here. Stan kissed her closed eyes, her cheeks, her forehead; he had not imagined it to be this way. He had only ever wanted to force his mouth to hers, but now he wanted to touch her softness, not frighten it away, and he wanted to taste her innocent sweet youth. When Briar did begin to stir Stan moved closer, then as gently as he could he laid himself over her body, his mouth searching hers just a little bit more eagerly. Briar found it hard to breath, she was so very tired and her head still pounded, her hands were stinging her frightfully, why? Then she remembered the master and his beating, and she could remember faint soft gentle voices. But where was she? Was night upon her and her body so very tired that she had trouble breathing, or even moving? Or was somebody trying to suffocate her? Somebody was. With the sudden realisation and the stark reality that somebody was laying on top of her holding her down and pushing against her hard Briar herself began to push, her slate grey eyes now wide awake, her senses completely alert. Her own moans of sudden distress echoed against the cold walls of her incarceration, her hands clenched into fists ready to fight her assailant to the end, only her own cry stole from her any strength she had left, and rendered her helpless. It was already to late for Briar to fight, the rhythmical thrusts that pushed hard between her legs were burning the pits of her stomach causing her to cry pitifully as Stan Lawson thrust himself just a bit harder, his own body on fire as he wilfully took the girl for himself. "Ssh lass, dunna fre', ssh, I wunna hur' yo', jus' lay still." Softly Stan spoke, his bright blue eyes warm with the affection he felt for this girl. "Dunna cry no more lass, yore mi girl now, it has t' happen sometime, aye yore mi girl now." Gently to begin with Stan lowered his mouth to hers, her tears salty on his tongue. As Briar tried to wriggle free, his mouth more forcefully bruised her lips. But Stan had meant what he had said. He did care about her and now that she was his girl he would let nobody change that, and he would make sure nobody hurt her again, including the master. Wrapping his arms tightly around her pulling her even closer to him Stan pushed himself deeper into her until he felt his whole soul explode within her, causing him to tremble from his own exertion, his sweat dripping from his brow, his chest pounding heavily from his own release of all frustration. Briar Rose lay rigid, her body shaking violently from sorrow, every pore she could breath from cried for her, but offered her no consolement. Twice this had happened to her, once by her cruel gang master, and now by a workhouse boy almost four years her senior, but a lad who had been put in charge of her, somebody who should have known better. Briar closed her eyes tightly in an effort to block out the world, she had been used once more, defiled for another's pleasure, and she had nowhere else to go. Or had she? As she lay so very still, with nothing else to lose in the world, something inside her screamed, forcing her to listen, to take a step forward, a step that would eventually take her out of this place, and that first step was to listen to Stan Lawson's words. Briar opened her eyes, her slate grey eyes penetrating sharply through the bright blue eyes that stared longingly into hers, even in her deep distress she could see the sudden warmth there for her, and she could hear the gentle softness in his voice. He was saying she was his girl, that he also had plans to leave here and that he wanted to take her with him. Would she go? Briar wanted only to raise her knee and cause him as much pain as he had caused her, she wanted to scream from the highest window of the workhouse that she would never go with him, she hated him, and oh how she hated him. But again a voice deep within her stopped her, telling her to wait, the door of any youth she had left had now firmly slammed shut on her, but a cold air was telling her to push forward, to listen on and not scream as she so wanted. As the gentle rain of kisses teased her trembling lips she shakily gave her answer. "I'll come wi' yo'."

"So yore mi girl now then lass?"

"Aye Stan…I'm yore girl." Again Briar Rose closed her eyes, she could hardly believe her own ears, but for now she had nothing else to lose. Stan smiled as he gazed down at the girl beneath him. He hadn't planned it this way at all, he had only ever wanted to forcefully kiss her, but he had wanted her to want him back. Briar was young, only fourteen, but he had no problem with her age, it could be a good thing she was so young, for she would settle with him much quicker he was sure of that. Affectionately he enfolded his arms around her; cradling her safe to him he spoke. "No more cryin' then lass, it'll be fine yo'll see." Once more he pulled her warm slender frame towards him, before pushing her legs apart, giving him the freedom to move more when the time was right. When he showered her with promises of the future, and sought her trembling lips that pouted the very second he found them, Stan chuckled softly and then he took her for himself once more. Briar didn't struggle, she no longer cared, what was the use? For he would take her anyway. The best she could do was to close her eyes and do her best to relax under the firmness of his body, even though her mind was in complete turmoil, and her senses reeled for the attack that invaded her very soul once more, taking another part of her, her body just used for the gratification of men. Yes she would rise above this; she would leave here with him when he left, for out there with him there might be a way open for her. He could prove himself to lead others, he would be useful somewhere, work would be open to him, and if she was with him, well she might be lucky enough to land herself as somebody's maid, where she could spend her nights safely locked in her own quarters. As Briar opened her eyes and stared blankly at the ceiling, the threat of tears began to shake her world once more. Was she only ever doomed to be with a man she hated? Why the hell did the thought of Ben Lawson creep through her mind now? Why was she shaking so violently now when she did think of him? Briar felt her heart would simply break as her first sobs choked her. But then she knew, she had seen a real warmth and kindness behind Ben Lawson's soft brown eyes, and something told her that he would not have hurt her, he would never have taken advantage of her the way Stan had, and was now. No, Ben would make twice the man his elder brother could ever become. As the hard rhythmical thrusts began to burn the pits of her stomach once more Briar began to sob even harder, she had never ever wanted to be used by a man like this again. Even the soft words that Stan tried to offer failed to make any difference for Briar Rose only sobbed even more pitifully, the image of Ben Lawson in her minds eye making what was happening to her so much harder to bear, destroying her world even further.

chapter six

As the heat from the summer sun turned the courtyard of the workhouse into a sundrenched blessing, the work doubled. June had remained dry, and July had been particualry good to them. August burst forth with the wealth of harvest from the workshop gardens, vegetable plots by the score, hidden at the far side of the womens fence were now left daily in small carts waiting for the younger lads. These lads had been handpicked by the master himself, lads that had great lack of any skill. It was their job to pull the carts to the main yard, wash them under the pumps, then to place them on large wired trays to dry, where they would then be weighed, ready for sale to the surrounding community of Crosshouses and nearby village of Berrington. What wasn't considered to be at its best was sent back to the women's side and down to the kitchens to turn into soups and stews.

"Put your back into it, there's more customers waiting. You cause me to lose money by wasting time; I'll beat you until you beg me to stop." The cruel voice of the master rang out over the heads of the lads in his care as they struggled under the heavy loads of the carts, but every solemn pale face knew that they not only worked to feed themselves, but the whole local community. More than that they also knew that the master prided himself on the fresh produce harvested there, and God help any man, woman, or child who forgot that. Every part of the Crosshouses Workhouse moaned or grinded under it's own unique task, from the sound of the hoe, to the smell of the iron as it was moulded into the shape of a horses shoe, and the whirr of cotton winders, as cloth was laid out ready for tailoring.

Every pair of trousers that was ordered, every turnip, or tomato, had it's price, every cart wheel, or horse shoe, every piece of furniture from the mill had a buyer waiting, a demand to be met, and on time. If it was not, it would be the fault of the lads, the men, the women or girls and each one would not know the mercy of escaping punishment however young they may be, or however brutal the master or mistress felt fit. Regularly the cry from a child would ring out from the inside, or echo against the whitewashed walls as the sharpness of a cane found young flesh. But once a child reached seventeen he or she was classed as an adult and punishment could often mean flogging, or if the act had been severe enough, the individual would be taken from the workhouse to face court and possible imprisonment. Whatever the age, meat and sugar allowances were often stopped, and milk was snatched from the hands of a tearful infant who hadn't been able to keep the rule of silence. "Usefulness, Virtue and Industry, remember those very words." Were daily bellowed upon the ears of every person who had walked under the archway of tears as they had entered the workhouse.

"Edwards, Jones and Brown, unload that cart, then on the double for the next. Drop one vegetable, I'll drop your meat allowance for one whole week." The master stood yelling his sharp brown eyes following each youngster as they hurriedly set upon unloading the cart. "Not you girl, get back to the mill, report to Lawson, there's enough work to keep you there until dusk." Sharply he addressed the girl, his face stern as he encountered the look of hatred behind her slate grey eyes. "If it's not finished, you miss out on supper for one week, understand?"

Briar Rose took a deep breath, the well of hatred deep within her heart, but when she spoke her voice was so very calm. "Aye master, I understand…perfectly." Offering her most grimacing of smiles, that immediately changed to a pout, Briar held her head high and marched straight back towards the mill, a clear stamp in her step. She could almost imagine his face as she left him, his eyes wide, and his mouth gaping open at her sheer rudeness. As a genuine smile lit up her eyes with amusement, Briar actually had the nerve to giggle, not caring who heard her, but she quickly had the sense to muffle her giggles in her hand, for he wouldn't think twice about using that cane of his, she already knew that.

"So cheerful t' see me then lass?"

"No, cheerful t' watch tha' smug look fall from the master's face, tha's all."

Briar's moment of happiness was gone as she stood face to face with Stan Lawson.

"Bes' ge' t' work then lass, theer's a pile over theer t' be sorted, the pieces wi' less knots in need t' be teken t' Ben. The res', smooth them down an' tek them t' Jacobs fur wheelin'." Stan watched as she eagerly turned her back on him to get on with the task ahead. "No' too quick lass, when tha's done Ben 'as some work fur yo'. When tha's done report t' me." He waited, but no answer. "Yo' 'ear me lass?"

"Aye, loud an' clear." Briar turned her face and pouted heavily, her slate grey eyes piercing as she was met with that wide grin of Stan's that annoyed her so. Stan's eyes sparkled with mischief at her attitude, there was just no telling what this girl would do or say next, and that alone caused a curious excitement within him, and kept his interest in her alight. He hadn't expected the master to keep her there all this time, but he had suspected that the master had also noticed just what a worthwhile worker this girl was. Though of course the master would never admit to that, in fact it had been the one reason to make her work even harder. Stan couldn't help the pleasure he felt by it all, for now he knew every move the girl made, and her very presence brightened up his existence, for now she was his girl, even if she was a temperamental spitfire. Behind his work bench, his latest creation of a dolls house well under way, Ben Lawson watched his brother closely. He didn't like the weird atmosphere he sensed between them, and he couldn't tell if he was right or not. All he knew was that the day Stan had carried the girl away; he had been an unnaturally long time. Ever since he had watched his brother and the way his eyes had followed Briar around, almost as a cat would a bird. Only he had seen a different kind of look behind his brother's bright blue eyes, one he recognised to be that of pure sensual lust. He had seen Stan almost playfully reach out to touch Briar, and he had noticed just how fast Briar had moved away. Ben had also seen Briar's attitude change towards Stan, she was still just as rude, and sometimes highly challenging to all in sight, but it was the times he had caught Stan speaking with her privately. For these times, it was clear that Briar had agreed with something he had said, for the fight had clearly gone from her, and her slate grey eyes that could pierce so fiercely, seemed so very distant and strangely sad. Ben wished the master would send the girl back with the women, even if it meant not seeing her every day, or having her so close, but exactly why he wanted her out of sight was hard for Ben to put his finger on. It was almost as if she was in danger around his brother, and that had to be crazy...didn't it?

"Yo' alrigh' our Ben?"

"Aye Stan. Fine, jus'fine." Ben forced a smile as his brother spoke, but his usually warm brown eyes remained as distant as Briar's had been. He should not feel this way, for Stan was his brother, his only kin, and Stan had always been around to help him in the past. In fact there had been times in his life that he would never have managed without him, but as far as the girl went, things were suddenly so very different, for he had never felt quite like this before. He longed for the first light of morning, just to see her heart shaped angelic face, to watch her with interest, and to feel the pound of his own heart when she walked into the room only to feel the dread that flooded his soul when she dared to put a foot wrong or speak out of place which she often did. He had watched Stan work her hard, where he had tried to shelter her, to make things easier, he had given her more interesting tasks that had not pulled on her back, and he was sure she had enjoyed them. He had stood over her, his stick giving him the support he so needed, as he had eagerly tried to explain the different joints in the dolls house and why supporting rafters in his delicate dolls house frames was so important. He had helped to show her the skill of smoothing wood down properly, and not leaving rough edges. "When yo' 'ave finished theer lass, yo' wanna 'elp me? I'm startin' the roof today an' I can teach yo' wha' rafters are for." He waited, but not for long.

"Aye Ben, I would, I'd liken that" Briar answered honestly, her slate grey eyes alight with her smile. There was nothing else she would rather do.

It was enough for Ben, his own smile genuine with affection. There was something he would ask her, something he had been longing too ask and had up until now pushed it to one side. But it couldn't wait much longer; he needed an answer from her. Ben had had an offer, one that was being sorted out at this very moment while he sat here. He had heard whispers that there were other positions available, and he had even had the nod from one very formidable customer. Now he needed to know if Briar Rose would be interested. Would she be interested enough to go with him and leave this place behind? If the answer was yes, then he needed to know just one more thing. Would she be willing to go as his girl, to put her faith and trust in him, to commit? Or, would his crippled short leg repulse her enough to turn her away? Ben had wanted to ask so many times, but he feared rejection the type that only a girl like Briar could give, for if she did, he would know that she considered him less of a man because of his crippled leg, and that he certainly was not. As Briar worked on, Ben smiled to himself, he didn't care how hard he had to work in the future, or how many candles he would have to burn throughout the night to finish off some cabinet, or rich child's toy. It would be worth it to him, if only she was there with him. Ben had considered their age, she was but fourteen, and he would not be fifteen for a couple of months yet, but neither of them had had the easy road in life, and he considered himself far older for his years. He considered Briar the same, the way she worked and spoke, the way she defended herself was hardly like a delicate girl of fourteen, she seemed far more worldly. "Be ligh' handed miss, watch. Jus' hold the edge between yore two fingers…fingertips lass, tha's better tha's the way, now jus' sand the edge upwards in a quick ligh' motion."

Briar tried as hard as she could, but the thin roof rafters slipped out of her fingers, and he wanted her to be able to slat them into place. "Eeh I canna do it."

"Try; come on concentrate jus' a little more, come on." Ben's voice had sounded firm but when Briar tilted her face to see him the smile was welcoming and quick to put her at ease.

"And if I mek a mistake? I'll be lucky t' ge' any supper t' night. Mi meat allowance 'as already been stopped fur another week. If I mess up yore work the master will 'ave me locked up an' starved." Briar Rose smiled as she handed Ben the tiny rafter.

"Well then miss, yo' finish this as I asked, an' I jus' migh' save yo' a piece o' cake…even if it is stale." Ben grinned, but gently pushed the work back into Briar's hands. "Come on now miss, wha' is it we say? 'Usefulness, Virtue an' Industry?'"

"Aye Ben, an' a bloody good beltin' if we dunna."

Ben spluttered with laughter, but gently held out his fingers, placing them to her lips.

"Ssh, yo'll ge' it if the master hears yo' swearin' liken tha', an' besides miss, if yo' speak liken tha' when I leave 'ere I wunna tek yo' wi' me. So yo' bes' mind yore manners." Again Ben smiled, but this time at the astonished look that had crept over the pretty heart shaped face in front of him.

"Yo' goin' t' leave Ben? Would yo' wan…"

"Back t' work lass, an' yo' Ben, theer's no talkin' whilst workin' remember?"

Stan's voice brought them both to a halt, but only momentarily, for Briar had not finished. She sensed that Ben had more to say and the master was not around to hear them anyway.

"Tell me Ben, wha' was yo…"

"Di' yo' 'ear me lass?"

A muffled echo of suppressed chuckles escaped the lips of the young workshop lads, only to fall hidden on a bed of sawdust that covered the mill floor.

"I said back t' work." Stan stood firm, his back straight as he cast a furious glance towards the other lads to carry on with their own work.

Briar Rose sharply stood up from the stool, carefully placing Ben's work down, she was furious to be interrupted. Had Ben real plans? She did not know, but the thought of leaving this place, walking back through that stony archway of tears and leaving the likes of Stan Lawson behind almost won the day. But she had to be careful here, very careful, for if Ben had but a whim, and no real plans at all, she knew it would benefit her in the long run to then keep in Stan's favour. She couldn't afford to burn her bridges just yet, for she may still need Stan. He was also a good worker, a leader, and with him, if she had too, she would easily find herself a place of work, and that would eventually be the start of her getting away from him for good. Conforming herself fast, she took a deep breath, before slowly walking up to meet his angry gaze. "I'm sorry Stan, I di' all tha' wa' asked. If theer's anythin' else, jus' say so."

Stan glowered, he wasn't fooled, she was trying to be polite, but her slate grey eyes gave her temper away and there she stood so very stiff, a pout covering those lips of hers.

How tempting, Stan ran his tongue over his own lips, his eyes tightly locked onto hers. How very tempting it was to reach out and grab her and to take her out of here for a while. Since the day he had taken her, he had not been given another chance for at nights she had kept a chair barricaded against the door. He knew, for he had tried.

"Yo' are mi girl Briar, yo' still know tha' dunna yo'?"

"Aye Stan, I still know." Her answer was quick, her voice soft and low so nobody else could hear. She had seen the look of lust clouding his eyes, and she had made damn sure she wasn't left with him a moment longer than she should be. In fact if he never came near her again, it would still be far too soon. Stan watched her carefully, he couldn't be too sure if she had meant it. She had answered him readily, she had even partly smiled at him, but her smile never reached her slate grey eyes, not like it did when she smiled at Ben. A rush of heartfelt jealously filled him with a spark of anger, such as he never felt towards Ben, and when he glanced his brother's way he was met with a look that struck him cold. Did he see contempt? Hatred? No it wasn't that strong, at least not yet. What he witnessed was an expression of bitterness, and maybe even jealousy towards him. And why? Because of the girl. Well that could soon be put right. If the path was to be a smooth one between them as brothers and Briar Rose was to be part of his life, then Ben would need to know that he himself had already made a claim on the girl, one he vowed to keep. When he gazed down and caught the slate grey eyes that pierced him, he also knew that to make life easier for all three of them in the future, the girl would need to know exactly where she stood with him. She was a worker, as hard as he'd ever encountered, and her strong mindedness amazed even him. But she couldn't keep displaying her will so openly, for it could lose them all work. When Stan did find a way to leave here, and he was certain it would be through Ben, then he would take the girl with him. "I dunna expec' t' hear a peep owt o' any o' you'. If the master wants me I'm sortin' owt a problem."

Not a murmur, just a sea of curious faces and the occasional glint of mischief from those who suspected.

"Go on lass, after yo'." His attention was now fully on Briar Rose, whose rosy complexion and wide eyed look gasped aloud for her. When she didn't move Stan looked over to where Ben now stood, his weight supported by his stick, realisation belting him cruelly in the face, his chest could clearly be seen heaving with emotion, anger evident in his face. For Ben could see the look in Briar Rose's eyes. The girl did not want to go and he could also see by the light of want that shone in his brother's eyes exactly what Stan wanted her for, but then hadn't he taken her down already? Any doubts he had had about that were now washed away.

"If the master finds owt our Stan yo'll be flogged or worse still imprisoned. Yo' know the punishmen' fur wha' yo' wan' from the girl." Ben took a deep breath, his heart pounding. "le' 'er go Stan, le' 'er go."

Stan bit down hard on his lip, a sneer curling up the side of his mouth. He did not need to be reminded of the punishment if he was caught. But any day now, if what Ben told him was correct, well then Ben would be called for at any time, and when he was Stan would be going with him. The threat therefore of severe punishment was not something that was hanging over his head. Roughly he reached out grabbing Briar Rose by the wrist.

"She's mi girl Ben, yo' may as well know tha'." Casting his eyes downwards he faced Briar. "Tell 'im I'm righ' lass, well go on." Stan waited, any smile he'd worn before was gone, his jaw line tense, his body rigid, and the smile he had seen between Briar and his brother had incensed him deeply. Briar Rose glanced quickly at Ben, how she wanted to scream, "No I'm nod, I ne'er will be." But she could not, for she did not realise that Ben really did have plans or she would have loudly declared it. What she saw was a look deep in Ben's warm brown eyes, a look that would protect her right now if she refused to go. But where would that leave Ben? The master would hear, and would thrash Ben as well as her for causing the trouble. Briar took a deep breath, how shaky she felt, how hard it was becoming, to hold on to reality of any kind, but the look that shaded Ben's face right now, that pitiful discarded look was almost to much to bear. There was only one thing Briar could do to stop Ben causing a stink, and it would save him from the masters wrath, only Ben would not understand the real reason behind what Briar was about to do. Slowly, she raised her eyes to meet the stern unsmiling face of Stan, his bright blue eyes held only harshness, and a certain threat towards her. As Briar began to speak she watched as the frown slowly faded and the harshness turned to a twinkle, and his sneering lips turned to a knowing smile.

"I'll come wi' yo', yo' dunna need t' mek me, I'll come." Without looking back Briar led the way out of the workshop, Stan close on her heels, she couldn't bear the thought of Ben seeing the look of despair that filled her young soul with dread. For if he did, if he saw the tears she was choking back, she was in no doubt that Ben would have stepped in, and to have to watch punishment brought down heavily on Ben's back was something she would not be part of. What Stan wanted from her she would now cope with, for she had been through it before, once with the gang master, and also Stan, so she knew what to expect. If she couldn't think of a way quick enough to get away, she would lie still, and refuse to acknowledge any abuse forced upon her, maybe then it would seem like it had not happened. "Stan I canna come wi' you', nod liken yo' wan' me too." Coming to a sharp halt Briar turned to face him, she had to try and get rid of him, for if she didn't try she wouldn't be able to live with herself. "I mean it Stan…" She hesitated, the menacing look was returning to his eyes, he really did class her as his own. "Looken Stan it inna tha' I dunna want t', bu' wha' if I fall fur a child? Yo' wouldna wan' me then. Yo' know I can work alongside yo', bu' nobody will tek yo' wi' me laggin' on an' a stomach owt 'ere." Expressing herself bluntly, she immediately saw Stan's attitude change towards her, he was grinning from ear to ear. She even smiled herself, how convincing that had sounded; it looked like she had fooled him.

"Well Briar, I though' yo'd forgotten yore mi lass, bu' I can see yo 'anna." Stan reached out and pulled her against him, his arms firmly around her as his lips sought hers. "Dunna worry lass, I wunna le' nowt 'appen t' yo', I promise." As his whisper vanished, his lips roughly finding hers, Briar gasped and closed her eyes. Her body trembled from repulsion, no she could not do it, she could not go with him, not to save anyone's skin, she had to get him away from her. As Briar wriggled in his arms, Stan mistook it for her wanting to be closer and pulled her even harder towards him, he had felt her tremble with expectancy and pleasure. How could he have ever doubted her? As Stan became even more earnest for Briar to follow him his eagerness bruising her mouth, his bands rough as they fumbled to reach inside her woven shirt desperate to feel the tenderness of her youthful breasts, Briar began to recoil. She could feel his hardness, the smell of his stale breath so very close. She tried frantically to push away the fumbling fingers as they now reached inside her shirt, so very rough against her tender skin. The nearness of him repulsed her, if something didn't happen now she would indeed be sick.

"Lawson, what is the meaning of this? Girl, come here immediately."

United in their efforts to pull apart, both Stan and Briar turned to face the master, a man of such a cruel reputation, who would now delight in making an example of both of them.

"Lawson, I'm disappointed boy, I thought you had more sense, you've let me down. You have set a bad example to every boy in the mill."

Stan stood so very still. "I'm, sorry master, it wunna 'appen again."

The master glared at the boy, a young man of just eighteen, and a boy who stood eye level to himself. He wasn't bloody fooled by his mumbled apology, the boy wasn't sorry at all, he was trying to take what was only natural, but even still he'd have him flogged by his own hand that very day, in the courtyard right at the front of the mill. There he would be on show for everybody to see, and those that did see, would heed.

But for now…he stared down at the girl, a rather tall girl for fourteen, with the most striking of eyes he had ever encountered, whose heart shaped face appeared so very angelic, but whose strong will was both unattractive and infuriating. "As for you girl, I regret the day you ever entered these grounds. You have no concept of decency, and going by what I have just witnessed you are still the field girl you came as."

Briar shuddered, but said nothing.

"Well I'll teach you once and for all. Lawson I'm going to flog you myself in front of the mill where every lad can watch and learn that nobody crosses me, ever. As for you girl." Taking a deep breath the master pulled himself even taller his sharp brown eyes piercing, his lean face so tense with anger. "You too will be punished in front of the mill." Not taking his eyes of the girl he snarled. "Lawson, fetch the mistress, tell her to bring a yellow sash for the field whore and tell her to bring the thickest cane she can come across…Go now."

Briar Rose cast her slate grey eyes towards Stan. He too looked afraid, he was red in the face and she could almost hear his heavy breathing. He could not help her now.

Staring at the master once more she felt a wild fluttering deep within her breast, causing her body to stir, to slowly waken and take its flight. There was nothing left to lose, she had done her very best to prove herself to her master. She had worked until her back had felt it would break, and her legs could hardly carry her weight. She had gone without meals and had been dealt many a beating, and then she had been cruelly raped by Stan. Nothing she had done meant anything to the master; she was just another urchin, wayward lass who would never belong anywhere. And did she belong anywhere? Lost in troubled thought Briar shook her head and stared forlornly at the floor, no she had nowhere, and who the hell would want her now. After all she was but fourteen, and had already had two men, even if neither one had been by her own choice. What she did know was she did not want to be left alone with Stan Lawson again; he thought he owned her body and soul. But he had taken it; she had never given any part of herself to him and never would. As for Ben, she briefly closed her eyes, it was best she did not think down that path, for no good could ever come of it. She had as good as told him she was Stan's girl, and by the look he had given her, well it said it all. As Briar saw the look of hesitation in Stan's eyes as he turned slowly to fetch the mistress his own cruel fate just ahead of him Briar glowered up at the master her lips a very heavy pout, and then she did what she had done when she came and found this place, she took to her heels and ran. Bellows snapped at her heels as the master ordered her to stop. She could hear Stan's voice somewhere behind her warning her she would make it worse for herself, and then she thought she heard Ben begging her to stop, that he would bear her punishment for her. Did she hear all of that? Or was it just some sweet fantasy that she hoped to hear?

Still Briar ran from the cold interior of the long foreboding corridor, back through the mill and out across the courtyard. She ran as fast as she could along the track that would lead her away from the men's side of the workhouse, and towards the main entrance that was shadowed by the stone archway. The archway of tears. Panting heavily Briar sobbed as the archway came ever closer, her tears blinding her, her heart pounding so heavy the pain inside gripped her chest, her fear of what would become of her now grasping her soul with sorrow, for no good could ever come her way. She had nothing in the world, just the boy's clothes that hung on her back and the hobnailed boots that would eventually slow her down.

"Watch owt lass, watch out."

Weather it was Stan's voice, or Ben's in the distance she did not know. All Briar could feel was the frightful pain that thundered against the side of her head, the startled whinny of a frightened horse and a sea of faces she knew so well, and those of strangers, as they hovered above her head. As the strong arms of a young mill hand gently picked up the twisted body of the fading girl another battle had begun. As Briar Rose lay motionless in the arms of Stan Lawson, her breathing laboured, her silvery blond hair drenched with her own blood by a deep wound to her temple, her master argued with vigour that he would not give up his best workers without a fight. Jonathan Hampstead stared down his nose at the workhouse master, disgust clear on his face, he had no real time for these masters at all, they were re-knowned for their cruel reputations. But for now he had his own mission foremost to the front of his mind, and with the talents of young Ben Lawson, he knew he would soon be known as the best cabinet and toy maker in Shropshire, given the right guidance of course. But he recognised the strength in the older lad, and he also needed a grounds man, one that could control those around him, one who would be eager to work. What better lad than a workhouse lad, for they certainly knew what hard work meant, and though at just eighteen the Lawson boy could be considered young, Jonathan only employed the young, for all his staff were trained by him, and he could train this lad to know how to handle those around him properly, firmly, but fairly. As far as this strange girl went who had ran straight under his horse then rendered herself unconscious, well he wasn't sure. But by the look in the Lawson boys eyes, both of them, they were making it known that where they went, she went. Whatever the relationship was between the three of them he was not interested. The poor class people were very different from his class. He could guess that their understanding of social moral would be as poor as the rags they wore. As he looked down, a deep frown on his face at the heart shaped face of the sleeping girl, no older than thirteen or fourteen, even he was left speechless. The girl was dressed as a boy, in hobnailed boots, and boy's clothes, but a worker he had heard. Well they were short of a scullery maid, and he had told Emily Bunting that she could have a girl to train, but a girl dressed as a boy? Oh well, under the guidance of Mrs Bunting she would be no trouble, and then he'd wait and see, if the girl did prove to be trouble, he'd throw her out of the door.

Glancing at the workhouse master once more Mr Hampstead simply dismissed him as he would one of his own servants. There was nothing that the workhouse master could do or say, for he knew that if he argued the point any further, this man Hampstead could call the constabulary and he himself would be arrested and tried, even flogged or imprisoned. For forcing a girl to work on the men's side of the workhouse was completely unheard off. He would be more than frowned upon. As the master cast the girl one last look of utter disdain, he secretly wished that she would never wake from her unconscious state. There she laid her hair drenched in her own blood, amidst old rags on her way to a new life, the kind of life she did not deserve. How he resented even taking her through his gates two years ago. If he had the chance now, he'd bring the whip down upon her back himself. Without a word to either of the Lawson brothers the workhouse master strutted off, his lean frame tense with frustration at losing the most talented young lad he had ever come across Ben Lawson. But, he had other lads, and he'd push them even harder and God help any of them if they did not meet his standards.

"Come on lads move it, hurry now, we have not got all day. The girl will be fine on the rags, so stop fussing." Jonathan Hampstead briefly smiled at both brothers. "Well I know you are both used to hard work, so we'll get on just fine. Though there are a few things we do need to discuss." Raising his eyebrows as he glanced at the girl he carried on. "So up on the cart then, no time to waste, no time to waste."

Obediently the brothers clambered into the back of the cart. Neither one spoke, their eyes thoughtful, full of unspoken truths and desires. It should have been a moment of great joy, of excitement, but their flight of what would have been full of youthful hopes had been dampened by their future prospects. For seeds had been firmly sown in their hearts by each other. Seeds that would grow and flourish into thorns of jealousy and bitterness.

As for Briar Rose, she didn't have the joy of cheering as the cart disappeared under the archway of tears and away from the Crosshouses Workhouse and it's community. She would never have to encounter the likes of it again. So unaware of what was happening around her, she lay peaceful oblivious that she too was on her way to a new life.

chapter seven

"Goodness me above girl, yo'll be the death o' me yo' really will. Eeh the mistress will 'ave us all skinned alive if them theer floors inna sparklin' liken the chandeliers."

"Calm down Emily, it'll be done, an' it'll outshine any sparklin' chandelier." Briar Rose grinned mischievously, then squealed with laughter as Emily raised her elderly hand slapping Briar hard as she did so.

"Mrs Bunting t' yo' young lady, an' dunna yo' furge' yore place. Eeh the mistress will faint at the sigh' o' tha' floor."

"I'm goin' t' do it righ' now Mrs Bunting, an' I wunna tek a breath o' air until it's done."

Emily Bunting waved her hand dismissively at the girl in her care, tutting loudly before scurrying away to make sure each girl was doing her duties competently. Briar Rose smiled to herself as she watched the short but full figure of the elderly woman leave her.

In the two years that she had been a chamber maid in Master Jonathan Hampstead's Estate house, she had been in service, under the guidance of Joseph and Emily Bunting. Emily was an elderly lady whose job was to fully groom and train six young girls who would eventually be able to maintain all household duties. They would all learn the art of cooking, cleaning, serving, and laundering, all with hope of serving a future master and mistress at the highest of standards. Briar Rose had learnt much, for once her young mind had been active, and she grasped every task given her, and paid great attention to the smallest of details that would leave a lasting impression. Very Quickly Briar had managed to impress Emily and

Joseph Bunting, and then her new master and mistress. She had been noted to work long hours always to the best of her ability, and had never been heard to complain. Briar Rose could not have been more than pleased anywhere else, for here in this very house she was finally learning a trade. She was a chamber maid for part of the week, but now she had been promoted to the kitchen for three whole days and there was little that she couldn't do. She delighted Emily with her obedient response, and could now even rustle up a meal for the servants out of the scraps without aid, even Emily had laughed when Briar announced that there would be plenty for the grounds men and the mill workers. Emily had gone on to reward her by allowing her to help with a special banquet that Master Jonathan and Mistress Blanche had held for their social circle. Briar had impressed all with her mouth watering exquisite canapés and sweet tasting dips. But today she had to focus on one task and that was the floor. Rolling up the sleeves of her starched grey chiffon frock Briar Rose knelt down and began. There were visitors coming this very week-end and Master Jonathan had stressed he wanted the library floor waxed until it looked like new, and she was the girl for the job. Lost in thought Briar set about her task eagerly, she was very lucky to be employed here.

Jonathan and Blanche Hampstead owned the large estate house on top of the Common, a pleasant area with few neighbours in the quiet country location of Bayston Hill, a tiny village just five miles outside of the Shrewsbury Town centre, just one dirt track passing through it. Jonathan's estate over-shadowed the few houses on the common, but the estate was attractive, and he had his own flourishing business adjoined to his premises that kept some of the able village lads in work. Those who were there considered themselves extremely lucky for their only other option would be to work down the quarry mines, digging for limestone. Jonathan Hampstead was considered a very fair man and those that found themselves in his employment seldom left. Joseph and Emily Bunting had been in the

Hampstead's employ for almost thirty five years, so long that Jonathan and Blanche would not consider them ever leaving. Joseph had always been butler, and doorman, and he took care of the household expenses as far as the servants wages went and money to maintain the servant's pantry. He considered it a great honour when Jonathan asked his views on the grounds men, and told him of future plans he had for his gardens, Joseph also made sure that all the servants, from the girls under his wife's guidance, to the grounds men and the mill hands if they approached the back door, knew their place. He too was considered fair, and would listen to a problem, but he could be sharp, and would stand for no behaviour that could be frowned upon. Emily his wife was in soul charge of her six girls; she had to train them in all aspects and knew the standards that would be expected. Jonathan Hampstead was content with his life, he asked for the highest of standards and as long as they were met, and tasks were done, he never asked for more. He was happy to relax in the company of his young wife, a girl almost twenty years his junior. At fifty five he was more than content to sit back and enjoy his days in the company of friends, a game of cards, and the comforts his wife willingly bestowed upon him. Jonathan had worked hard to accomplish the business he had now established, and the fruits of the work mill and its workers gave him time to do whatever he wanted with his days. The grounds of the house were beautifully kept, even if it was a little bit on the plain side. Lawns covered a vast area, with just the occasional weeping willow tree, or a small ornamental pond with the stray statuette to break up the monotony. But there were no flower bed or rockeries for that in the past had taken up too much time, but now, maybe he would think about that as well. At the one side of the neatly kept lawns was a large orchard, where fruit trees and bushes grew. Here the fruit was harvested and sold to the local people or taken to the Shrewsbury Town Market. Jonathan employed four lads to maintain this whole area and one lad who acted as foreman, whose job it was to make sure the lawns were kept to a maximum of an 1inch in height. To guarantee that not one piece of fruit rotted, and to make sure he managed to get the best profit available. That young lad was called Stan Lawson, a young man of almost twenty years of age who could be as firm and as ruthless as a man twenty years his senior, but a lad with the head to lead those around him, and be able to gain and keep their respect. Then, came his largest asset of all, his wood mill. A very large mill adjoining his grounds which held ten lads, all of them working to order, their work the highest of standards. Jonathan had an eye for talent, for that alone would bring him money, and each of the boys in his service had a rare gift of fine craftsmanship, whether it came down to toy making, cabinet making or for being known to make the best cart wheels around. Just the sound of the saw as it cut each length brought music to his ears, for it was one length closer to getting the job done, the smell of the steam power as it turned logs into planed up sections of timber or trimmed it as thinly as veneers for fancy furnishing, ready to be piled up on one of the work benches. It was a great delight to Jonathan Hampstead for it all had a gentle melody to it and that sang money. Jonathan would openly cheer his workers and show his appreciation as thin veneers were cut down to paper thin to give a better appearance, often the false sense that would make the work look like oak. Every cast off was calculated and given to one lad of almost seventeen years to craft into whatever he found fit in his own time. And that lad was Ben Lawson.

Just the thought of that lad made Jonathan want to rub his hands with glee, he could almost smell the money floating in. How many cabinets had he made and sold since that lad had come to him? How many wooden ducks painted in bright colours and toy carts and not to mention the decorative dolls houses had Ben sat and made? Mostly way into the night under the glow of flickering candles. Who could be accurate where this lads talents ran, for he had never seen the likes of it, and the lad had never had no training. The skill was there embedded in his fingers, silhouetted deep in his mind, images of wooden toys ready to live in reality. Jonathan Hampstead had relished in the successes of Ben Lawson, the most gifted mill hand he had ever come across. Yes, life for Master Jonathan was going well, very well indeed.

"Yo' nearly finished ye' Briar Rose?" Emily Bunting had reappeared once the floor was waxed, now it was ready for Master Jonathan's guests an then if it had been done adequately there was work for Briar in the kitchen.

"Aye Mrs Bunting, I can see me face on the floor, looken." Briar smiled up at the elderly woman, she was still on her hands and knees, but she was confident the floor would pass inspection. Peering downwards Mrs Bunting stared hard. The girl had done a grand job, and she would have said herself that the floor did indeed look brand now.

"Nod bad, no nod bad at all. Now, less o' yore bloomin' cheek lass, or yo'll have mi Joseph t' answer too."

Briar Rose dutifully answered, "Aye Mrs Bunting." A smile lighting up her slate grey eyes. Without another word she gathered up her cloths and beeswax, and followed Emily Bunting to the kitchen. She liked the elderly woman, and so did the other girls in service there, and Briar held no fear of Joseph Bunting the butler. The Buntings were both fair and treated the girls kindly, though Joseph had been known to raise his voice and would not think twice about treating cheekiness with a sharp rap across the offenders knuckles. But then it would be forgotten and he was swift to hand out a hanky if he did cause tears, and that was seldom. In the Buntings the girls found a source of parenting, a bond of trust was quick to reach the hearts of the girls in service, none of them older than seventeen, often missing their own parents. To Briar Rose the special yet working relationship was one that she welcomed, for she had never received anything resembling parenting in her life. As for Emily and Joseph, they made sure the girls were well turned out, that each starched grey ankle length frock was clean that each white pinny was tied into a neat bow, and each mop cap kept every stray strand of hair out of sight. They gave each girl the comfort of a decent meal each day, a bowl of hot oats each morning and a mug of hot mushed tea. They had an allowance of a quarter mug of milk every day to themselves and even shared the luxury of a piece of soft fruit cake once a week. They were taught skills of the house, they would not have otherwise known, and they all understood discipline in the kindly nature. The girls shared a large room in the wing just of the side of the parlour that overlooked the yard and water pump, and Briar being now one of the first there as other girls had moved on and new recruits taken on, she had the luxury of a small room to herself. It was furnished nicely with a bed, a small table and she had her own wash bowl and a rail to hang her few frocks. It was also part of Emily and Joseph's duty to educate the girls in religious structure, and so each girl dressed in her better frock on Sunday to join the Buntings in the nearby chapel, that stood proudly on the Common of Bayston Hill. Briar never complained, she was happy with all that had happened to her since her fortunate turn of affairs. She was thankful that she had been taken on at Jonathan Hampstead's estate, for she had never had a room of her own, or had the comfort of knowing when the next meal was, and she had never known kindness from any adult, especially men, something she had severely lacked her whole life. Here she did not fear her master, for even though he held great authority, he was renowned for his kindness. He never raised his voice to her, and the threat of punishment from him and the mistress Blanche was not evident anywhere she had looked. Nothing ever went any further than the fatherly rap over the knuckles from Joseph Bunting who had been heard to call the girls his 'house daughters' at least while they were in his and his wife's care. As if it wasn't enough to get used to, Briar looked forward to her half day off a fortnight, for then she was given time to spend as she wished, and she would often catch the midday cart and hunt the Shrewsbury town market for remnants of material, or a length of bright ribbon for her hair.

"Go an' wash yore 'ands lass, well an' good mind. If the smell o' wax touches mi pastry, eeh yo'll be facin' mi Joseph."

"Aye Mrs Buntin'." On a giggle Briar left the kitchen, swift to make her way across the yard towards the nearest pump. Always the same with Emily Bunting, fast to give the idle threat of Joseph her husband, but what would she have done without either of them?

Sighing Briar took a long deep breath, an air of sadness clouding her slate grey eyes as she glanced back over her shoulder towards Mrs Bunting's parlour. She could see the elderly woman through the window her mop cap covering her white hair. What would she have done without her? A question that Briar often asked herself. Would she ever gain the common sense that Emily tried so hard to install into her? Would she ever see her own path clearly in life, the way Emily told her she should? Probably not.

With a vengeance Briar splattered the water from the pump over her hands and scrubbed, making sure that any left over bees wax was gone. She was as prepared as she could be to go back into the kitchen and work, oh yes she was. "Oh damn it." Looking down at her frock she gasped at the soaking wet patches.

"Are you having difficulties young lady?"

Briar gasped aloud and turned quickly to face her master Jonathan Hampstead; almost stumbling over her own feet as she did so. "Oh no master Jonathan…excuse me…I'm so sorry fur wha' I said…eeh" Squealing Briar gave a full curtsey as she'd been taught to do by Emily. "Excuse me master, I mus' go now." Without further ado she lifted the bottom of her hem and ran towards the kitchen full pelt ahead, much to the amusement of Jonathan Hampstead, who found the silvery blond haired girl with the slate grey eyes as interesting as a new untamed colt. He had known from the start that the Bunting's would turn this girl into a passable young servant, and he had been right. The girl was indeed pleasant to the eye, polite, but with an air of wildness that no longer offended.

"Miss Briar Rose, is tha' the way fur any young lady t' act?

Dunna le' me see yo' run again. A young lady never runs." The stern voice of Joseph Bunting echoed firmly across the courtyard and Jonathan Hampstead watched as the girl stopped immediately and once more gasped aloud. His laugh could plainly be heard as he walked away.

Briar stood sullen as she listened intently once more about not running, something that Joseph would not tolerate. "It causes accidents and chaos, an' neither are ever far from yo' are they Briar?"

"No mister Buntin', unfortunately not." Briar pouted heavily as she always did when she found herself questioned, the colour of bright pink raising in her face.

Joseph took a deep breath and firmly but kindly lowered his voice as he stated.

"Now it's no good poutin' at me young lady, wha' I say is true. Now yore no longer a child or a lass tha' knows no better. In a weeks time yo'll be responsible fur yore own, an' I dunna expec' t' 'ave t' remind yo' then o' such thin's." Joseph stared down at the girl as she slowly raised her eyes to meet his. He'd had many girls here over the years, but none had managed to pull at his heart strings the way this girl had. She'd been severely concussed when she'd arrived, and had been somewhat of a wild young creature who had often tested the patience of all around her. But under the guidance of his dear wife Emily and himself, she had blossomed into a striking young woman whose silvery blond hair shone with life, and whose slate grey eyes that he had seen pierce with fury, but could spark with mischief of her youth often clouded with a sadness he was yet to understand.

"I try 'ard Mr Buntin'."

"Aye lass yo' do, an' a man t' the end o' his patience. Yo' remember lass, remember wha' we taugh' yo' an' yo' wunna go far wrong. Yo' run around liken a leave dancin' on the breeze yo'll face another mans wrath, nod mine, an' nod all men will tek kindly t' it."

Briar nodded knowingly, she did not need to be told that. She knew only too well how most men, well all other men had been towards her in her life.

"Off yo' go then lass, back t' Emily…an' walk."

With the reprimand over Briar Rose dragged her feet as she entered the kitchen quietly.

When Emily looked her way Briar forced a smile then quickly turned away to start her task of making pastry. Emily Bunting filled a large saucepan with water; she sensed a pot of hot mushed tea was needed. She had heard the words of her husband, and knew that Briar Rose had taken everything to heart. They had both spent many hours grooming this girl well, and they both took great pride in her ability to work hard and never to complain. But there was one thing she felt she had failed, and that was preparing Briar for the hurdle she must cross on her next half day off. For on that day she would finish with any childlike notions she had for life, for something else would fill her days, and with that she would finally finish growing up. Marriage. At first the girl had refused the man in question, she had actually screamed her refusal and had upset the relaxed atmosphere in the whole household, and Joseph had had to take her to one side fast in order for Briar to conform herself. Emily herself had been fast to speak with the upset girl, in the bid to make her see sense. "Eeh lass, yo' may nod love him, an' by yore noise I see yo' dunna, bu' thinken on. Love is something tha' flies owt the window very fas'." Emily nodded knowingly, "Respec' love is wha' yo' need t' begin wi', respec' fur yore man. Wi' tha' yo'll learn t' care, an' in the years t' come yo'll find owt yo' loved 'im all along." Emily smiled to herself as she remembered Briar's reaction.

"I dunna even liken 'im." She had wined pitifully.

Dear me, it had certainly not been easy.

"He is a good lad, a worker, one wi' standin'. Yore luckier than a lo' o' lasses, eeh yo' even 'ave a cottage t' star' yore married life in." Emily was not the only one in the kitchen pondering over past conversations, for Briar struggled to find anything good at all in the forth coming event, and found little comfort in anything she had been told. She was sixteen years old, ripe for marriage so everybody had said and both her and her husband to be had good positions on the Hampstead Estate. That much was true; she knew that, there was a small two up two down cottage, a grounds man's cottage that had been empty for years. It was run down, but could soon be put right, and she knew she should be grateful she was in the company of people that cared enough to want to help her. But even still; the very thought of sleeping each night with a man she did not even care for filled her with fears and sheer dread.

"Come on lass, si' down fur five minutes, tell me wha's on yore mind, bu' speak sensibly." Emily pointed to the chair by the hearth and watched as Briar immediately sat down, glad to take the weight of her feet, eagerly taking the tin mug of hot mushed tea that Emily now placed firmly in her hands.

"Oh Emily, I know I should be grateful bu' wha' abou' the rest? Have I go't' be grateful when every nigh' I'll be in pain fur the res' o' mi life?" There she had said it, and bluntly, she did not want to sleep with him.

Emily spluttered, and then chuckled loudly as a pout covered the girls face. "Goodness gracious girl, the thin's you' say." Emily pulled a mocking frown, but sat down herself when those slate grey eyes that searched hers looked so very forlorn. "Eeh lass, jus' go wi' the wind, tha's all I can tell yo'. Yo' wunna be in pain fur long, bu' dunna refuse 'im lass, nod yore husband, men dunna liken t' be refused."

"No Emily, o' course nod." Standing up Briar finished her tea and placed the tin mug in the sink. "I'd bes' ge' on eh? Theer's an evenin' meal t' thinken off."

"Aye lass yo' do tha'."

Emily smiled warmly; convinced her talk had eased the girl's troubled mind.

Little did she know the full turmoil Briar was really in. She was only getting married because of the strain being pushed on her that it was the right thing to do, and not many girls married for love, it was a way of life, and did she want to end up an old maid? But to belong to a man she would never respect was as daunting as going back to her childhood days and belonging to a gang master. As for not 'refusing' him, she could only think of extreme ways to save herself.

Just set to the side of the Hampstead Estate in the work mill, another sat filled with dread at the thought that he would never again see Briar Rose for what she was now. She was a free highly spirited girl, whose temper could still rise and send those slate grey eyes of hers piercing into the very soul of the one who had annoyed her. Ben Lawson had spent two years on this estate, working to order, pleasing his master immensely with his various designs of cabinets and dolls houses. Just lately Ben had found enough cast offs to make a dozen trinket boxes, each one with an engraved lid of various tiny patterns. He had often worked way into the lonely hours of the night, pushing himself on, his skills forever amazing those around him. He had but one outlook, and one amazing achievement on his mind, to establish himself, a partnership maybe, enough to give himself his own roof, his own income, and not to rely on a master or to share a room with other boys. Ben sighed as he remembered his recent conversation with Jonathan Hampstead. Jonathan had actually said that he was thinking about sending him on his way, for he knew of properties for lease, places that would suit Ben, and of course suit him, for there would be a large percentage of Ben's work he would cash in on.

Everything had sounded so very perfect, for then Ben would have been able to approach Briar Rose, for he was more than ready to ask for her hand, and he would be able to support her himself without her looking for work. But not now, as if his very thoughts had wheedled their way into the mind of another, Ben had sat back and had not said a word, for he had been stunned into complete silence to learn that Briar Rose had accepted a proposal already. She would never be his wife, for she was going to marry another in less than a week's time. His own brother. Stan. Ben had found it impossible to share his brothers excitement, for though he had little doubt in his mind that Stan did actually also love Briar Rose as he himself did, Ben had to wonder about Briar. For he had seen himself the animosity that oozed from her and sparked fiercely from those slate grey eyes of hers every time Stan approached her. Marriage in Ben's eyes, and he was sure it was the same with Stan, was a sacrament not to be taken lightly, and Ben truly felt that Briar Rose had accepted Stan's proposal flippantly. Of course he had mentioned this to Stan who had laughed aloud, and had queried Ben's jealously. Never in his life had he been filled with such raw emotion as he felt now, for he would gladly take Briar Rose to one side given half the chance and shake some common sense into her. As for Stan, he didn't blame him for loving the girl, for Ben himself knew how the very sight of that heart shaped face that could look so angelic stir within him a feeling of great power. The want to capture her wholly, just to dream of touching her soft silky skin could cause a man's heart to burn with lust, until the pounding within him was threatening enough in itself. But now, as Ben stood in the doorway of the workshop, his stick in his hand, his back forced to stand as straight as any other man's he felt his body tense as he watched his brother Stan run across the grounds. There he was his frame young and strong; his legs powerful, Stan could have had anybody he chose. His bright blue eyes and shock of red hair made him stand out from the crowd. Stan had the ability to hold authority over those under him, and his cheerful boisterous outlook on life was enough to woo many a girl, especially with the gift of charm he could turn on at a moments notice. So why Briar Rose? Ben quickly returned back to his work bench, he had things to do, and like it or not, it was no good beating himself up over it. Briar Rose would very soon become Mrs Lawson, but not to him, she would belong to his only brother. There was only one thing he could do, so as not to hurt his own brother and force a wedge between them. He would have to learn to accept it, like it and lump it...even if he did hate it.

chapter eight

In the small scenic village chapel in the heart of Bayston Hill, Briar Rose took her vows. She promised to love honour and obey the young man beside her, and all the servants of Hampstead Hall were there to witness it. Master Jonathan and Mistress Blanche had been most kind, allowing all of the staff the morning as their half day off. Now, back in the parlour in the company of Joseph and Emily Bunting and five other serving girls and Ben Lawson, Briar stood silently as she listened to the speech her new husband was making on her behalf. "I'll raise a toast t' mi new wife, an' thank yo' all fur the 'elp yo' 'ave given us. An' now t' mi wife, Briar Rose." Stan turned and faced her; his bright blue eyes sparkled with life, his smile warm and genuine as he slightly bowed his head to her. "I promise I'll mek yo' a good husband Briar, an' I wunna ever le' no 'arm come t' yo' lass, yo've made me as happy as any man could be." A soft ripple of 'aah' echoed around the parlour as Stan cheerfully held his glass in the air. "Health and happiness t' all o' us."

"Aye, aye, t' all o' us."

The gentle clink of glasses rang in unity as those that were there savoured the full bodied taste of the rich red vintage wine, a gift from their master sent up from his cellars especially for the occasion. Not a moment did Briar waste, drinking back the rich liquid that caused her to splutter immediately, she held out her glass and very bluntly announced. "Aye, t' all o' us, an' I thinken I'll 'ave another."

Giggles from the girls quickly past as Joseph Bunting cast them a look of fierce warning. Emily tutted aloud and had to wonder if Briar had listened to anything they had tried to teach her. She quietly vowed she would give the girl a real piece of her mind later.

As for Stan, it brought a broad grin to his face. So, she still had that outrageous will of hers, daring to tread where angels would only fear. But it was Stan that quickly diffused the sudden atmosphere of shock and laughed aloud. "I thinken lass one is enough fur any o' us, after all theer's work t' go back too." Gently Stan took the glass from Briar's grasp, his smile lighting up his bright blue eyes. Where she was concerned she'd never fail but bring light into his life. He knew at times he himself would have to 'quietly' remind her of her outbursts, but he had no intentions of breaking that wayward spirit of hers, for it was that that had attracted him to her in the first place. Standing back Stan watched silently as Briar over eagerly took a small parcel offered to her by the other girls under the Bunting's care. How different Briar Rose looked out of her grey frock and mop cap. Here she stood in the softest of blue he had ever seen, a frock that touched her highly polished black laced boots. How neatly the dress clung to her waist, revealing her slim youthful figure perfectly, its long sleeves and high neckline giving her an appearance of angelic qualities. Again he grinned, she was a wild flower his Briar, as wild as the rambling rose that grew along the roadside.

When Briar gleefully thanked the girls for the hand embroidered table cloth, her slate grey eyes shone with laughter, her pouting lips for now wore a genuine smile that turned her heart shaped face into that of an angel. As her silvery blond hair hung gallantly down to her waist just a length of ribbon tying it gently into some source of obedience, Stan began to wet his lips. The sooner he got her out of here the better they both had to get back to work before long, and he wanted to take her home first, to their cottage across the grounds.

"Now this presen' is fur yo' lad, an' dunna ge' any strange ideas. It's from upstairs." As Joseph Bunting stepped forward handing

Stan a wooden case, Stan frowned with surprise, this was most unexpected. As he laid the wooden case on the table and opened the lid to reveal its contents, a grin immediately lit up his own face. There lay a gun, an old gun, one that the master had long since finished with, but a gun just the same, that Stan would never have afforded otherwise.

"Fur me?" Stan's delight was evident.

"Aye, it's a gun tha' 'as been given t' every grounds man tha' 'as lived in the cottage over the years. Now wi' tha' comes the righ' t' hunt over the Lyth Hill, and cover the fields at the back o' The Common. Theer's many a grouse over them fields." Joseph stood as tall as he could, he was pleased with the delight the present had brought this young grounds man, he obviously knew gratitude. His own smile broadened as he watched the seeds of thought in Stan's face bloom into realisation.

"Oh aye, o' course no more food from 'ere fur me eh? Now I go' mi own wife an' house, I 'ave t' provide fur mesel'."

"Aye lad tha's righ'."

Briar watched her new husband as he ran his fingers so gently over his new toy, so very carefully as they roamed over the barrel, exploring every curve on this spotless gun, before replacing it back in its box as if it would break. She had to wonder if he would be as gentle with her, and then she gasped aloud and closed her eyes at her own sudden thoughts. It had to be the effect of the wine.

"It's alrigh' lass, it wunna jus' go off, bu' yo' bes' stay away from it, understand?"

"Aye." Briar was quick to answer, he had misunderstood her gasp.

When Stan smiled appreciatively at her she had to wonder if she could one day learn how to respect him and maybe even like him. Stan was tall and very lean; his stomach firm, and his arms strong. His eyes were of a good oval shape and the brightest of blue, and his lips were wide, offering a very attractive smile. Standing there dressed in his one pair of black corduroy trousers, a grey flannel shirt and a black jacket he had borrowed, he certainly was attractive to the eye. His bright crop of red hair had been cut and was combed neatly to his head. Many a girl would have been willing to have been in her boots, especially with a cottage thrown in. Briar smiled back as radiantly as she could bear too, her thoughts had returned to the gun laying there in it's case. It could come in very handy indeed.

"Before yo' both go theer's somethin' I 'ave made, it's a gift fur yo' Briar, a gift t' welcome yo' as mi new sister." Ben had stood back until now. "I hope yo' dunna mind Stan?" Facing his brother squarely, Ben waited.

"No Ben, nod me, le's see it then." Stan now waited. Why should he mind? After all Briar Rose was now his own by law, and he would allow no man ever to put that to sunder. Gingerly Briar stepped forward until she stood just inches from the warmest brown eyes she had ever encountered.

"Fur yo' Briar." Softly Ben spoke, his voice a mere whisper as he passed the brown paper parcel into her hands. Without the eager ripping of the paper as she had with the girls present, Briar placed this package on the table and carefully undid the string, taking great care with whatever it could be that was so well hidden. As the paper fell to one side she stood so very silent gazing down at her gift. There it laid her very own possession, her very first true gift in the world and the choke that escaped her sounded like a muffled sob. Fast to raise her hand to her throat so it should not happen again Briar took a deep breath. Why did she have this strange urge to cry so very suddenly? She could not answer, but she could feel the tears welling up fast until her gift became a blur. No, she must not cry. 'Conform yourself' in silence Briar's own thought reprimanded her. Then, as if it would fall to pieces under her touch she gently reached out and picked up the small wooden chest, a tiny box with two exquisite drawers crafted out of wood. So daintily she ran her fingers over the engraved lid. "It's beautiful." Her own words almost fell lost on the gentle breeze that now teased her through the open kitchen window. "It's a rose."

"Aye lass, it is." Ben watched with pride as Briar ran her finger over the engraved rose. It had taken him hours, almost as long as it had to make the box itself, but her response had been well worth it. "Looken inside lass."

Glancing up momentarily Brair spoke once more. "Inside?"

"Aye."

Slowly she lifted the lid, and there it laid a small wooden pendant in the shape of a cross. Such a fine piece of workmanship, the small cross was engraved with the tiniest of delicate leaves.

"Theer's no chain…I hope yo' liken it?"

When the prettiest of heart shaped faces turned his way her slate grey eyes damp with unspoilt tears Ben smiled with a deep pride he would never be able to explain. If she had been his, he would have made sure the pendant was linked to the finest of chains, but he had to be very careful that nobody saw behind his gift. For it had been made wholly with her on his mind, and every exquisite pattern he had engraved had been done with his own love, just as she was engraved in his heart, and always would be. Briar gulped as she faced Ben. There he stood, his stick helping to keep his body straight. How handsome he looked in the same black corduroy trousers and grey flannel shirt as his brother. Only Ben had no jacket, but what did that matter? He stood only a fraction taller than her, but much shorter than his brother and his hair was a dull shade of red unlike Stan's but was also combed back neatly. What Briar saw in Ben's kind face was a quality, a rare quality that had aged his youthful face, for he had not yet reached seventeen, but his crippled condition had always made him think too hard, and had given him the air of a somewhat older man. As she first had when she had burst into his life that day at the workhouse, she saw something different in his warm brown eyes, and Briar knew it to be concern, a look he always held whenever he neared her. "Thankyo' Ben, thankyo' so much."

In a rush of unpredicted emotion Briar threw her arms tightly around his neck, firmly planting a kiss on his lips before stepping back. Tutts from Mr Joseph Bunting could clearly be heard for her brash behaviour, as giggles from the girls were quickly hushed by Emily who was fast to threaten them with her broom. Ben couldn't help but smile, would this girl never cease to cause a stir of some kind? But he guessed not. Stan was probably the only person in the parlour who stood tense, his body rigid, and all laughter gone from his bright blue eyes. He had given Briar no gift at all, and he had no idea that Ben's gift would have been so personal, to have made her a small table, or a chest of drawers for them both would have been a different matter, but a trinket box, and then a pendant? No, Stan didn't think much of it at all, and one thing was certain, there was no way he was going to buy any chain for it. As the sharpness in his eyes caught Ben's attention, a fierce silence echoed from the eyes of each brother, each one of them learning so fast what it was like to bear a grudge, until it was becoming bitter with jealousy. Stan's silent threat was well matched in his brother's eyes, for Ben would always watch over Briar, even if it had to be at a long distance. Stan could sense so plainly his wanting, for Ben's urge was every bit as strong as his own, only now he would be able to use that wanting and take it. "Le's tek the gifts 'ome lass, we 'anna go' long now, an' yo' need t' change owt o' tha' frock." Just the sound of listening to Stan suggesting getting changed made Briar flush terribly, the colour racing into her cheeks. Silently she picked up the wooden chest tucking it safely under her arm as she made towards the door with her new husband. As she briefly glanced over her shoulder and took in the forlorn but warm look in those brown eyes of Ben, her heart began to pound, until her whole stomach fluttered with butterflies. Why even now just an hour after she had taken her vows did she feel so light headed with just the sight of Ben? But she needed nobody to answer that question for her, for she had been in love with Ben for over two years, it was just a shame he hadn't felt that strongly towards her, or otherwise he would have asked for her hand himself. As for Stan... "I'm waitin' Mrs Lawson." Stan's impatience was becoming clear.

Oh why was she thinking of that gun again?

chapter nine

For the first two months after Briar Rose's marriage to Stan Lawson, life at the Hampstead Estate nestled on the Common of Bayston Hill proved to be anything but peaceful. The sight of the girl with the waist length silvery blond hair and slate grey eyes in what could only be classed as a field peasant in a patched frock became the talk of the villagers. Who had seen the likes of it before? Not many, for the girl couldn't even be bothered to tie her hair back in a dignified manner, never mind being seen often running down the Common and towards the dirt track that would take her to the local beauty spot of Lyth Hill. But every evening after Briar's own work on the estate she would change from her work shift, take the gun and stalk the local fields, around the Common and on towards the Lyth Hill on the look out for grouse, or rabbit. The tiny community of Bayston Hill had always been one of tranquillity, a pretty village, safe for the wandering child, or peaceful for the roaming courting couple, a very close nit community. Local folk were aghast, for it was unknown for a mere lass to roam freely with a gun, and just not care if she was seen or not. Oh it was different for a farmer's wife to be able to shoot, but even she kept to her own fields, and didn't run around without a care in the world. Yells and crude remarks from the slate miners were often heard as they left the nearby quarry for a well earned drink from the local inn, and though they cursed the girl under their breath, most of them would happily admit they found the strange young girl with the most piercing of slate grey eyes interesting, mysterious even, for not once had she spoken to any of them, and their fascination grew. Older men in the village wondered if she was mute, a bit daft maybe, but nothing was voiced to the girl, most kept a safe distance, for the way she held that gun clinging to it as if for dear life, sent a shiver down the hardest of spines. Back on the Hampstead Estate however, those that had taken Briar into service were not going to keep silent for much longer, for disgust was running high. Briar Rose was heard regularly, her tongue had begun to run as wild as her spirit and the once happy establishment was becoming threatened by her outrageous behaviour. The girls that were also still under the Bunting's guidance that had once cheerfully worked alongside Briar began to give her the cold shoulder, fearful that her bursts of mad temper would lead them all into trouble, even though the occasional giggle of one of the girls could be heard. As for Emily Bunting, she had taken Briar to one side and had almost shaken the life out of her. "Eeh lass, it's common knowledge wha's goin' on, an' dunna looken liken tha'. Eeh lass 'ave yo' no shame? The whole damn estate 'as heard yo', it's shameful, an' you'll only brin' trouble t' yoresel'." It was a day that Emily had also made herself heard, something she seldom did, and the rest of the girls in her service had ran for cover when the elderly woman had actually shouted the word 'damn', a word that the likes of the Bunting's never used. Joseph Bunting had been incensed, for he had also that same day been sent for by Master Jonathan who had queried in great lengths the unsettled atmosphere on his estate. He had also gone on to question Joseph in menacing detail why it was that Stan Lawson was seen regularly with a new bruise to his face, a swollen lip, or puffed eye? What could Joseph tell him? That Stan Lawson's young wife fought with him daily? Yes, fought with him, on the ground like a lad if he would believe the tales the young grounds men under Stan's care told him. It was an outcry, no girl acted this way, not here, not anywhere, and certainly not one of the girls in his and his good wife's service. That very afternoon the atmosphere of the Hampstead Estate became even more cloudy than a summer thunder storm for Joseph

Bunting did something so severe, something he had never known to threaten, never mind actually doing, and it sent the other girls in his service, including his own wife fleeing from the parlour and cowering in their own rooms. Joseph was desperate, he had never known defeat in all the years he had worked for the Hampstead's, and he was as proud as any man could be of his trusted position in this house. He would not expect his own kin to endanger his position, but the girl had actually caused Master Jonathan to have words with him, and now he had to stop her silly nonsense and fast. Joseph Bunting had stormed through the parlour without a word, only to return just as bluntly with a riding crop tightly in his hand. Without a word of reprimand or warning he had grabbed the girl in question and had leathered her there and then in the parlour until her cries of distress rang out across the courtyard and towards the ears of the grounds men. Stan Lawson had stood rigid, his whole body tense, his spade so tightly grasped in his hands, until his knuckles turned deathly white. He knew the sound of a thrashing only too well, he'd never forget the sounds of pounding flesh and fretful cries from the workhouse, and he also knew that it was his wife on the end of this fury. But what could he do about it? She was still employed and under the service of the Bunting's, to interfere would guarantee his own dismissal and without papers, and then what? He also had the brain to know that Joseph Bunting must have been at his wits end to do this, for he was known to be a firm, but a very fair man who fathered the girls, and never had been known to raise his hand in anger. Did he really blame him for this? No, Stan did not, for he too was at his own wits end, although he wasn't that desperate yet. Marriage was nothing he had expected the very instance he had taken her to their new home she had pointed the gun at him, and had refused him bluntly. In fact she had been very fast to learn just how to use it. Oh the cottage was fine, she was a hard worker which he had always known, and in no time at all their entire home was a tiny palace of cleanliness, wild flowers were daily placed on the table and nothing was out of place. There was always water without him having to fetch it, and wood for the fire, he hadn't had to raise a finger to help in any way. Briar was proving to be a pretty good hunter too, for rabbit or grouse had been the main course on his table now for almost six weeks, and she had proved she knew how to use the house keeping wisely. No, he wanted for nothing, she did everything any other wife would do and gracefully, but that's where it ended. When the last flickering glow of the candle began to die she became hostile towards him, the gun was never far from her side. He had not been near her since his wedding day almost two months ago, for if he did step too close she fought with whatever she could lay her hands on and had regularly marked his face when he had tried to get just a little bit closer. Stan had been patient, he hadn't wanted to wait, and at times he didn't see why he should, for he was not a stranger to her, for he had actually taken her once before, back at the workhouse, so she could hardly be scared of him. But he hung back and he waited, for though he wanted nothing more than to feel her softness next to him in the heat of the night, he wanted one thing far more. For her to want him back. All Stan could think of doing was to prove that he could be as good a husband as she could ever desire and not push, for his own needs. He had to allow her space she so obviously needed. Only now it was becoming so very hard, for with the regular beltings he was receiving from her, he had been turned into an obstacle of ridicule from the young lads who worked under him… "Ge' back t' work the lo' o' yo' or dunna thinken I'm too sof' nod t' tek a strap t' any o' yo'." Stan had tuned to see three curious faces as they stopped work and had stood and listened to the commotion coming from the parlour of the Hampstead House. Subconsciously Stan had reached up and had touched his face, the latest bruise to his cheek still painful. They must have heard up at the house how he was getting his bruises and had decided to punish her for it. "Back t' work." Stan's bellow immediately set the lads on their heels. He would put up with no slacking. For now he had the lawns to cut, the brushes to prune, and Mistress Blanche had suggested a few flower beds would be a good idea. Yes he had work to get on with, but later…later…he touched his head, he just could not think.

In the heat of the work mill Ben Lawson was hard at work, his greatest piece stood in front of him, something he was so proud of. "Dunna overheat tha' veneer Robert's, the minute it's done I need it on the double." Oblivious to those around him Ben lost himself in the world he knew best, where he stood taller than most men. The gentle sawing that hummed perfectly in time with the tapping of a hammer and the clanking of clamps as timber, piece by piece was so carefully and perfectly placed, gradually finishing off some grand jigsaw. "Pass me tha' hammer, the small one, an' dunna knock mi bleedin' bench."

"No Master Lawson."

"Eh…Master Jonathan…I'm sorry sir…I wa' too…"

"I can see Lawson; let no man stand in the way of a craftsman and his work eh?"

Jonathan smiled in contentment as he ran his fingers over the cabinet, a drinking cabinet for a gentleman from the well refined area of Kingsland, the grand houses just over the river Severn that towered over the town of Shrewsbury. "Pleasing boy, very pleasing."

"Do yo' liken it master?" Ben dared to push further.

"Very much Lawson, yes very much." Jonathan checked over the work as if his own life depended upon it. The craftsmanship this young lad turned out was indeed without fault. The decorative veneer had given the cabinet an appearance of old oak, and the engraved detail around the edges was of sound precise perfection. Jonathan eyed the work even more closely, no he could not find a single fault, and as always he was left in awe by the beauty of this lads work, a lad so very young. "Have you given thought to my offer Lawson?"

"Oh aye master, an' a generous offer it is."

"And?"

Ben gently closed the cabinet door and faced Jonathan Hampstead full on. "It's a mighty generous offer master, yo've offered me mi dream, an' I'd be a fool t' turn it down." Taking a quick breath Ben quickly carried on. "Bu' I'd liken t' discuss the business side o' it jus' a bi' more." He waited, he could see certain surprise in his master's face, "Bu' I am grateful master, oh aye I'm very grateful."

"Then we shall discuss it further Lawson, later when work is done call for Emily Bunting to have one of the girls bring you up to my study. Maybe that young sister in law of yours, keep her out of trouble eh?" Jonathan winked at the lad in his mill, a real fine lad with a talent that would take him far and also be a good little business on the side for him too.

"Aye master, I will…an' thankyo' again."

"Until later Lawson." Without another word Jonathan turned and left, he had the other lads work to check over, and work had to be distributed between them, and any orders that had been taken that morning seen too. Ben downed his tools just for a short while and watched the others around him thoughtfully. How strange life was becoming, who would have thought that a gentleman like Jonathan Hampstead would have been interested enough in him, to even think of a business deal? But in the two years that Ben had been with him he had come to know his true worth, and he had made it plain that one day he would have his dream. His own workshop with living dwellings where he could be his very own man. Now, with the help of Jonathan, it looked very promising, for though he would not own the property, not yet. He would be his own man. It was turning out perfectly, except for one thing that was worrying him. Ben had heard certain rumours concerning his brother, and though deep inside Ben would never accept the fact that Stan had gone and married Briar Rose, Stan was his brother just the same. He'd seen the marks on Stan's face, and he'd also heard about Joseph Bunting having to discipline one of the girls, something that was unheard of here. Yet Ben knew in his heart that the girl had to be Briar Rose, for he knew no girl who could push a soul to frenzy the way she could. After his meeting with his master Ben would make his way over to Stan's cottage and take his brother out to the local village inn. They needed to talk seriously, brother to brother how they once had. For before Ben could venture further with Jonathan Hampstead's kind offer, he had to offer his hand of friendship and steady the ground between himself and Stan. Then maybe, just maybe, he'd get the chance to have a quiet word with Briar Rose himself, a firm word.

"See yo' firs' ligh' lads, an' dunna thinken we're in fur an easy day. Her ladyship 'as plans, an' by the looks o' it, the pond is on the cards t' be gone." Stan flipped his cap at the three lads that worked under his supervision. Stan was happy in his job, and content to do all that Blanche Hampstead asked of him, it was more up his street to work outside in the grounds, and though the gardens were not the most decorative, they were kept to perfection, and there always seemed to be plenty of work to fill up his days. Stan glanced around the outside of the freshly cut lawn. Good, no stones, it was the one thing Blanche was so particular about, stones, woe betide them all if a stone was found on the lawn. Stan grinned to himself as he thought of the Hampsteads Blanche was a good mistress, kind and mostly polite, but never did the order for work come directly from her. They were given through her husband, while she stood quietly by and simply offered a slight nod from time to time. But today had been very different, when Stan had been ready to call it a day, he had been called to his master's study, and then he had seen a different side to Blanche Hampstead. Jonathan had kindly told him that his work on the estate was satisfactory, and his leadership good, he was happy with Stan and hoped he would stay with him for many a year. But the talk had turned, and there was far more on Jonathan's mind which had to be said, and it made Stan's blood boil. To add insult to his frail emotions, Blanche had gone on to say openly that she would not have her servants upset. She had told Stan that the sound of Briar Rose's voice screaming and the distress caused to all in her household by Joseph Bunting's punishment that day had nearly caused her to faint. The blame could not lay with Joseph Bunting; it had to lay with Stan. Jonathan had firmly told Stan that he would not have this type of thing happen again, and seriously suggested that Stan took his family life in hand, and fast. Stan had bowed his head as he offered his mistress his sincere humbled apologies, and promised his master it would not happen again. To make matters even more embarrassing, when Stan had been excused from the study he had walked out of the door only to find himself face to face with Ben.

"Stan."

"Ben."

"I'll be over later Stan, if tha's alrigh'?"

"Aye." Was all that Stan could mutter. He knew that Ben must have heard all that had been said, for why the sudden visit to his cottage? Ben had not been near there since his marriage to Briar. As the fierce heat from the brilliant August sun blessed the land with a shadow of reprieve from her scorching rays Stan crossed the grounds; slowly. He was on his way home, exhausted, emotionally drained and embarrassed; he had much on his mind. He was glad his cottage was private, right away from the house, almost out of sight as a large hedgerow shielded the windows almost from view. Before he even opened the door, the aroma of stewed rabbit and chopped onions gently wafted through the air settling nicely causing his mouth to water wantonly. It was almost welcoming, how perfect this could all seem to a passing stranger, his own cottage, a meal waiting for him as he finished work, and a pretty young wife inside making their home a comfortable place. Stan sighed, for everything was almost right, except for the welcome. For he sensed at most times that Briar would have rather not had him there at all. But even now, after the humiliation he had suffered at the expense of the young grounds men laughing at him, at hearing the commotion at the house that very morning, and then the stern talking too he had just received over her, Stan was still ready to try and ease his wife into his world gently. He had requested the same half day off as her, and he would do his best in that time to make her relax with him in the hope that his married life would take the normal path. Briar gasped as she heard the door close, had she misjudged the time? Stan was seldom home this early, it was hardly six o'clock surely. "Dunna come in, I'm…I'm on mi way, dunna come in."

Stan immediately grinned, his humiliating show down with the master and mistress briefly forgotten. He could hear the gentle splash of water behind the curtain at the far end of the parlour, she was bathing, just inches from where he now stood, a simple curtain separating them.

"Theer's a cauldron o' water heatin' over the fire, I wunna be a minute an' then yo' can 'ave the bath." As fast as she could Briar stepped out of the tin bath, grabbing her towel to cover herself, just in case he should happen to see her, or worse yet, dare to try and walk in.

"Dunna yo' worry lass, yo' res' yore aches an' pains, I'll wai'." Stan stared at the closed curtain, she was silent, and not even a subtle splash of water broke the sudden peace.

Briar Rose also glared at the closed curtain, her slate grey eyes flashed with annoyance. So he knew. Well he could be kept guessing the rest, for she would tell nothing about what had happened to her that morning. Quickly she took her cotton undergarments almost stumbling as she struggled to make herself decent, winching as she did so. The freshly laundered cotton always made her skin feel so soft and clean, only today all it made it feel was the bruising to her flesh where the riding crop had stung her.

"Stay theer." Loudly Briar spoke, just in case Stan did have any ideas of walking in. Hurriedly now she pulled on her clean frock, a dress she had made herself of pale green cotton with three quarter length sleeves. It held no nonsense, but fitted snugly into her waist before falling to her ankles, in a very generous flow. "A very serviceable frock" Emily Bunting would have called it. "Damn it." In her hurry to dress, she had forgotten her petticoat, reaching out frantically she made the last rush to dress herself properly, finally brushing down the front of her frock to let any creases fall out naturally.

"Yo' le' Joseph Buntin' hear yo' speak liken tha', he'll thrash yore arse again."

Silence. So he did know. Grabbing the curtain that divided the space between them Briar sharply pulled it back and faced Stan, a heavy pout turning her pretty face into a sour scowl. "Aye well be tha' as it may, theer's water if yo' wan' it, otherwise mind yoresel', I 'ave a meal t' ge'." Rudely Briar pushed past him, rubbing her hair dry with her towel as she did so. Stan watched her carefully, he had no intention of bathing just yet, and he could see he had already annoyed her. But shouldn't it have been him who should have been enraged with her?

"Anythin' yo' wan' t' tell me lass?"

"No."

"So yo' 'ad a good day then?"

"Aye I di', an' yo'?" Briar snapped her answer. She had told herself she would try very hard to stop her sharpness, but she had started already. The lecture Joseph Bunting had given her after he had dealt her the riding crop had chilled her to the bone. He had given her a few home truths about herself, and had bluntly told her what was what. He had succeeded in making her feel like a ridiculous child, and had reduced her to sobs before he sent her to see Emily, only for Briar to receive another sharp reprimand. "I'm sorry, I jus' feel…tired…I didna expec' yo' so soon. I 'anna se' the table ye'."

Stan took a deep breath and slightly nodded in response as her slate grey eyes flashed his way. He too had one aim, and that was to stop all of this and try to make things better between them. "If yo' wanna talk t' me, well 'ere I am. If nod tha's alrigh' by me too, at leas' fur now." Sitting down on the easy chair by the hearth he watched her more intently. She was slowly calming down, her eyes had stopped piercing him so violently, and in fact she was watching him too, though the pout on her lips was still very evident. He had to tread carefully; she was still in a mood. "Si' down a minute lass, leave tha'." Stan pointed to the cauldron of hot water she held, then pulled a chair up closer to him. "Si' down, I wunna bite. I've been doin' some thinkin'."

Briar placed the cauldron down and without a murmur obediently sat down opposite her husband waiting to hear what it was that had left a heavy expression on his face. He didn't look angry, his bright blue eyes held a certain warmth, but she could sense he was tense for he was sitting bolt upright, something he never did unless he felt upset. He was about to ask her something, tell her something she was sure of that, and she somehow knew he would only want to hear one answer. "I thinken we need some time t'gether lass, an' nod 'ere. I've teken mi half day wi' yo', so how abou' me an' yo' tek the firs' cart into' Shrewsbury Town an' do a little shoppin'?" Stan smiled as he saw a look of surprise cover her pretty heart shaped face. The sullen glaze in her slate grey eyes held that certain spark of curiosity.

"Yo' wan' t' come an' help me banter fur the price o' a piece o' fish?" She waited, he nodded. "An' I wan' t' wander the market fur material." That would put him off going for sure, but just another nod. "I wan' some ribbon fur mi hair." Again Stan nodded.

"I'm sure yo'll find somethin' mi lady." In a mocking tone he carried on, for he could see he had her interest. "An' when mi lady's through, we could stop by tha' stall jus' at the end o' the market square an' ge' a hot potato."

"Wi' butter?"

"Now yore pushin' yore luck." Stan grinned broadly, if she wanted the luxury of butter he'd make sure she had just that.

Briar Rose turned her back for a few long moments as she quietly set the table for tea, passing a small warm loaf over to Stan for him to cut. She enjoyed her half day off by herself, but would having him with her be so bad? She glanced at him, and was met with bright blue eyes that smiled with interest at her. Briar remembered all that Joseph Bunting had said to her that morning. How angry he had been with her, and she remembered Emily's firm words. "He's yore husband lass, nobody forced yo' t' marry him, an' believe me yo' could do far worse. Eeh t' thinken wha' some men would do t' yo' lass if yo' marked their faces the way yo' 'ave Stan's."

Briar frowned, lost in sudden thought. She did everything for Stan that any other wife would do, he wanted for nothing. That was except the one thing she knew he wanted, what made a marriage whole between man and a woman. But maybe with everything she did do for him, she did have respect for him, in some way, though what way, she was still undecided.

"So then daydreamer, shall we go owt? Me an' yo' t' Shrewsbury Market, and find tha' ribbon fur yore hair?"

Briar answered with a smile, and tried very hard to mean every word she said when she softly spoke. "Aye Stan, I'd liken tha', I'll looken forward t' it." Stan graciously took the pot offered him placing it in the centre of the table." Looks real good lass, yore the envy o' all the men owtside wi' the smells tha' come owt o' this parlour." Stan helped himself first to a large plate of hot rabbit stew, and then offered a smaller helping to her. She had accepted his offer to take her to the market very pleasantly; he hadn't had to try very hard at all. It was a start, maybe then she may learn to relax in his company. It was the first meal in their two months of marriage that they sat as any other husband and wife, speaking to each other sociably. Stan told her all about Blanche's ideas for the new flower gardens and even caused her to titter when he tried to mimic her sweet talking voice pronouncing every word perfectly. Briar found herself interested in what Stan was saying, and for the first time since she had known him realised what a sense of humour he had. In fact sitting there laughing and joking, his manners towards her impeccable, she found herself thinking that maybe she had been too harsh on him. Perhaps she should try harder. He was tall, and very lean with a shock of red hair that made him easy to see. He had the brightest of blue eyes, and wide lips that parted into a radiant smile leaving crease marks at the corners of his eyes. He was in fact very pleasant to the eye, she just hadn't noticed. "More tea?"

"Aye lass, please." Stan carried on talking as she stirred the mushed tea several times before pouring it. Her hair was still very damp, leaving patches on her frock, but she moved so gracefully as she served him the hot mushed liquid before gathering up the empty plates. When she smiled as she did now, he considered her most pretty, with the face of an angel and eyes that could melt a man with their childlike glow. When she pouted and screwed her nose up at him however she became that wildcat he had very first fought with, her temper was dangerous, and her slate grey eyes could pierce through any man's soul and leave him quivering. It was as Briar cleared the last of the dishes and Stan sat by the hearth that the tap on the door startled both of them.

"Oh I furgo' tha', mus' be Ben."

"Ben?" Briar immediately stood up straight, smoothing her frock down to get rid of any unseen creases.

"Evenin' Stan…Briar."

Briar watched as Ben stepped into their parlour, the two brothers shaking hands, though Ben's eyes fastened tightly onto her own.

"Hello Ben this is a surprise." She noticed Stan gave a brief frown, her words had come sharp. She hadn't meant it, but Ben had not been near the cottage since their marriage, and he had not been within an arms length of her.

"Yo' look well Briar."

"Aye I suppose so."

"Shame our Stan 'ere keeps walkin' int' walls though. Bruises on a man's face ge's folk talkin'." Ben quickly winked at his brother, he did not wish to patronize Stan, but by the grin that appeared on his face Stan had taken it all in his stride. Only Briar Rose held a look of defiance. Her heavy pout had returned and she looked tense, her slate grey eyes had lost any warmth and now they pierced straight through Ben, and then Stan. She was furious. As Stan made Ben welcome, both brother's relaxing in each others company Briar sat up the far corner by the table and fumed. This was planned, she could tell, and Stan had told her nothing about Ben's visit. When Stan excused himself on a laugh, and disappeared upstairs to change Briar Rose pouted all the more, but when Ben limped towards her, his stick steadying his frame she felt that familiar turn of somersaults in the pit of her stomach. As he stood just inches from her, she gulped and found nothing to say. Why did Ben have to turn up on their doorstep tonight? Hadn't she tried over the past two months to forget him? But now here he stood, in reaching distance, just a heartbeat away, but he may as well have been a million mile away for what good it could do her. Ben gazed deep into the prettiest face he ever wanted to know, the most striking of grey eyes he would ever encounter. How he had tried to push her to the back of his mind, to keep his feelings well hidden, for he had no right to want her any more, she was his brother's wife. How he wished he could turn the clocks back just two months ago, for he would then have pushed himself forward, he should have told her his true feelings, but now he never could. There would have been so much he could have made for her, he would have gladly surrounded his world just around her, and he would have needed nothing else. Now, here she stood, so very close to him, and to make his heart feel even more wretched he could feel the sense of longing between them, he could see an echo of hidden secrets deep in her slate grey eyes, and he knew that she too was fighting to keep her reality in line. For if she didn't, her whole world would stumble and crash around her. Ben could feel fire between them, a dangerous liaison that could never now take place, and he would help make sure it didn't, and maybe help her as well accept his brother better than she had. Ben had made up his mind to take his master's generous offer, and though his own heart would ache for a while, his conscience would be clear and then Briar would maybe be the wife to Stan that she should have been.

"I've heard rumours lass."

"Oh aye."

"Aye, an' I dunna liken wha' I'm hearin'." Ben stood as firm as he could, for once he was glad of his stick, for his fist clenched as tightly on it for support he suddenly desperately needed. For though his heart would never hurt the girl in front of him, his common sense told him he had too. "He's mi brother lass, an' yore nod givin' him a fair crack o' the whip." Ben swallowed, he could see she was flustering, the colour was rising in her face, and if he didn't know better he swore he could see dampness in her slate grey eyes. "Yo' married 'im lass, nobody made yo', so why the big fuss eh?" Ben watched her take a step backwards. He hadn't quite planned this form of questioning, but he had been hurt by her marriage to his brother which had just grabbed control of his own emotions on sight of her, destroying the common sense he'd entered the cottage with. "Yore mekin' a real fool o' our Stan an' he deserves better than yore givin'. Bloody hell lass it's nod as if yo' dunna know 'im, yo' laid wi' 'im before yo' were wed; remember?"

Remember, how could she have forgotten the only time she had laid with him. She had been but fourteen, and had been beaten by the workhouse master until she had fainted, and what had Stan done to her? Raped her, not once, but twice. Briar pouted heavily, her slate grey eyes pierced through Ben, her anger beginning to surface rapidly. Her only experience with men had not been good, and here stood another man, a very young man, but a man just the same hardly a year older than her, and daring to tell her that his brother deserved better. Ben could see the agitation building up in Briar's face, her slate grey eyes pierced him fiercely, and he could also see that at any moment she'd lose control and lash out marking his face too, so before she did, he'd finish what he had started.

"I'm leavin' 'ere pretty soon Briar, bu' before I do, I wan' t' see mi brother happy, an' yo' livin' an' actin' liken the wife yo' should be. Grow up Briar, yo' inna a little lass any more, yore a married woman now, star' actin' liken one."

Briar gasped, the coldness in Ben that now faced itself squarely at her visibly made her tremble. Taking another deep breath she stepped backwards, how hard it was not to let the flood gates open. Did he really say he was leaving? And his hate towards her was clear, but what did she expect? She had known where his feelings lay a long time ago, for she had seen it in his warm brown eyes, but she had seen the wall quickly build between them the day she had turned in the workhouse and had left with Stan. But that had only been to save Ben's skin if he had stepped in, the workhouse master would have beaten him. But through her actions it had led them here, to this estate. Briar knew she had one chance left to make him see why she was so unhappy with her life; she either had to take it or keep her mouth shut forever. Her voice shook as she began to speak, but she spoke as clearly as she could, and her bottom lip ever ready to pout quivered, her tears just a second away as she began. "Maybe I shouldna 'ave married Stan, maybe I wa' waitin' fur another, maybe I'm married t' the wrong brother."

Ben struggled, his body leaning even more heavily on his stick, how hard it was trying to hold onto the man he sounded like, so harsh. How easy it would be for him to declare his own passion, the feelings he had kept locked away for so long, how very easy it would be to destroy his own brothers marriage here and now. He had been more than smitten with this girl, and Stan had known that and had openly taken her for himself. He could do the very same, how easy it would be. But even still, Ben had a loyalty to Stan, a loyalty that was bound by blood, so when he spoke, he knew it would finish any dreams he had ever held onto, and would plainly let Briar know exactly where she had to stand.

"No lass, yo' didna marry the wrong brother. If I'd wanted yo'

I'd 'ave spoken fur yo'. No lass yore wi' the better man, fur if yo' 'ad treated me the way yo' 'ave our Stan, I'd 'ave skelped the hide o' yo' mesel', bu' ne'er would yo' 'ave raised yore hand t' me." Ben hardly knew his own voice, a voice so hard it could have sounded from a man double his age. He could see by the reaction he got he had hit home hard with his sharp words. Ben took another step back when the tears did begin to fall, and she stared at him, so forlornly, her slate grey eyes lost in a sea of tears, and when she visibly shuddered at the sound of his voice, he was left with just one desire. To hold her, and tell her that none of what he had just said was true. How right they could have been together, and he would never have done anything to hurt her even if she had belted him the way she had Stan. And yes, Ben wholly agreed she had married the wrong brother, but he could never tell her that.

"Wha's goin' on 'ere then? Wha's the fuss?" Stan now stood at the foot of the stairs, his one pair of decent black trousers on, his shock of bright red hair combed in place. Not a smile evident on his face, his voice questioning. "Yo' made mi wife cry Ben?"

"Aye, I'm afraid so, didna mean too." Ben turned away from Briar, his voice a false tone that appeared jovial. "Told 'er if she marks yore face again, I'll skelp 'er mesel'."

"An' tha' made yo' cry Briar?" Stan was not convinced, some girls maybe, but not Briar, she was usually so…

"Aye it di', because he's a nowt. I inna puttin' up wi' him an' 'is mouth. He can go back t' 'is ugly tree." Briar finished on a scream, and silenced them both. For as she always had in the past, when there was nothing she could throw in her defence she always went back to highly childish remarks she had used as a small girl. Ben gave a quick glance of contempt; he had no intentions of passing comment to such a silly remark. Stan however was not quite so forgiving. "Enough o' tha' Briar, yo' watch tha' temper o' yore's lass."

Stan watched the heavy pout cloud her pretty face and decided it was time for him and Ben to leave when insults were hurled their way, followed by a plate that Briar had grabbed, narrowly missing them both as they fled out of the cottage.

Following the narrow lane that led them from the Common and down onto the one dirt track that led into Bayston Hill, Ben and Stan crossed over and made their way towards The Three Fishes, the one inn that was always packed with local villagers, farmers, and miners alike. It was the first time in months that the brothers sat and talked as most brothers did, and how they once had. Each one enjoyed the slightly warm ale, and neither of them complained about the smoky atmosphere or the loud brash jokes that echoed from the miners. It was a man's pub, a time for relaxing and saying just what they felt without their women folk present, a time when, whatever their job or social standing, they were one of a kind, the working class folk who needed to drown their fears deep in a tankard of ale, or celebrate it's glory.

"I knew yo'd mek it Ben, an' though I dunna say much, I'm proud o' yo' lad."

"Aye I know, bu' I'd ne'er 'ave done it wi'owt yo' by mi side. Theer's times I dragged yo' down Stan when yo' could 'ave gone on, bu' yo' didna." Ben spoke softly and honestly. He could see the look of pride in his brother's eyes, pride by his success, and he could feel the warmth of brotherly love pulling them back as close as they had always been. Stan reached out and laid his hand on Ben's shoulder, something he had always done when there were no words left. Not to have Ben on the same property as himself would leave a gaping hole in his life. They hadn't had much to do with each other since his marriage to Briar, but Stan knew where Ben was, and he knew he was safe. He was only three years Ben's senior, but he had always looked out for him in times of great strife. He had taken beatings for him as a small boy and he had held his toddling brother in his arms, being hardly more than a toddler himself when Ben had screamed out in agony as the polio had struck him down, and had slowly and cruelly crippled his leg. He had never thought of a day in his life when Ben would not be close by, for Stan had grown up fast where Ben had been concerned, he had not just been his brother, he had been his mother and his father. And now, as if Ben was his son telling him about his great offer, and his chance to move on Stan's heart pounded with a pride so strong it made him feel quite sick. "If yo' ever need me Ben, wha' ever it is, yo' come t' me lad, I'm the one yo' come too."

Ben grinned, "Aye an' yo' come t' me too our Stan, an' if yo' wan' me t' sor' yore wife owt, I'll skelp the lugs o' 'er, yo' see if I dunna."

Stan roared with laughter, the serious side of them gone. It was good to laugh, and Stan having never heard Ben speak this way spluttered even more so at his not so quiet, not so thoughtful younger brother. Way into the evening the Lawson brothers sat, ale flowing freely between them, each one feeling the warmth of the liquid, relaxing them even further. They had much to celebrate, at least Ben did. "I'll only be in lease fur the firs' three years, wi' the master, then after tha' I'll be able t' suppor' mesel'."

"A partnership o' kinds?"

"Well…nod really." Ben went on to explain that he could not afford a business property with living accommodation of any kind. But, with the master's offer of leasing the property to him for a very reasonable profit on Ben's crafts for himself Ben could take the first step into the big world of industry. Of course Jonathan Hampstead would not lose out, it would be a business on the side for him, he'd not only get profits from what Ben could take on himself, but he already had orders that would be passed Ben's way that his own mill lads would not handle so well. "Bu' I'll be mi own man. I can si' all nigh' wi' mi toy mekin' an' tek a break when I wan'." Ben could not hide his enthusiasm. Toy making was something he wanted to venture into even further. He had a new design in his minds eye, a child's rocking horse, for a very small child, where it could sit safely without the aid of its mother. Ben had many ideas; he could hardly wait to put into practice. "An' yo' Stan? Yo' goin' t' mek it work wi' yo' an' Briar?" Ben watched his brother turn very sullen, the light gone from his bright blue eyes. The ale was having its full affect, and Stan was looking more down as the evening went on. "Is it really tha' bad "Oh aye it is, the rumours yo' 'ave heard, well they're all true." Stan bit down on his lip, lost in thought, but he carried on, "I 'ave a wife who can handle 'ersel' better than me. A real mean swing she's go' Ben. She's fas' t' bel' me, and even quicker t' reach fur tha' gun. The sigh' o' me meks 'er feel sick."

"I'm sure it's nod tha' bad." Ben nudged his brother in the hope that he would see that silly grin of his light up his eyes, but nothing.

"Aye it is."

Ben placed down his ale.

"I'm a laughin' stock wi' the lads Ben. She bel's the livin' daylights owt o' me, an' she 'anna once shared the same bed as me." Stan stopped only momentarily. By the look on Ben's face he hadn't expected to hear that, and the sudden hush from a small group of nearby miners, who were beginning to find the conversation about the silvery blond haired girl interesting only made Stan feel worse. But what the hell, everybody knew anyway. "Well tha's me Ben, yore big brother who's always looked owt fur yo', canna even handle 'is sixteen year old wife." As the smoky atmosphere took its grip and the laughter of men's crude jokes fought through the murky atmosphere, Stan had sat and had spilt out all that was troubling his heart. There was nothing left to be said, for he was already the laughing stock of the estate, and now most probably the whole village of Bayston Hill. Ben gently took the tankard from his brother's hands.

"Time t' go our Stan, tha's if we can both stand up." Nobody paid attention as the brothers stumbled towards the door, both of them the worse for wear, with nothing else left to say. No secret was now held between them, each brother trying to support the other, whilst trying to walk straight himself. Stan had a thumping head from all of the ale, and Ben was thankful once more for his stick. "Yo' keep yore 'ead up Stan, an' dunna le' life ge' yo' down, it will all work owt yo'll see."

"Aye, it will, aye." Stan waved his hand and lifted the latch of the cottage door, just a lowly candle was left, ready to flicker its last fading light. Briar was not there. As Stan's sharp eyes gazed into the darkness of upstairs he shook his head, she would not be up there. Rubbing his hands together with a sudden chill that took hold of him Stan sat down for a while and waited, when she still didn't appear he decided to go and look for her, it was late, and she shouldn't be out in the dark by herself.

Ben had quietly made his way from the cottage and towards the mill. He shared dwellings above the mill with four other lads who would probably by now be sleeping. At first light he'd go to the master and finalise their arrangement. Whistling to himself, Ben ventured on in the darkness, he had to get on with his life and move as far from here as he dare. Why he should suddenly turn, he would never know, for he had heard nothing, he just sensed before he ever got to the mill that somebody was close by in the trees that kept the cottage of Stan's from view. "Briar, wha' the hell are yo' doin' owt lass? Stan will wonder where yo' are."

"Will he?" Briar stepped forward away from her shelter of the oak trees. Since they had gone out she had sat alone in the trees and had waited her heart heavy. She feared she would not see Ben again, and she was ready to risk what she had once more. "Di' yo' really mean those nasty thin's yo' said t' me Ben? I mean' wha' I said, I di' marry the wrong brother, bu' I thinken yo' know that really."

Ben faced the girl head on, the gentle breeze of the warm August night air relieving his mind of earlier turmoil, placing a new worry in its place. As the girl with waist length silvery blond hair and slate grey eyes pleaded tearfully with him to listen, Ben had to fight within himself. Clutching tightly onto his stick, he tried to steady himself, if he did not have the stick right now, he would undoubtedly fall. "Yo' shouldna be owt by yoresel' lass, go home t' yore husband."

"I'll go in a minute Ben, bu' nod until I've said somethin'. I've ne'er loved Stan, I married him thinken I could learn too. bu' I canna, I married the wrong brother."

"An' yo'd 'ave married me would yo'?" Why Ben had said that he did not know, again he had to steady himself.

"Aye, I would 'ave, bu' yo' didna bother wi' me di' yo'." Briar snapped, her answer accusing. Her comment brought Ben reeling back to his senses.

"I didna ask, fur I had nowt t' give. Bu' I would 'ave, when I go' mesel' sorted owt t' tek a wife on an' looken after mi own properly. Now I 'ave the chance, bu' nod wi' yo'Briar, fur yo' couldna wai', yo, up an' married fur the sake o' it." Ben wobbled as he glared into the slate grey eyes that began to pierce through him. "Aye dunna liken the truth lass? Well neither do I. Wha' do yo' wan' t' 'ear Briar? Tha' I wa' too bloody tongue tied t' tell yo' wha' I really fel' fur yo'? Well now yo' know lass, I've loved yo' since the day yo' broke int' the mens side o' the workhouse, an' tried t' steal mi boots, an' every day since yo've teased me wi' those damn grey eyes o' yore's, getting' between me an' me wits until I canna breath." Ben stopped momentarily, his heart pounding so heavily, why the hell had he just told her that? Drink had made him lose control of his senses. "Well lass theer's nowt I can do abou' it now, so go back t' yore husband, mi brother, yo' made yore bed, now go an' lay on it."

Briar had heard more than enough, how dare he blame her, he had no right, he did not know what she had gone through, and now he blamed her. Ben didn't have time to step back before Briar was on him, her slap sharp as it sliced against the side of his face. Just as quickly she raised her hand a second time, but Ben was just as fast, grabbing her wrist to hold her as steady as he could. "Stop it Briar, I inna lettin' go until yo' stop it." Ben's voice carried on the warm night air, but Briar struggled more violently against him, her pride shattered, as tears streaked her face. Never had he been so cruel, and here she stood fighting against his grip, the last person on this earth he had wished to distress. Again Ben felt the effects of the nights drinking session as he wobbled precariously almost losing his footing. But then Ben did move, fast and knowingly as he let go of Briar's wrist and grabbed her by the shoulders, pulling her close towards him, something he had wanted to do for so long. Roughly Ben forced his lips hard against hers, his arms circling around her holding her steady and tight against him. Briar's first instinct was to fight, to escape the sudden embrace that only ever meant pain when a man did hold her this way. As she tried to push Ben from her, she felt the warmth, as his arms held her less firmly and his mouth sought hers for pleasure, then her face, until his kisses gently roamed over her tearful eyes. Taking a deep breath Briar began to relax, her fight over for now, she sensed Ben was not going to hurt her. When Ben felt the struggle cease, he let her go, only to pull her straight back in his arms, his kisses of fire being met with a burning desire of promise from the girl he had longed to hold for so long. There was no wedding band, or man made law, or promise to obey any husband as the torn young couple who had battled between their loyalties and what should be right, began what they had both wanted to do for so long ago. Ben knew in that moment only the touch and gentle caressing bond he could feel with the girl in his arms was not wrong. It was a love they had both been denied, and one they could no longer keep hidden. He had loved Briar from the time he had set eyes on her, when he hardly knew what his own feelings meant, but now he would do anything to protect the girl that should have been his wife. For Briar it was a release of built up tensions that she had held for so long. She had been in love with Ben since a fourteen year old lass, only she had been too blind to see that his love had been just as strong. She had always sensed his warmth towards her, and now being held so closely by a man, she did not feel the terror she had only ever known before, she knew what it was like to be wanted, to want back, and if Ben had the urge to take her now, she would willingly be ready to give.

"So looks liken I'm the las' t' know, even mi own brother's

tekin' me fur a laughing stock. No wonder the other men mek fun o' me, wha' a bloody fool I am."

As one, Ben and Briar gently released, and stood apart, but not leaving each others side. Ben kindly glanced at Briar protectively pulling her to the one side of him.

"It inna wha' you'may 'ave wanted t' see Stan, bu' it were me tha' took advantage, Briar wa' on 'er way 'ome, righ' lass?" Ben caught Briar's confused stare, but he slightly nodded, he could think of no other way tonight, Stan was in drink, he had to smooth things as fast as he could.

"After yo've finished wi' 'er eh? No wonder she ne'er comes near me, bu' I would ne'er 'ave believed it o' you' Ben."

Ben took a step forward, his stick suddenly giving him the extra support he needed.

"Dunna come near me Ben, nod now, nod ever. Keep away from mi wife, or God 'elp the pair o' yo', I'll tek the gun t' yo' both." Stan glowered hard at them and shook his head; no he would never have believed this unless he had seen it himself, as he just had. As Stan stared deep into his brother's warm brown eyes that locked tightly to his he felt a burning hell rage up from inside of him, burning through his veins, boiling his blood until the pain ripped straight through his heart. His only brother had knowingly deceived him, his only blood kin. Never would he be able to trust him again, and now, he wanted Ben as far away from him as possible. When Stan looked down at his own wife, he saw her startle, her slate grey eyes pierced through him with anger, fury at having been caught out. Stan's fury turned to pain; a deep trodden in hurt that shook him to the core. He'd only ever had pride for Ben, and he'd been proud of his wife, the way she could work and even handle herself, for never had he met a girl before her with such qualities. Only now he felt shame, he had been let down by Ben, and he was disgusted by his wife's actions. With the stark realisation of what Ben and Briar meant to each other Stan's love for Briar grew dangerous and highly destructive. There would be lessons that each one of them would one day know the true meaning of, for there is a thin line between love and hate, each emotion as strong as the other, each one able to take a life and destroy it.

"Briar ge' home now." Stan spoke sharply, but Briar only moved when Ben gently pushed her ahead and said.

"Go on lass, it's bes' yo' do, thin's will sor' owt in the mornin'." Ben watched, his heart sinking deep within his soul as Briar nervously walked towards Stan, but fear paralysed him when he saw the look of coldness penetrate from his brother's eyes as the girl slowly passed him, making her way home alone.

"Dunna yo' 'urt her Stan, it were mi faul' nod 'ers, an' I'll leave at firs' ligh', only dunna yo' 'urt her."

"I wunna touch 'er as long as yo' ge' off this property, an' I ne'er see yo' near mi wife again."

It would be the last that the Lawson brothers would speak for a long time, for by first light the next morning Ben would be gone. In the coldness of the cottage Briar sat and waited with just the glow of a lowly candle. She had to try and speak with Stan. If she sat and told him exactly how she had felt for so long now, maybe he would find it in his heart to forgive her and let her go. Maybe in the future the brothers would be speaking again, but she had to speak up for Ben, for it was really her fault he had kissed her that way, for she had chased him, and was secretly glad that she had. Briar wasn't to be given the chance, for Stan was far too furious to listen to her whims, or to see common sense, or to wait until the morning. He had no intentions of being made look a fool any longer, and he'd never allow her to flash those grey eyes with contempt at him again.

Briar startled and stood by the hearth as he stormed back into the cottage, slamming the door behind him. "Stan..."

"Shu' up...jus' shu' up." Spitting out his words he threw his arm out in a motion for her to leave him.

"Stan if yo' jus' listen."

"Listen t' wha? Another pack o' lies, t' thinken theer I were ready t' mek yo' feel at ease wi' me, when all the time…" Stan bit down hard on his lip, he could hardly speak, he was shaking violently with an unleashed anger, and with every word she muttered he found himself hating her more so. Briar pleaded helplessly on deaf ears for him to listen, and when Stan ignored her, continually waving his own dismissive gesture, Briar's own temper began to rise. "See wha' I care anyway, I dunna care wha' yo' believe or say. If I wanna see Ben, I'll do so an' nowt yo' can do will stop me, I love 'im yo' hear tha? I've ne'er loved yo'; ever." Briar screamed her words, truthful words that she had a right to shout. Stan stood very still and glowered, her words had wounded him even further, for if he was honest with himself, he had to admit he had known that all along. But she had married him, and now he was not going to let her go, he would keep her with him, one way or another. Before Briar had time to think, Stan was upon her, the slap he delivered knocking her straight to the ground. Briar immediately began to kick out and scream, for she had fought him so many times before, but not like this, for she was suddenly faced with an enraged husband, and one heavy under the influence of drink. As Briar struggled to get up, she felt his strong arms push her, holding her shoulders hard against the floor, his mouth rough against hers, bruising her lips as she tried desperately to breathe under the sudden weight upon her. Forgetting her insults, she began to plead with him to get up and leave her, that they could talk in the morning, but nothing made him listen, and when she felt his hands roughly pulling her frock up, bruising her legs as he did so, Briar began to struggled even harder. As she felt her petticoat rip, she frantically pleaded with him to 'stop', but when his fingers dug deep into her flesh causing her to winch, still with a sense to fight on Briar did all she knew. She did what she had done to the gang master when she had been just twelve years old. She spat in her husbands face. Stan momentarily stopped, stunned by the venom she really felt towards him, briefly he relaxed his grip, what was the point? She did not want him at all; it was a battle he had frightfully lost. Stan was ready to get up and let her go, but Briar could not wait. Feeling him relax his grip gave her the chance she needed, as hard as she could she bit deep into his arm, only releasing when he yelped in pain. "Ge' off me, I 'ate yo'."

Stan winched himself as he glared down at his own wife, her eyes filled with hate, and then he slapped her once more, he had had more than enough himself. With a grip even tighter than before, he pushed her hands above her head, holding them tightly in his one hand, before he forced his mouth hard against hers again. Briar struggled as before, and when she could, screamed abuse as loudly as she could. Only as she felt her underwear tear from her, her screams became that of sudden dread, and when Stan paused only to pull his own clothes off, she froze, then began to cry pitifully as her young body fell subject to violence under a mans touch, her cries turning to deep despair when realisation fully hit her once more, and the burning deep inside her stomach tore through her as Stan ripped into her as painfully as he possibly could. It was an August night that the three of them would never forget for many reasons. Ben and Briar alike were aware of their love towards each other, and try as they might over the coming months, they would not forget it. Ben would also find out for the first time what it would be like to be out alone in a world of industry, with no kin to stand by him, or no real friend. Though Ben's great talent to craft wood would guarantee him a place in the world, he would question himself endlessly over his love for Briar and his broken loyalties towards his brother, something he would find very hard to deal with. As for Stan, while he held his wife down so forcefully, his own tears mingled with hers, tears of frustration and deep hurt, yet immediate regret. For he knew that after tonight she'd never raise her hand towards him again, for she would hold a certain fear of him, something he had never wanted of her. For he had fallen in love with the wild highly spirited girl, and now he had taken that spirit and had brutally broken it. As for Briar, she would never forget that night for as her screams had turned to sobs, and now she cried needlessly into her husband's naked chest, it was the night that she would conceive her son.

chapter ten

"Yo' di' well lass, real well, I'll mek yo' a cup o' tea. Would yo' liken tha'?"

"Aye Stan…I would…thankyo', an' thankyo' too Emily."

"Nonsense lass, yo' res' a while now, dunna attempt getting' up ye'. Yo' los' a lo' o' blood lass, I'll call by later." Emily Bunting who had looked after this girl in her service until recently, kissed the top of her silvery blond head before turning and leaving the room.

"Yo' tek care o' 'er Stan, she'll be a little weak fur a while."

"Aye I will, an' thankyo' Emily."

"Yore a good man Stan, an' dunna worry she'll be up in no time at all…an' congratulations."

Stan cheerfully saw Emily Bunting out, and then made his way back upstairs a tray of hot tea and biscuits in his hands. "Yo' heard wha' Emily said lass, yo' res' now." Stan smiled warmly as he entered the bedroom. It had been agreed that she should have the bedroom while she was with child. It had taken a lot for him to persuade her too, but here she lay, looking so peaceful a small babe in her arms. Briar smiled back, her slate grey eyes so heavy, but bright with the new life that had just entered her world. Whatever she'd endured the last nine months had found its worth. Any feelings of despair she'd felt as the movements deep inside her grew ever stronger had vanished forever. As she gazed down wearily at her newborn son, a tiny child with a glint of bright red hair, Briar found something she had never known before. The love of her own kin, a bond that would always last whatever the test of time could display upon them. Stan's joy was evident, he too had kept his great concerns quiet, for he had wondered if she would discard their child and not want it near her, and he would be entirely to blame if she had. But his concerns were no more, for Briar could hardly stay awake, but her slate grey eyes were as soft as he'd ever seen, as she gazed down at their sleeping child so slowly she ran her fingers over his tiny face, stroking his head as he lay so peaceful.

"He's so beautiful Stan, so beautiful; I'd 'ave ne'er believed it." Whispering to her babe, Briar sat a while longer until sleep did engulf her, smothering her soul with a well earnt peace. So carefully Stan took the sleeping child, so as not to disturb his wife, and placed him in the wicker crib by the bed. Stan's own world looked bright in the future ahead. For with this tiny baby in their lives, they both had a mutual interest that would bind them wherever the road led them. Their son.

The month of May in the Lawson household found a calm that had not encountered it for so long. Briar no longer worked in the parlour of the Hampstead's estate house, and had made it plain she was happy to spend her time at home with her son. As the weeks went by she openly told everybody who stopped her to see the child, that she wouldn't change things for the entire world.

* * *

"C'mon Danny, theer inna a cloud in sigh', jus' me, yo', an' maybe a rabbit or two." Softly Briar spoke to the red headed baby that was strapped to the front of her. Every day as Stan left to work she would take this route, down The Common, up the lonely dirt track that would lead her past open fields and the occasional farm, and towards the open landscape of the Lyth Hill. Only now did she stop and take a breather, gazing all around her at the meadows below, the occasional cart going to goodness knows where, and listening to the sounds of a child in the distance as it gaily laughed. Briar had come to love this place, she seldom saw a soul there, unless it was a hopeful hunter as she was herself, a knapsack on their backs ready to home any catch, and a gun clasped in their hands. Briar sang to herself cheerfully as she slowly walked across the top of the hill. Today she would be lucky, she just knew it, for if she didn't go back home loaded down with rabbits, well she'd go back loaded down with blackberries, and have the biggest pie she could make that very same evening. Briar smiled down at her sleeping infant. August was with them once more, she could hardly believe at times just how quick the past year had gone, and with them once more was the promise of scorching sunshine, something that she always welcomed openly. "When yore old enough t' toddle, I'll strap yore back wi' a knapsack an' yo' can 'elp me carry back the hunt." Cheerfully Briar spoke to her son, how peaceful he always seemed for a child of just three months, he seldom cried, and when he did wake, he just lay, contented to hear the sound of his mother's gentle voice. Again Briar stopped and gazed all around her, there was just a hint of a soft teasing breeze as it touched her soft skin and ruffled the bottom of her petticoats, but she was on much higher ground and in the open, how very good it felt to be able to feel so free and happy with herself. She always kept her dress simple, plain and serviceable, and wore good walking boots, she could move freely that way, and when she did shoot a rabbit, the occasional stain of blood did not worry her too much. Only now she was not in service, she never wore a bonnet or scarf around her head, neither did she tie her hair back, she allowed it to hang loose down her back, reaching her waist with no effort at all. "Eeh Danny this is a sigh' yo' will love one day." Stopping again she looked all around her, she was at the highest point of the hill. On the left she could see Haughmond Hill, and the dark shadows of the Wrekin very clearly. To the front of her she could see just the hint of the Black Clee Hills as they trailed away to pastures unknown. To the right she could see the start of the spectacular Stretton Hills, that dominated the landscape and appeared to call to her whenever she was up there. To the far right she could see the outline of the magnificent Stiperstones, and the dark rock formations that made up the Scattered Rocks and the Devils Chair. As always Briar felt a great joy up here, she was untouchable to the world she lived in and free to take in the air and scream aloud if she so wanted, for nobody would hear if she did. "One day Danny, we'll walk them hills, all o' them. I dunna know how we'll ge' theer, bu' we will."

After what turned out to be an uneventful morning, and just a knapsack full of blackberries, Briar decided it was time to leave her hill behind her and call it a day. Danny was becoming fretful; he was hungry, and probably very damp. Sighing Briar reluctantly made her way back over the top of the hill, down the dirt track and towards The Common of Bayston hill. Here she did see the occasional villager, but she never paid any attention to anybody, only offering a simple 'hello' when they spoke first. "Oh well Danny yore Da' will 'ave t' ge' by today wi' lef' over broth and blackberry pie. An' if 'e dunna likes it, then yo' can bawl the place down an' tell 'im yoresel'." Briar smiled warmly as the small face turned to her, staring at his mothers face, offering her a toothless innocent grin. "Eeh, yore liken yore Da' t' looken at, yo' go' 'is blue eyes, an' 'is red 'air. Bu' yo' ever grow up liken 'im Danny lad, I'll kick yore arse straigh' owt the door." Again Briar smiled warmly as she watched her son, his eyes alight at the sound of her voice. Not for the first time she wondered at her own feelings. How strange it was to look down and love this child so very much, so much, that she could burst wide open, when he looked so much like his father who she hated with a vengeance. Things would never change between her and Stan she knew that. She kept the cottage spotless, and its small gardens, and she made sure that Stan never waited for his meals or lacked the comforts the cottage gave them all. But as she first had before the night he had so brutally raped her, Briar did not share his bed. She slept on a small eiderdown she had made herself, downstairs in the parlour. The main difference in the Lawson household was that there was no more screaming or shouting, or fighting with her husband. She never raised her hand to him, and no longer did she throw plates at him. Then neither did she speak to him, or hold any form of lasting eye contact. Briar was just thankful that Stan had seemed to lose interest in her, for he had not attempted to take her against her will, or to coax her into giving what she did not want too.

Stan nodded his head in acknowledgement. "Aye master, consider it done sir." Turning towards his mistress Stan bowed his head with respect. "It's a grand idea Ma'am, it will be down immediately."

"Dismissed then Lawson, there is nothing else." Jonathan Hampstead politely but directly dismissed his grounds man. He could not find fault with his work, or his ability to lead those around him, and whenever he checked, Stan Lawson was always busy, as the lads in his care were. In fact the grounds had never looked as good as what they had since Stan had been there, and with every new whim of his good wife Blanche, for requests of trellis and clematis growing down the sides of the estate house Jonathan knew that the trellis would indeed be ordered and made that very day. Stan would see to it himself. Jonathan sighed as Stan left the room, he could not tell quite what it was, but since Stan's brother had taken his offer and upped and left a whole year ago, Stan had been somewhat preoccupied, almost to the point of being rude. Jonathan put it down to jealousy, for there was no other explanation, what ever though, he would make sure that Stan Lawson did not get above himself. After leaving Jonathan Hampstead's study Stan sent orders down to the work mill by one of his lads, and changed all his own arrangements to suit his Mistresses latest requirements for the grounds. Stan was happy enough in his work, for a while now he had the respect of the lads under him, and was no longer the laughing stock of anybody there. Stan had learnt how to harden himself to the grounds men, and the local lads who had heard all about his fiery young wife. In return they had all learnt not to push Stan too far, for Stan had actually complained about a couple of the grounds men under him who had been relieved of all duties. He had then gone on to render a young lad a beating himself for a joke he had made concerning his wife. From that time onwards, manners were minded when Stan was around, and nobody argued over their duties he implied. All day Stan attended the grounds of the Hampstead Estate, only returning to his cottage at the far end of the grounds when his working day was through. His home was a place of rest, to wash and to feed and to have his laundry done for him. But after that his home life lacked many things. Oh he always had a decent meal waiting for him, and the cottage was spotless, fresh flowers never failed to be centre of the table and he never had to worry about fetching water, it was there. But that was it; he had a wife, a girl still so very young with the face of an angel, and the most slender of figures around. She looked as fresh as an unpicked daisy with her waist length silvery blond hair and those slate grey eyes of hers, a girl many a man would have gladly taken. Stan sighed as he thought of her. She no longer fought with him, or pierced those eyes of hers at him with defiance. In fact where he was concerned they held no life at all, Just an indifference that clouded over her the moment he walked through the door. Then there was the child, his son who smiled openly at him, a child he loved dearly who would one day work alongside him, learn from him how to show leadership and one day in the far off future would carry his name forward. But the one thing lacking in Stan's life was the comforts of a woman, for he had none, nobody shared his bed; there was no woman's gentle laughter or the soft tender touch teasing him lovingly. He had no intentions of ever forcing a lass again, he had broken his own wife's spirit because of it, and the tears he had cried in the darkness of night by himself because of what he had done to her that night had killed part of him also. Stan felt he had nothing else to offer any woman. It would have been easy to have taken a mining girl for relief on the side, many were willing for a farthing or two to help feed their families, but no, Stan would only hate himself further if he did. He had a pretty wife, and if it meant not being able to touch her, then he would forget his own pleasures just to keep her close to him. "I'm home Danny boy." Cheerfully Stan picked up his tiny son as he entered the cottage.

"Hello Stan, theer's nowt much fur supper, vegetable broth an' bread...bu' theer is a blackberry pie." Quickly Briar spoke of the blackberries, before hurriedly laying the table. She was a little behind herself today.

"It's fine Briar, dunna 'urry so much lass, I'll wai', I dunna mind." Stan watched her scurry about around him, her eyes not resting on him for a moment. Sadness filled his heart; never would she have scurried about like this in the past. She resembled a wife used to taking a beating if things were not ready, but Stan knew what he'd done to her was far worse than if he had have beaten her. "It smells good lass anyway, an' wha' abou' Danny 'ere? Has he been a good lad?"

"Oh aye, as always, he's such a happy baby."

Stan smiled a smile that was briefly returned. It was the only time she resembled the Briar Rose he had fallen in love with, and that was when she talked about or looked at their son.

In the very heart of Shrewsbury Town a young man was ready to close shop for the day.

"And you can promise me you will have it ready for my daughter's birthday?"

"Oh aye mister, res' assured. I'll mek 'er the bonniest dolls 'ouse yo've ever seen, an' the fines' furniture a little lass would ever wan'." Ben winked at the small girl in question as she held her fathers hand tightly. A small girl dressed in the very finest of calicos, her laced bonnet allowing her curls to bob gently down her back. The gentleman was obviously delighted, and firmly shook the hand of the young man he'd heard so much about. Ben Lawson was fast becoming known as one of the town's finest cabinet makers, but a craftsman who could also make some of the most decorative extravagant toys the town had seen. Ben had thought he'd have time for himself, but in the first year since he had left the Hampstead Estate, Ben had worked well into the night sanding and shaping, his thoughts and inspirations taking form as he shaped the wood held tight in his grasp, often under fading candle light. Ben had made considerable profits and once he'd paid his percentages to master Johnathan Hampstead who visited him regularly, often with more orders, Ben had been able to build himself a decent nest egg. He was bound to the lease for the next two years, but after that he'd have enough to take it over on his own grounds, or look for a property that he could take on. Looking all around him as he locked the front door for the night he smiled with a sense of satisfaction. The shop front was small with just four cabinets on show, a small child's rocking horse and a dolls house. But inside on shelves all around him there was much more, small toys from wooden dolls with moveable painted arms, to a pull along tiny child's cart. He had sets of brightly coloured wooden ducks, and had just recently made some geese. There, just inside the doorway hung a wooden chime that clinked gleefully in the whisper of the wind when a customer did enter. At the far end of the shop was another door, here lay Ben's workshop, an array of sawdust, chisels, and saws. There was a long workbench, and an area where his wood was stored neatly. Candles were safely placed around his walls, everything placed perfectly to give him the maximum room in which to work. Again Ben grinned to himself, he had time to rinse down and grab a piece of bread and dripping before he carried on. Slowly he hobbled up the steep flight of stairs that would take him over the shop. Here he lived in one large room, but a room that kept him adequately comfortable. He had a large feather mattress that he had made a base for, and a small table with two chairs. He had an easy chair that had seen better days by the hearth where he sat and waited for his water to heat. Here he could cook for himself when he wanted, and that pleased him, for there was one large window where he could see out off, a window that overlooked the busy shoppers in the towns square below. On the wall next to his bed he had an old wardrobe and a large chest of drawers that was all he had, for he needed nothing else, his few material possessions with just him in mind. He ate, slept and regularly used the tin bath, all in one room, but he didn't mind one bit, for his life was downstairs in the workshop, long after shop hours where his imagination found life, and his time meant money. Only tonight Ben was going to do something for himself. He had thought of it, and he had started to make it, now he would fix it and learn how to move with it. Staring down at his crippled leg, he nodded. "Aye I may always 'ave a sligh' limp, bu' after tonigh' I'll hold mesel' as straigh' as any other man." Ben nodded with pride, for his creation would give him an added three inches at least in height, and then he'd discard that damn stick and never look at one again. Whistling loudly to himself with nobody to hear him Ben set about making a fire large enough to give him the water he would need. He was certainly going to be busy, busier than he'd have ever believed and for that he was thankful, for it kept his mind from the past, and a past he could not see ever being reunited in his future. Jonathan Hampstead had told Ben that things had appeared to have settled down with his brother Stan. He had often remarked to Ben what a fine worker his brother was; and had the respect of all beneath him. Ben had been pleased, for the rumours had obviously stopped then? When he'd heard the news that Stan had fathered a son, Ben had felt a mixture of emotions. He was pleased for Stan and would have cheerfully congratulated him. But deep down Ben fought with a bitter disappointment...if he had only spoke for her first. Briar could have been his wife, and he would have been the one to have fathered the child. But Ben had to be realistic in many ways. He had wanted to support a wife properly, and though he would have given anything for the child to have been his, he knew that at hardly eighteen, he was not yet ready to take that responsibility on, though if he was honest with himself, he would have jumped at the chance as long as it had been with Briar. Ben had tried to push Briar far from his mind, and mostly when he did work she seldom crept through his thoughts, when she did, or when he did awake startled in the night for no reason, it left him in turmoil. For Ben knew until he could honestly say he no longer loved her, he did not stand much chance of meeting another. As for Stan, Ben missed him, he was his brother, one who had watched over him as a father would when he had been a child, but he hadn't seen or heard from Stan since that night they had been drinking together a whole year ago. If he could guarantee a half welcome Ben would take himself back to the cottage up The Common of Bayston Hill and offer his brother his hand. He would also dearly love to see his young nephew. Sadly Ben sighed, he'd just finished a small child's bed, a bed he had spent chiselling his own unique design on, with a headboard engraved with all the letters of the alphabet. It was not an order, it was a present, a gift for his nephew, and though quite how he would present it to him he had yet to think about. Little did Ben know the same heart rending search for unity of a brother lost yet still loved was causing another the same dull pain. Stan had spent many an hour considering how to contact Ben. He did not know quite where he was for he never ventured into town and Jonathan Hampstead had not offered the information. Stan had found himself more and more just lately wanting to know how his brother was faring, hoping that against all odds Ben would walk up to the cottage and tap on the door. Stan often smiled to himself; Ben would be tickled pink to know he was an uncle. Stan did not need to worry how Ben was faring, or the difficulty in finding him for Ben Lawson's name was becoming widely known and his name was displayed above his shop door.

chapter eleven

"This early in the month lass? Theer's three weeks lef' ye'." Stan reached for his heavy overjacket and black cap. "Eeh it's turnin' mighty cold owt theer, yo' sure abou' goin' lass? It is early yet." Stan stood by the cottage door, it was almost six, and there was no sign of daylight attempting to show her face. He was ready for work, but Briar's sudden announcement had thrown him. "Yo' didna say las' nigh', bu' then yo' dunna say much anyway."

Briar heard the note of sarcasm very plainly and answered him simply. "Well seein' as we were both in the house, it seems tha' yo' dunna speak much either. I dunna need t' go t'day if it upsets yo'. It was jus' an idea tha' were all." For once Briar held perfect eye contact, something she had refused to do for many a month. For a long moment Stan appeared to hover by the door, his bright blue eyes watching her carefully. It was true, he had been there all night, but every time he had tried to talk things over with her, she used Danny as an excuse to get out of his way. But her announcement to go into Shrewsbury shopping wasn't that unusual, for he'd heard some of the workers wives already discussing Christmas, and there was bound to be things that Briar wished to get herself.

"Aye, anythin' yo' wan' lass. Theer's extra money in the tin nex' t' mi bed if yo' wan' it. Even if yo' dunna tek some an' buy yoresel' some material fur a new frock eh?" Stan smiled a pleasant smile that would have lit his bright blue eyes with life at one time, but now they held a certain gloom. If only she had tried to forgive him he would have bent over backwards to make her life as happy as possible. If only she had listened to his heart felt apologies she may have found a little peace within herself. But though he had tried so many times, Briar would have none of it. She stared straight at her husband and nodded, her voice quiet as she spoke. "Thankyo', I will tek a little if yo' dunna mind. I could ge' maybe a length o' crushed velvet, an' a decent length o' corduroy. Tha' way I can mek yo' some trousers an' some dungarees fur Danny." Almost excusing why she needed the money or the visit she carried on speaking her words beginning to roll into each other. "I though' I'd buy a gift fur Danny fur Christmas, an' look fur a decen' butcher down on the Row, I can place an order for a goose or a duck."

"Either would be fine, I didna mean t' query it. Enjoy yoresel' lass, wrap the babby up warm an' then tell me all abou' yore adventures later." Stan now smiled warmly, in so many ways she was the wife he'd dreamed she'd be. If only she could have loved him the way he still loved her. Briar bid him a 'pleasant day' and watched as he gently closed the door behind him so as not to wake up the sleeping child that lay by the smouldering fire on his mother's makeshift bed. Briar sighed deeply after he'd gone. In so many ways he was a generous husband, never pulling the purse strings too tight on her, always ready to give whatever he had. Briar wasn't blind to him; she could see what an attractive man he had become. In his twenty first year his face had matured somewhat, and his short crop of shocking red hair would be classed as fashionable. He always held himself well, and when he did smile, his bright blue eyes shone with life. Briar felt a strange sense of sympathy towards him lately, for he sat every night just watching her with their son, a certain sadness about him. She had tried so hard to be a bit more pleasant towards him, but when he did stand too close she had shuddered. She just couldn't help it, when she looked at him she could still feel his hands roughly tearing at her clothes and brutalising her body, the smell of ale rich on his breath. She could not forgive that attack, ever, he had repulsed her and still did, and that was the bottom line of it. One thing still surprised her though, and that was the strong love she felt towards her son. For if it had not been for his fathers brutality he would not have been conceived, she was sure of that. Stan had given her the greatest gift he could have ever bestowed upon her, and she would happily admit that. But it didn't stop her from hating him. With a burst of energy, Briar began to tidy her cottage, she needed to clean the hearth, make Stan's bed, and drag the dolly tub into the parlour. There was bed linen to clean and mangle before she sat down and took her child to her breast. Then, she would be able to get ready and catch the nine o'clock cart into town. She wanted to be there early to catch the very first trader.

"Clear the decks wi' boughs o' holly…" Ben Lawson winked mischievously at two mature ladies who glanced his way, chuckling to himself as they tutted loudly and strutted on by. It was a very busy time, every day rolling into the next, but today was Wednesday the first week of December, and the market traders had begun to set up their stalls as early as eight that morning. The usual shouts were heard as carts were unloaded and horses were safely tethered and left in the quieter side street. It would be a day of hard work for all, where traders and local farmers would loudly declare their produce to be the best, where reams of cloth would be displayed and where ragged barefooted children would run freely waiting to pounce on a fallen apple or better still warm their hands over the steel like container that kept hot chestnuts aglow. All walks of life became one on these market days, gentry alike bartered for a decent bargain, and all who sold wanted a decent profit. Ben cheerfully cleared his front window, and placed his latest piece of work right inside it for all to see. A large wooden toy train. Master Hampstead had given him a picture of a train and had told him that trains were a large part of life down in London, and one day they would be all over the country. Ben had been fascinated and had spent hours drawing his own design. Now here it stood, a large wooden train with red painted wheels that actually moved, and Ben could not be more proud if he had tried. Back inside the shop, he made sure that each cabinet was dust free, and easily accessible for a would be customer to inspect more closely. On the far side of his shop, lined on shelves sat an array of various sized dolls with painted faces and jointed arms and legs. Each doll with its own unique markings, and brightly coloured cheeks, dolls for children of the gentry, for they fetched a decent price. On the bottom shelf Ben kept a selection for the less fortunate, but even still, these toys too were finished to perfection. Small wooden ducks and cats, all in various colours. Hand sized trinket boxes, each one different, and each engraved pattern on the lid marking it as a unique gift. Ben was more than pleased with himself, for not only had he finished the grand train, he had met the deadline for a rather special dolls house for a young girls birthday, and he had been rewarded handsomely. More than that, he had orders for six more, starting in the New Year, and the price he would pick up on those alone would cover his expenses for almost a whole year. With his mind on the day ahead and his imagination never far from his next design, or what he would indeed make Ben cheerfully opened his shop door. It was December the month for gift buying, and he was sure to make a tidy profit.

"Mind yore step lass, an' remember, the las' carts around four o'clock, miss tha' yo'll be walkin'."

"Aye I wunna furge', thanks mister." With her child strapped to the front of her Briar Rose graciously took the hand offered to her as she stepped down from the cart and onto the cobbles of the Shrewsbury Town Square. Shivering against the cold crisp air, the light dusty glisten of sharp frost so very evident Briar took a deep breath and stared up towards the grey skies. Snow was in the air, she could smell it. As a child in the field gangs she always knew, and now she still knew, snow was not far away. "Well at leas' yore warm." Gazing down at her son, she pulled his woollen hat further down. "Canna le' yo' ge' cold now." The square was already a bustle of activity as Briar stepped towards her first stall. It was almost ten and the banter between stall owner, and customer was colouring the air, as an annoyed housewife loudly stated she'd get cheaper at the next stall. Kypes of apples sacks of potatoes and turnips stood proudly by rickety tables as jars of homemade pickles and jams took centre place.

"C'mon sweethear' tek this back t' yore man, sure t' spice him up a bi'."

"No thankin' yo'." Briar glared as the man tried once more to push some type of chutney into her hands. When he winked, Briar immediately pouted heavily then stormed off red faced and furious when she was met with a wolf whistle. But today was her day, and nothing was going to upset her. It didn't take long before she was caught up in the atmosphere, and found herself loudly bartering at a cloth stall. "Wha' else yo' go' then? I wan' black corduroy an' I inna payin' a big price fur it." Briar made herself very plain. She had the extra money that Stan had told her to take, but she had no intentions of spending it all, and she only wanted bargains. Nobody was going to sting her, and that meant this harsh sounding tall woman who stood as straight as a beanpole, and loudly told any street urchin to "Clear off." Briar stood her ground, her slate grey eyes piercing into that of the woman opposite her. "A righ' cold little fish yo' are, an' a sharp tongued young skit at tha'." The woman stared deep into the girls eyes. She'd not encountered eyes such as this girls, such a strange startling colour of slate grey, and piercing at that. She glanced at the sleeping babe in the girls arms, she wasn't very old this girl, probably too young to have birthed the child, but she certainly had guts. Briar held her head high as the woman rudely looked her over. She was about to give her a real piece of her mind when the woman half smiled. "If yo' wan' tha' corduroy yo' pay the price. Bu' I 'ave go' this." Reaching under the table and rummaging around in sacks the woman produced a length of charcoal grey corduroy. "I dunna know 'ow much yo' wan' bu' this is the end o' the ream, an' yo' can 'ave it fur half a crown."

Briar ran her hand over the material; it was good quality, better than what was on the table. It would be enough just to make Stan some new trousers, and hopefully her child.

"I'll gi' yo' sixpence an' I wan' some grey thread."

"Oh do yo' now?" The woman nearly spluttered over her words, but her loud cackle filled the air, as she took a reel of thread and wrapped them both in brown paper. "It's nod everybody I'd do this fur, bu' I liken somebody who knows jus' wha' they wan'. Yo' 'ave a bargain theer yo' little cold fish, an' dunna yo' furge' it." Briar hurriedly paid the woman, took her package and strutted off, her head held high. Nobody had ever called her a 'cold fish' before, and she had not liked the sound of it. Next Briar stopped at a stall full of ribbons, lace and table cloths. Here she toyed around and picked up the table cloths, her fingers running over the fine embroidered patterns.

"Dunna touch if yo' inna goin' t' buy. Grubby fingers lose sales."

"Well I 'anna go' grubby fingers, an' I wan' t' look before I buy." Sharply Briar addressed this woman before she carried on picking up each cloth before placing them down. "No, I dunna thinken I will, I can mek mi own, bu' I wan' a length o' tha' deep red ribbon."

The woman tutted loudly before measuring a length of ribbon along the table. "Tha' will be threepence...please."

Briar reached into her purse and paid, taking the small package and placing it safely into the brown package of material.

"It wunna hur' yo' t' learn a few manners lass."

"An' it wunna hur' yo' t' know tha' nod every customer 'as grubby hands." Briar glowered at the woman before storming off to the next stall. She wasn't doing bad with bargains at all, but she'd already felt fit to burst at the seams with temper at three people, and she'd only been past three stalls. Her next stop however proved far more friendly. Here a rather plump middle aged woman cheerfully cooed over Briar's sleeping child.

"Eeh wha' a lovely babby, an' looken at tha' red hair."

"Aye it is brigh'." Briar answered as she pulled her child's hat back over his head, "he's liken 'is Da'."

"Now lass, red velve', eeh, le' me see." The woman fiddled around with different reams of cloth on her table after Briar's adamant request. She had all matter of different textures, but the lass that stood waiting in front of her looked hard struck for money, and she was barely more than a child herself. Gazing over Briar's slim figure she frowned then with a loud 'hhmm' she reached out under a certain pile of heavy cottons and produced a red crushed velvet. "Now this one will look grand against tha' blond hair o' yores, an' it will fetch owt the colour o' yore eyes." Standing back the woman allowed Briar to pull out the ream a little so she could see the quality for herself. What a pretty girl this youngster was, and with that silvery blond hair and striking grey eyes of hers, she'd be as bonny as a picture gowned in this velvet.

Briar smiled warmly, "I'm too scared t' ask 'ow much."

"Well its one crown lass, bu' dunna looken so sad. I'll tell yo' wha'." The woman clearly saw the look of disappointment cloud the girl's face, a pretty face that now looked so very forlorn. "The one crown it 'as t' be, bu' I'll gi' yo' yore thread, and a length o' red lace an' six pearl shaped buttons t' help yo' mek yore frock."

Briar's face changed, a radiant smile lighting up her slate grey eyes. "Oh aye, I'll tek it yo' 'ave a sale." Both were pleased, the woman because she had lots of bundles of left over ribbons and lace and Briar, because with the extra lengths, and the buttons she'd be able to make herself a dress that would be pretty and not just practical. Cheerfully Briar slowly made her way towards the cobbled road, she would be back later to look for something small for her child for Christmas, but first she'd make her way to Butchers Row and see what she could find. As Briar happily strutted away from the square her brown packages under her arm, her sleeping child strapped to the front of her she was completely unaware of a pair of warm brown eyes that had followed her sadly, watching her every move. Ben Lawson had seen the girl haggle for a ream of material at the first stand just in front of his shop. To him she had looked as grand as any lady who had walked into his shop dressed in the finest of rich clothes. But there Briar Rose had stood, dressed in an ankle length blue jersey frock that settled neatly on her black boots. A frock that wasn't too full in the skirt, its colour slightly faded, telling of better days gone by. She wore a black shawl over her shoulders and wore no bonnet as she probably should have done. Her silvery blond waist length hair was tied loosely back with a show of pretty blue ribbon, and all in all she held herself proudly, her faded clothes spotlessly clean. She looked what she was, a working girl, a farm girl maybe, but to Ben she was so much more. He couldn't see the child's face from where he had stood, but he had seen the shock of bright red hair when the child's hat had been briefly removed. How easy it could have been to approach her. But by the time Ben had made up his mind to call out, he had instead waited, for she had approached the second cloth stall and had seemed so preoccupied with red velvet. Now he stood alone as if she had been just some sweet vision that had faded before him, for she was gone. Briar hummed merrily to herself as she slowly made her way up the Pride Hill. Her eyes scouring every window. She watched a cobbler proudly place a pair of brown leather boots in the window, offering him a smile as he waved 'hello' to her. She pulled a face, screwing up her nose as she past a leather shop full of riding saddles and fine leather crops, the smell almost overpowering to her. There were people everywhere, gentry parading down the street, women in the finest of long warm coats, small children with thick hats and fur muffs, fine leather boots on their feet, and thick fancy stockings. She saw desperate mothers, a baby strapped to them as their flock of small children followed close by, taking the chance to beg from a passing stranger, moaning as they rubbed their red fingers trying to keep warm from the cold air. Briar kept well away from the passing horse and traps, her loving glance frequently checking her sleeping child. Every so often a small child would smile up at her, and Briar would smile warmly back, but very often she would catch the distained look from a child of the gentry or its parents, and Briar would know why. She was working class, her clothes were worn, and she had no bonnet which alone was classed to many as being disrespectable. Gazing up at the black and white buildings of the town shops and dwellings, Briar forgot about the people who had stared at her. She found the buildings fascinating. She had always liked the tiny window panes, and smiled as she offered a wave up towards a small child that was peering down on the streets below. How homely they appeared, keeping everything safe behind large oak latched doors, canopies protecting any wares that slightly split onto the cobbled streets. Briar took another deep breath. Oh yes, snow was definitely in the air. As she turned into the narrow street of Butcher Row, her cheerfulness disappeared, her humming stopped. Here the terraced houses seemed to want to topple down upon her, lines of washing hung above her head, as strings of sausages, and raw hides hung on just about any space that a hook could be put. The smell of the back yard cesspit mingled with the smell of freshly butchered meat and even in the cold of winter, flies swarmed around the dead carcasses. Immediately Briar struggled to pick up the hem of her skirts, the blood from slaughtered animal had left its stain against the white frost, and she shuddered to think of having to wash it out of her clothes. Here she took no notice of the street urchins as they played in their stockinet feet, their hair home to a hundred knots and dowdy with lice. She held tightly onto her child and kept his face against her all the way, she could not risk him getting any disease that any of these children may be carrying. As fast as she could she pushed her way through the lower end of the Row making her way at great haste to the top of the alley. Here the Row widened and a few butchers stood with canopies over their shop fronts. No washing hung over these shops, and the smell of cess pits was left behind in the lower end.

"Hello theer lass, an' wha' may we ge' fur yo' then?"

Briar looked hard. "Well I'd liken t' order a small goose fur Christmas."

"Fur two eh lass?"

"Aye fur two." Briar smiled, one that was immediately returned. She waited patiently and when the price was given, she nodded. "Aye tha' will do fine, I'll be in the market Christmas Eve."

"Aye well I'll be 'ere lass. Now wha' name shall I pu' on the goose?"

"Briar Rose."

"Well I wunna furge' a name liken tha'."

Briar smiled again, she never gave her surname as Lawson, in fact she hadn't used the name yet.

"Anythin' else lass?"

"Aye, I'll tek a quarter o' bacon spits, an' if yo' split those sausages in half I'll tek them too, an' can yo' cut me some black puddin'? Oh, I'll tek two o' them pies over theer."

"Meat and potato them lass."

"Aye they'll do."

Briar watched as the meats were wrapped in separate paper, and then bundled in one large wrapping and neatly tied. Another package to carry and she still hadn't got any vegetables, or the gift for her son. Pleased to leave Butcher Row behind her Briar took the short cut down a narrow passage that stood at the top end of Fish Street going once more at haste to return to the square below. Now she would finish her shopping and then look for somewhere warm where she could take the weight of her feet. Her child was sleeping now but he wouldn't be for long and then she would need to feed him. Loaded down with all she could carry Briar started to search for her son's gift. It was proving more difficult than she could have imagined for she had no idea what it was she was looking for. It had to be hand sized and safe for him to place into his mouth. There was a young woman selling teddy bears, and Briar happily gave sixpence for a small brown furry bear with ribbon around its neck, but she wanted something else, something more..."Oh my ...eh looken at tha'." Talking aloud to herself she swiftly made her way to a shop window, pressing her face close to the glass like any small child would. "Oh tha' is so..." Briar gasped it was far too big and she knew just by the look of it she could never afford to buy it. The workmanship was far too grand for her pocket, but still she gazed at the wooden train with the bright red wheels that stood so proudly by itself. It was a toy any boy would love to own at any age. "Theer may be a small one inside...eh come on Danny le's tek a look." As her child began to stirr Briar Rose gently opened the shop door, and an instant tinkling of a bell alerting the owner that somebody had just entered the premises. Briar had been so excited at the sight of the wooden train and what could be inside for her son that she hadn't stopped to think, or she would have recognised the craftsmanship. If she had just looked above the shop doorway she would have clearly seen the name. 'Ben Lawson Cabinet and Toy Maker', but Briar had her mind on just one thing, her son. Once inside she marvelled at the dolls houses, the tiny window frames, the miniature front doors, bending down she peered into the small rooms and gasped with delight at the exquisite way each room was like that of a loving warm home. She moved on picking up wooden dolls, all with various painted faces, no two the same, and giggled to herself when she moved the jointed arms and legs. She had never been inside a toy shop before, and she found herself wanting to touch and pick up everything in sight. She liked the figures of wooden cats and ran her fingers gently over the soft wood; yes she was hopeful she would find something in this shop. As she made her way over to a selection of trinket boxes, each one with a neatly engraved lid she blinked and paused suddenly. They were not quite the same, but they were very much like a certain trinket box she had been given on her wedding day, looking around her once more, seeing the shop with eyes that were now open she studied the workmanship more carefully. She had hoped to make roof rafters back at the workhouse, but that did not mean... and then she saw something that took her back to the very first week she had spent in the workhouse. Something that she had held onto so tightly in her hands all in sheer hope that she would learn about 'Industry'. So carefully she picked up a figure of a wooden duck, it's brightly painted body so catching to the eye, and now she placed it in the palm of her hand and marvelled at the work. Oh yes, she knew this work, only too well, there could only be one that could carve and shape wood so elegantly as this. As Briar peered over the family of ducks she stood so very still, wanting to run, but unable to even move, the only sound in the shop was the loud pounding of her heart and it sounded so very clearly, echoing from the very walls.

"I hope yo' inna thinken o' puttin' tha' in yore bag then mekin' off wi' mi tools lass? Yo' wunna ge' by me if yo' do." Ben Lawson had watched with interest in the shadows as he had so long ago on a cold dark night, his memory of her so very plain to behold.

Briar hesitated, not knowing if to turn around and face him or not, but when he had finished speaking she found herself spluttering nervously with uncontrolled giggles, and had dropped her packages onto the floor, startling her small son as she did so. Ben grinned as she faced him her cheeks flushed with embarrassment. Here she stood, Briar Rose, and within seconds of entering his shop, there was chaos all around her. Her packages were just lying in a heap on the floor, she was obviously having trouble to speak through her giggles, and now the child in her arms was wailing its head off.

"Yo' goin' t' pu' mi duck down lass?" Ben mockingly frowned, but his smile was quick to light up his brown eyes with warmth.

"No, I mean aye...no, I wan' it. Can I buy it fur mi son?"

"No lass, yo' can tek it, its yores."

Briar smiled radiantly, but 'ta' was all she could mutter. So this is what had become of Ben, she wasn't surprised, he had a unique gift with wood, and anybody who saw his work knew that. Again Briar was at a loss for words. "Ssh," gently rocking her child she blushed, "I'm sorry Ben, I mus' go an' find…"

"Yo' can see t' the child 'ere lass, go on upstairs wi' the pair o' yo'. Tek the only other door through theer in the workshop, an' yo' canna miss the stairs."

Again Briar giggled; there was something different about Ben, very different. "Well go on then lass, go an' see t' yore son, I canna allow wailin' in here." Ben stood aside and pointed to where Briar was to go. "Leave the packages, I'll ge' them ready. Go on I wa' abou' t' mek a mushed tea, an' yo' looken like yo' could do wi' one."

Slowly Briar crossed the shop floor, but in silence, her giggling had stopped, her slate grey eyes just staring deep into the warm brown ones that locked onto hers. Yes he had changed, he was a young man in his own rights, and nobody was his master. He was his boss in every way, and appeared very upfront with her. Briar had only known the Ben who would have stood quietly back hoping for her to go about what she wanted, but he had simply told her to see to her son there and then, and he had not given her the chance to back out. As Briar got closer to Ben she felt the strange fluttering deep inside her heart, and she wet her lips to stop them from getting too dry, her stomach churning wildly with butterflies. As she stared deep into his warm brown eyes she swallowed. If she had fooled herself over the last tedious months that she'd left Ben behind in her life, she knew now how very wrong she had been, for there had only ever been one who had made her heart pound with joy and want, and that somebody was Ben. Ben gazed down into the slate grey eyes that stared longingly into his and he too swallowed hard. To think he had nearly worked himself into a grave to try and forget her, to rid his memory of her was a joke in itself. He could no longer have forgotten her than he could have got up and flown through the air. But here she stood after all this time, a bit skinny if anything, but still she held him entranced by that heart shaped face of hers and those striking grey eyes. "Go on lass, mek yoresel' comfy, I'll follow shortly."

Briar Rose smiled, she still was struggling to see what was so very different about Ben, and it was far more than him just being in control of his life. Looking all around the large room Briar found herself in, she took off her shawl and unstrapped her distressed son. "Ssh theer Danny, ssh." It was a large room, with a low ceiling, and black beams, the walls whitewashed. There wasn't much to echo comfort; just the basic needs faced her, like the one rickety chair that stood by the window alone. A single bed was pushed against the far wall with a tiny table next to it, and a candle that held not much hope when darkness did arrive. There was a large sink near the chair and a hob stove, but not even a table to lie. That was it, just the bare necessities, but one thing the room did hold was light, lots of it, for there was two windows in this room, both of them over looking the busy market square below, a sight Briar found fascinating for here she could clearly see all of the stalls, and as the people below her moved as one large group, she could hardly see the ground beneath their feet. Smiling at the sight below her Briar turned and settled down on the one chair, she had to feed her son before he screamed the placed down. Undoing the button of her frock she held the child to her breast and immediately began to hum softly, something she always did when she held him so very close.

"Yo' comfy theer lass?"

Briar startled as she quickly pulled the shawl about her, hiding her suckling child and concealing her partially naked breast.

"Dunna worry lass, I wunna tek no notice, I jus' brough' up a tray o' tea. Yo' wan' some sugar in yores?"

"Oh aye, I do...please." Briar blushed as she stumbled over her words, the tea was very welcoming, but even still suddenly being faced with Ben in the room and her feeding...well, it was something she had not expected to happen. Ben grinned, he bet sugar was a luxury to her, and he bet that she would have expected him to at least knock the door. But this was his home, and he was a man in his own rights now. Quietly he poured the hot mushed tea, placing a tin cup on the floor by her chair as he did so, no he wasn't a fool, he had been only to eager to offer her a place upstairs to feed her child, but now she was here he would keep his distance. He had wanted so badly to see her, to stare into her slate grey eyes that had always captured him, but just the sight of her holding her child so hidden from him, from the nakedness that was so very close had began a deep stirring within him, that was warning his irrational heart to be careful.

"Ben."

"Aye lass." Ben had turned to leave, but now he faced her at a safe distance and smiled. Again he could see her eyes wide with questions she wished to ask him. "Wha' is it lass?" Playing with her curiosity he waited, for he knew what was going to be asked.

Briar struggled for words. She knew now what was puzzling her over Ben. He was standing far straighter, his limp was not so prominent, in fact he was a few inches taller, and he was no longer using the stick he had once relied so heavily upon.

"Yo' dunna need t' si' theer wi' yore mouth wide open lass. I'm nearly as straigh' as any other man, an' I can walk wi'owt no stick." To prove a point Ben pulled up his trouser leg, and proudly let her see the wooden clog he had made and built up inside his boot, to make him stand more evenly. He smiled warmly, his pride evident in his warm brown eyes as he gazed back at Briar expecting a mouthful of cheek to meet him. Instead she looked embarrassed, and had nothing to say to him. When she gazed down at her suckling child she had so carefully hidden, she looked beaten. She did not resemble the girl he had known, that girl would have had much to say. "I'll leave yore tea theer lass, yo' tek yore time. If yo' need me, I'll be back downstairs."

"Aye, an' thankyo'." Briar smiled meekly as their eyes met. She would be as quick as she could, and then she would be on her way. Being here under this roof, so close to Ben was doing her no good. For it only reminded her of what she could have had, and what she had instead settled for. After Ben had left the room Briar pulled her shawl from her son and gently ran her fingers over his face and across his shock of bright red hair, and not for the first time she fell into thoughtful silence. How could she love this tiny boy so very much, with a possessive fierceness that only a mother can know? A tiny child that resembled his father, a man that made her feel physically sick with hate. Ben was also in deep thought as he slowly made his way back into the shop. Maybe she had just grown up; after all she had the responsibility of not just a home and a husband, but of being mother to a child. That had to be the case, but Ben shook his head. No, the disbelief was creeping through his veins just too fast and laying uncomfortably on his soul. He had seen a certain look in her slate grey eyes that had been ingrained there since he had last seen her. Ben had recognised fear. Briar did hurry, she fed her child and straightened her frock. She was soon ready to say 'thankyou' and go. But before she did she took one more longing glance around the sparsely furnished room. How basic it all was, but she had sensed warmth here, and she knew that there could also be laughter. Gazing out of the window once more she smiled at the bustle of the market place below her. She could have been happy in this room with her son. Gasping at the realisation of her own thoughts of deceit, Briar scurried across the room, through the door and down the stairs. She must leave, leave now and never return. As she entered the workshop she stopped, her parcels had been left with Ben and now she would have to wait for she could clearly hear Ben with a customer. As she peered through the shop door, she could see a stout gentleman, very finely dressed with a large black hat on. Briar watched in astonishment as he brought two wooden dolls, two trinket boxes and not only enquired about the large wooden train in the shop window, but ordered it to be delivered to his home. "I must have it wrapped, and delivered to Mustleworth Grange in Kingsland by Friday, understand?"

"Oh aye sir, I'll see t' it mesel'." Ben was smiling warmly, "An' thankyo' sir."

"Thankyou, the pleasure will be all mine."

"Six pounds an' three shillin's, eeh tha's more than I'll see in a year. Six pounds an' three shillin's." Briar had spoken aloud as she had entered the shop through the work shop door.

"Aye lass, it's called industry, industry o' the gentry. Yo' mek or sell anythin' tha' the likes o' me an' yo' canna afford, tha's wheer the industry will always be, rich men an' their pockets."

"Well yo' inna doin' t' bad owt o' it." Briar snapped her answer back, and watched as a dark frown clouded over Ben's warm brown eyes, but only momentarily for a smile was quick to light up those eyes with mischief.

"Well lass, see yo' 'anna los' yore tongue altogether. Tha's more liken the Briar Rose I know, fas' an' snappy. Wha' I saw before wa' a meek lamb, an' tha' yo' inna." Ben watched intently as her straight back slumped, and the look that had just sparked into her slate grey eyes had now lost its piercing glow. He saw it again, the wild spirit that had been so radiant in the girl suddenly gone. She had almost backed away to the tone of a man's voice. Was she as down trodden as she looked? Or had she just lost interest in herself? "I mus' go now Ben, 'ave yo' go' mi parcels?"

"Aye, tha' I 'ave lass, all 'ere packed up easier t' carry. Bu' before yo' go, I wan' yo' t' do somethin' fur me." The smile returned to Ben's face as he now saw the slight spark in those eyes again.

"Wha' is it?"

"Le' me look at mi nephew, le' me hold him jus' fur a minute."

Briar gasped, she hadn't even told him the child's name. "Ben I 'anna even..."

"It's alrigh' lass, yo' dunna 'ave t' say nowt, can I hold him?"

"Aye, aye yo' can." Expertly Briar undid the harness in front of her, and as proudly as any mother would she handed her child over. "Ben this is Danny, Danny this is yore Uncle Ben." A long moment was spent in silence, as both of them stared into the others eyes before looking at the small child. Ben held the boy in his arms and chuckled as the child gave him a broad toothless grin. The child had his brother's broad shaped mouth and full lips; he also shared the same bright blue eyes. "Hello Danny." As the child smiled, Ben saw a glint of mischief, of sheer wonder from the small boy's eyes that shone with the promise of the life ahead of him. Gently he removed the woollen hat and laughed aloud when he saw the shock of bright red hair forcing its way through the child's scalp. "Eeh lad, yore a righ' chip o' the old block himsel'. I can see yore Da' as plain as if he were standin' righ' next t' me." Briar stood back quietly as Ben cheerfully spoke to the child in his arms. How different her life could have been. She didn't mind Ben handling her son at all, she trusted him, and she could see her son liked him too. When Stan picked the child up however Briar was left feeling so frustrated with an overwhelming hatred towards her husband, that often her child would sense this and cry. "Yo' alrigh' lass?"

"Aye...oh aye." Stumbling over her words Briar forced a smile. She had hoped that with time her love towards Ben would become just a faint flickering light that would die. But being here with him and seeing him had made it all so very difficult, for she knew that life with him could have been so good, a sweetness she would never now know. Briar eyed Ben cautiously, she could still detect a slight limp with him, but now she could see more so the confidence that Ben had found and wondered if it was due to the wooden clog he had made himself. He had once lacked in height so badly, but now he stood almost as straight as any other man. He would never be as tall as his brother, but Ben had had to rely on his arms so much to carry his weight as a small child that his shoulders were slightly broader than Stan's. Briar smiled to herself as she watched Ben's warm brown eyes light up with laughter. How thin his face had once been, but now she stared into the face of a young man who had suddenly matured, and what a fine looking man he was with the warmest of brown eyes and the dullest of red hair. Nothing escaped Ben's attention for he too had never been able to push his love for

Briar to one side. Having her here was also proving difficult for him, for he'd had fond memories, but now she resembled just a ghost of the girl he had once known to kick up and fight. With a sadness that lurked behind her slate grey eyes, Ben found himself in a whole new world of worries. "Are yo' alrigh' lass? I mean alrigh'...yo' an' Stan? How is mi brother these days?"

"He's fine thankyo' Ben, bu' I really mus' go now, if I can 'ave mi parcels..."

"How are yo' lass, wi' Stan? Yo' 'anna answered me."

Rudely Briar snatched her son back, and as fast as she could strapped him back to the front of her. "I'll ge' mi parcels now." She couldn't stop here another moment, for being in Ben's company was proving too painful. Had he forgotten all she had tried to tell him the night she had waited for him in the undergrowth, the very night Stan had so brutally raped her until she had fallen with child? Well she hadn't, the memory of that whole night had scarred her mind for life. She would never forget how the man she had loved had told her to go home to her husband, pushing her love aside, while the other man, her husband had stripped her of any dignity she had ever been left with. She had not felt the same inside since; a great part of her soul had withered. Ben frowned, his troubled heart growing even more concerned. In her rush to leave here he could see the sudden temper turning her pretty face crimson, her slate grey eyes suddenly piercing with annoyance. She looked just like the wild cat she'd always been. But when she had past him, he would swear those same eyes had misted over with unspilt tears, and so he asked her once more. "I asked how yo' are lass? How are yo' an' Stan? Are thin's better than they were?" Ben waited, his tone had been as soft as it could be to try and help her relax. All he really wanted to know was how Briar really was faring with his brother. He himself had never thought that Stan and Briar were compatible; both had a wild streak running through their veins, a streak that often wanted full control of all others around them. Briar pouted heavily. Were things better? They couldn't have got much worse. Briar remembered once more the last night she had seen Ben, the lecture he had given her before he had gone drinking with Stan about how 'Stan had deserved better'. Did he still feel that? Ben saw the pout on her lips, her slate grey eyes piercing him with anger. But if she did fly into a rage, well he'd handle anything she could throw at him, for he had grown up completely in the last sixteen months since he'd seen her. Briar held her son close to her as her words spat out towards Ben. "If yo' wanna know 'ow Stan is, well go an' see him, he misses yo' I know it." Taking a deep breath she pulled her shoulders back, her head high as she slightly raised her voice. "Bu' dunna ask me 'ow I am. I hate yore bother, I hate him so much it meks me sick. I told yo' once before, an' yo' cu' me off dead. I married the wrong brother. Bu' wha' do yo' care eh?" Clinging to her child even more so Briar ended on a screech. Ben was just standing there staring at her with a frown taking any hint of a smile away from him. Now, her child began to cry, frightened by the sound of his mothers anger. "Yo' told me I came between yo' an' yore wits, tha' I'd made mi bed an' t' lay on it, so dunna ever ask me 'ow I am again fur the answer will always be the same. I married the wrong brother." The deathly silence that now stood between them was only broken by another loud wail from the child. Briar could take no more, her day had turned into a complete disaster and still she did not know where her parcels were. How she wished she had never walked into this damn shop. She was trapped and would forever be so in her lonely unloving world, where the dark cloud would always hang over her head. Almost fit to burst, Briar turned away from Ben to get out of the door. She'd leave her parcels behind, and think of what to say to Stan later, only now she had to get out of here, and fast. Ben's frown had deepened. Just as he had suspected. There was trouble, deep trouble that was holding fast onto her ready to swallow her deep into a hole. She had reared up at him, and looked ready to hit out as she once would have done, but the look in her eyes again had given her away. Whatever had happened Briar Rose had been pushed to defeat. Never would those wild eyes of hers have clouded over with tears otherwise. Yes, she was right, he had walked away from her sixteen months ago, and he had regretted it ever since. But deep down Ben had clung to the strong loyal bond that he had shared with his older brother since birth. Briar was still Stan's wife, but if he could just reach out maybe there would be a way to help them both, for Ben loved not just Briar, but his brother as well. If he could start with Briar, then maybe he could help stop whatever it was that was tearing the girl in front of him to pieces. As fast as Ben could he pushed forward just managing to get to the door before Briar could, blocking her from leaving. "Briar, I 'anna come t' see Stan because it's bes' fur now tha' I dunna. As fur me ne'er askin' after yo' again tha's somethin' I canna promise. I heard every word yo' said tha' nigh' an' no' a day goes by when I dunna remember wha' yo' said, believe me, I'll always regre' no' movin' fas' enough." Ben spoke softly as Briar kept her head bowed. "When yo' married Stan I could 'ave easily walked righ' away an' ne'er se' eyes on yo' again." Ben paused as eyes that were so forlorn gazed deep into his. "I've always loved yo' lass since before our Stan, bu' I know wha' ever 'is faults, he loves yo' as well an' tha' meks it damn tricky."

Didn't he think she already knew just that? Hadn't she fought within herself knowing that if anything did happen it would finish any brotherly relationship that Stan and Ben had ever had? Wasn't it after all through her that the relationship had already been severed enough? "I know its all mi fault, I know...now please le' me go...I made mi bed as yo' once told me an' I'll mek the bes' o' it wha'ever."

Ben swallowed hard as her tears did begin to fall. He'd never been the cause before for so much unhappiness, and now he hated himself for it. As he watched her bow her head once more, her tearful face hidden against her child, Ben turned quietly and locked the shop door. Briar heard the sound of the turning key and raised her tear soaked face. "Ben…"

"Yo' inna goin' nowheer lass, nod ye'."

As the first flakes of snow kissed the Christmas shoppers and snuggled down of the ledge of the shop windows with a pure innocence, a loyalty between two brothers finally crumbled into the dust. Ben had fought a battle within himself and had now given into the temptation and lost. As Stan had once taken the girl to himself in the cold basement of the Crosshouses Workhouse, Ben now gently took the hand of another man's wife and guided her through the shop and his workshop and up the steep flight of stairs back to his dwellings. Not a word was uttered between them as Ben took the child from her, placing him safely on the floor. When he turned back towards the girl and firmly took her into his arms he felt no resistance as a sob escaped her lips. Ben simply tilted her face towards his and tenderly kissed the lips that had pouted at him so many times. As the child cheerfully played on the floor, Ben took his brother's wife for himself, his soul soaking in the pleasure he had been denied for so long, a pleasure he would be denied no longer. Briar Rose felt not a scrap of remorse as she softly began to moan under the gentle touch of Ben Lawson. Never before had she been willing to give herself to any man as she so wanted too now. As Ben's warm kisses turned to a fiery fever, his mouth pressing firmly against her own, Briar made no attempt to struggle as he pushed her down onto the bed, his fingers playfully undoing the buttons on her frock pausing only so he could strip himself of his own shirt. As he gazed down at slate grey eyes that still echoed tears, he saw a light had re-entered them, offering him a promise of good things to come; Ben gasped aloud before pulling at the tiny bows of her cotton petticoats, his eyes resting on her youthful delicate nakedness beneath him. As Briar reached up and touched the side of his face, he knew she wanted him as much as he did her; as she reached out and held his face so tenderly, a smile now touching her lips Ben sought them even more feverishly until he felt breathless by his own desires. Briar had only ever known the terror and pain that a man could bring her as rough hands tore into her, searing pain through her body until she had screamed. But that very afternoon she found the deep longing inside of her find a lease of life. She felt how soft a man's hands could be, she found the pleasure of a feverish kiss and lastly the wave of ecstasy as her soul at last united her with a man she had loved for so long, until her head spun wildly out of control leaving her quite dizzy. Ben pulled Briar closer into his arms and held her safe beside him. How he had longed to bestow a love upon her that he had held for so long, to keep her happy and safe, to give her all he felt she deserved. From this moment on he knew he would never again see her as his brother's wife. He'd see her as she was, the girl he had always loved, who had been taken from him. Turning over Ben gently began to shower her pretty heart shaped face with more kisses. As he felt her tender fingers run down his back Ben lay over once more, his warm brown eyes drinking in the look that now lit up her grey eyes with expectancy. Being part of Ben's life would be enough for Briar, for now. There was no screaming or crying with pain as Ben once more released the rush of pure love through her. There was the strong bond, the loving caring bond between a man and a woman who had longed to be together since they had first set eyes on each other, and were now left gasping for more.

chapter twelve

"Wash off under the pump lads an' we'll call it a day eh?"

"Aye Stan, aye."

Stan whistled loudly as he also stood under the pump washing the sodden soil from his hands. He had a good understanding with the four young lads under him. It was simple; they did all he asked without argument, and he made life as easy and pleasurable as he could. But if they strayed from their duties in any way causing the Master or Mistress to complain Stan came down as hard as any man could for it also looked bad on him, and that he refused to stand for. His voice could clearly be heard on these occasions, and it had meant nothing to Stan to seek permission from his Master and then send a lad packing, for there was always young lads looking for a job as garden hands. Stan was happy in his work, he knew that he had only been there to begin with because of his brother Ben, but Stan himself had gained a certain respect also with his Master and he knew when he was comfortably off. As the lads bid him 'goodnight' Stan peered around him checking for faults, but there was nothing out of place for he had already checked. "Goodnigh' lads, an' dunna be late tomorrow." Stan nodded his head, and half grinned, they were never late. With all being quiet on the Hampstead Estate, the stable doors being closed for the night, and the distant calls telling him that the wood mill was also closing Stan briskly began to make his way across the grounds towards home, pulling his cap down as he did so to help stop the sleet from stinging his ears that had now began to pelt down from the heavens. January had certainly given her fair share of unpredictable showers of sleet and snow amidst the rain, and as always he was glad that his cottage was just across the grounds for he was cold and very weary.

"Tek yore boots off, the baths ready, bu' yo' inna sittin' down sodden liken tha', an' dunna pick Danny up, he'll catch his death o' cold."

"My boots are already off if yo' looken lass, an' mi hands are clean...see."

Briar Rose casually looked her husband over, her slate grey eyes searching him more closely finding there was nothing she could grumble at, all he was was very cold.

"So, am I allowed in then lass?"

"Aye guess yo' will do."

Whistling loudly Stan threw his over coat onto the easy chair warming his hands over the fire as he did so. It was good to feel the heat from the roaring flames. "Yo' had a good day at the marke' lass? Smells good in here."

"Aye I have, now yo' goin' t' tek tha' bath? The water wunna stay warm forever." Briar forced a smile; one she would hope would fool him enough for him to leave her alone and get on with his own business and take his bath. Stan stood by the log fire, the heat fast to warm his soul, glazing his face with a healthy glow. Things had improved between them greatly since Christmas. She still refused to share his bed and bluntly, insisting on sleeping beside the hearth with just the comfort of a rag mat and a blanket, but she was more...he almost had trouble explaining it. She spoke more, and smiled more often, and sometimes at him. In fact he had even caught her singing when he had come home unexpectedly. Stan smiled to himself, getting out weekly to the Shrewsbury Market was doing her the world of good, and he couldn't complain about the meals she was making out of her weekly visits either. "Well then lass, I'll tek mi bath, come on Danny boy gi' yore Da' a hug before yore mammy grumbles at me again." Taking his small son in his arms Stan loudly chuckled as the child reached out, his chubby hands playing with his father's face squealing with delight as his father held him high in the air.

Briar took little notice, she was too busy scurrying around the table placing the warm plates down, laying the knifes and forks neatly beside them. "Come on now Danny." Wiping her hands on her pinny she took hold of her son, "Yo' le' yore Da' tek tha' bath, for I inna boilin' up more water, an' I wunna be very happy if the broth boils int' nowt."

Once more Stan grinned as he gazed down into the slate grey eyes that held him in reprimand. He couldn't wish for a better wife in so many ways. The cottage was kept so neat and tidy, and there was always a small bunch of wild flowers to decorate the centre of the table. Whenever he did come home these cold winter nights he was always met with a roaring fire, and the tin bath behind the far curtain ready for him. The smell of vegetable broth, or boiled ham and sweet potatoes, the warm bread that could be smelt way before he ever reached the front door. More than that she was as good a mother to their son as he could have possibly wished for, where the child was concerned he had seen the gentle sweet nature within her that would have made her wild side seem like some far off imagination deep within his mind. Cheerfully Stan had released his son, winking at Briar before he disappeared behind the floral curtain. Briar took a long deep breath and closed her eyes in sudden relieve. She had almost missed the last cart home, and had had her work cut out to fool Stan into believing she had been home a fair while. She was thankful that Danny was such a happy child who was content just to crawl behind her, for otherwise she would not have found the time to tidy the cottage, or build the fire up, or come to that prepare a meal of any type. What was more she had managed to take the new wooden train that Ben had given to Danny, and had hidden it alongside his other gifts without Danny becoming too fretful. Gasping aloud to herself Briar placed her hand over her mouth. Eeh she'd have to be more careful or Stan would surely notice that things were not quite as they appeared. "Eeh Danny wha' will become o' us? Wheer will it end up?" Softly she whispered to her son as he sat happily playing with a wooden spoon. Briar smiled at her child warmly, she would not change having Danny for all the world whatever happened in her life, or where the path may lead her; she would always be thankful she had him in her life. But how different her life could still have been despite being married to Stan if she did not have her child. Closing her eyes she could see Ben's face dancing in her minds eye. She remembered every soft sentiment he had whispered that very afternoon. She could almost feel his gentle hands roaming lovingly over her body as they tenderly caressed her skin. Oh yes, how different things could have been for she would have simply left Stan and her home behind her without a second thought. She could have lived with the shame of deserting her husband and moving in with his brother. She could have faced the looks and sneers of sheer disdain at living with a man in sin, for she would be with Ben and that would be enough. How Ben had pleaded with her before she left to do just that, he wanted her whatever the consequences, and he was willing to take the child on as his very own. Her child, Briar smiled once more at the small boy with a crown of bright red hair, whose eyes were as blue as his fathers. Whose childlike smile lit up those very eyes just as Stan's did. "Eeh lad." Sadly Briar shook her head; why she should keep a loyalty to Stan she could hardly understand her own reasoning. But she did understand Stan's love for the child. He was a good father a loving father, and just lately her child had actually muttered 'Da'. Did she really have the right to break up the father and son bond that was in its most important phase of becoming a life long friendship? No, she did not, for if she did, one day her child may grow up and hate her for it. For now she had to think of him, she did not just have herself to think off. Maybe one day when Danny was much older and she could leave, she would, but until then Ben had said he would wait if that was what she wanted. Well she would have too. But fate knows of no love pact, and some would believe that those that did wrong would unwittingly write their own destiny, changing those very hands of fate that could offer any sympathy. In the months that would follow, Stan, Briar and Ben would all come to understand loss and grief, each one losing part of their life's that help them to breath so easily, eventually leaving just one of them to carry the burden of their chosen destiny alone.

chapter thirteen

"Yo shouldna ge' the cart int' town t'morrow lass." Stan spoke with conviction. "Yo' bes' tek it easy, theer's enough in t' ge' by surely, no other lass goes int' town every week, an' sometimes twice." Stan frowned as she sat down at the table, taking the bread himself and slicing it.

"I'm alrigh'." Briar Rose snapped, her voice sharp causing her son to whimper as he held his arms up to his distraught mother.

Stan immediately stood up taking the child himself, his gentle words coaxing his son. "I mean it Briar, carryin' on..."

"I said I'm alrigh', gi' Danny t' me. If yo' wanna mek yoresel' useful a few logs fur the fire wunna come a miss." Briar glowered; she didn't have the time for this, not now. She had to get into town tomorrow however bad she felt, and Stan was not going to stop her. As he had done just lately so many times Stan fell silent. What was wrong with her just lately he did not know, for she had gone back to hardly speaking to him. She had appeared to change somewhat over Christmas, her moods had almost vanished, and she had been civil towards him. But suddenly for no reason he could think off, she'd become even more distant than she'd been previously, only now she had began to snap wildly at him, her temper returning how it had been once before. To make matters worse she had been hit with a stomach bug that had caused her to vomit frequently for over two weeks. No, he wasn't keen on her going into town, for she wasn't too clever at noticing a bad butcher when she found one. And the meat pies she'd brought back a couple of week ago had not tasted too good, though lucky for him they had not made him ill.

"Dunna looken at me liken tha' lass." Stan saw the heavy pout covering her lips. "I can see yo' inna goin' t' tek any notice o' me bu' wha; I will say is dunna bring any o' them damn pies back". Stan waited for a response but was met with none. Shaking his head at her stubbornness he left the parlour without another word, if she wanted logs he'd get them for her. Briar was left alone, her young mind in complete utter turmoil. Her life was such a mess, and now things were about to become far worse. In fact she wanted nothing more than to put her feet up and rest just as Stan had suggested. But she had to see Ben tomorrow. It just could not wait.

"Hello Mr Lawson."

Ben chuckled as he opened his shop door to be met with a sea of small faces. "Hello...now le' me see...Artie, Jack, Charlie an' Harold, an' no' forgettin' yo' Emmylou." Ben winked, then laughed as the small group of ragged street urchins fled to cling to their mother's skirts, as she bartered loudly at the cost of a bag of flour, a small baby in her arms. Ben shook his head, how one managed with so many small children he had to but wonder, but he was used to seeing far worse than this on market days. He'd seen as many as fourteen offspring hanging onto their fraught mother. Whistling loudly Ben placed his sign near the shop door.

"Good mornin' Mr Lawson."

"Same t' yo' Mr Smithers."

"How's business lad?"

"Lookin' good, real good."

With a polite nod of his head Ben turned and walked back into his shop. He had spent most of the night finishing his latest creation, a beautifully painted rocking horse. It had taken him weeks and endless nights, each engraved mark he had chiselled deep into the wood giving the toy its own authenticy, and now, here it stood, its rockers giving perfect balance. Ben ran his hand across the horse's body, how fine the features on the face were, the long snout and long graceful neck. He marvelled over the painted saddle and black painted mane. It was a beautiful work of art; even he for once could not find fault with it, for Ben only ever wanted perfection with anything he made. He had been guaranteed a tidy sum for this extravagant toy and even with Master Hampstead's percentage taken out Ben was set to make his largest profit yet. He nodded to himself. "Aye, oh aye." Deep in thought Ben smiled at the masterpiece, "A profit yo'll brin' me alrigh'." Ben had made plans concerning his work from the time he had shaken Jonathan Hampstead's hand, plans that could not fail. He'd saved just about every penny he could, living as basic as he could in-between time. But it was worth it, for the way things were going, Ben would easily have enough over the next couple of years to put down on his own place. His own shop and living dwellings, when at last he would be his own man completely, a man in his own true right, who would own property, and become the County's best known toy and cabinet maker around. Ben whistled even more loudly to himself as he began to sweep the shop floor, there was never any dust on his floor, for it would rise and settle on his work, his wooden toys and cabinets were his pride and joy, that not too far in the distant future would reap him his just rewards. At hardly nineteen Ben was ready to support another, and not only that he wanted to do it so very badly, a beautiful thought that kept deep within his mind whatever he was doing. But even now, even after he had expressed his true feelings towards Briar Rose, feelings that he had had since before she had married his brother, a part of Ben would always feel a dreadful guilt. For he knew every time he laid down with the girl he genuinely loved, Ben was without doubt that his brother Stan also loved Briar Rose, even if in the past he'd had strange ways of showing it. Pushing the willow broom with more force to rid him of the glum air that now clouded him Ben finished sweeping the floor. He had customers to welcome, and later he had his young lady and her child visiting.

"I know, I know, the las' carts always the same time." Briar snapped her answer as the cart man gave his usual warnings for the last trek home.

"Well then missy as yo' know then mekin' sure yo' are on time because I wunna wai' fur yo' this time."

Briar Rose glowered as the cart man sharply addressed her, but still took the hand offered to her as she stepped off the cart and onto the wet cobbled street of Shrewsbury. The trek into town this time had been frightful. Briar and her ten month old son had been jammed against the sides of the cart the whole way, as other villagers had clambered on behind her. She had held her child as close to her as she possibly could to stop the chill of the March air, and the continual drizzle settling its chill onto him as it had her. With every jolt of the cart as the horses had trudged on relentlessly Briar had heaved, her insides churning with every movement. By the time they entered the town centre it was all she could do to stop herself vomiting. When the old woman sitting next to her cheerfully began to roll up a quid of tobacco Briar ensured she was the first to get off the cart, or she would not have kept her dignity. Now here she was amidst the market traders and shoppers alike, the bustle of early morning already in full swing. So many times she had found this exciting as she too had searched for bargains herself. But not today, Briar ignored the enticing calls from the nearby traders and shivered violently. God she felt so cold. Clutching her child close to her she took the deepest breath she could. Maybe, just maybe it would clear her head, rid her of the tangled mess that had cut short her thinking and clouded her life with the darkest of grey clouds that had now left her so cold. But what could possibly help her out now? Certainly not the crisp cool air. Whatever path she chose to take today would destroy something she held so very dear, and she knew deep down the path she had to take that would not destroy them all. She would carry on and live with just the love of her child, but her heart would forever last only for the love she had held onto for so long. Ben Lawson. A love she would have to sacrifice. Not a murmur did her child make as his mother slowly made her way across the busy market square. It was almost as if he too shared her turmoil, sensed her despair, that had iced over those slate grey eyes of hers, causing them to penetrate fiercely into the unsuspecting gaze of anybody who dared glance her way. Ben Lawson had watched with amusement as she'd stepped down from the cart arguing with the cart man as she did so. He had folded his arms as he stood in his shop doorway waiting patiently as she'd stood for a while daydreaming. As she made her way slowly towards his shop her child tight in her arms a smile of simple pleasure crept over his face warming his brown eyes as it did so. Just the very sight of her made his heart pound with joy, the sight of her silvery blond hair hanging loosely over her shoulders and falling down to touch her waist that shone in the morning madness that had captured the Square. She was dressed very simply in an ankle length dark blue frock with long sleeves and a black woollen shawl over her shoulders, her black boots always so very clean. So very plain and serviceable, just how she always looked, but even still, she out shone any girl that could have ever pass his shop doorway, even the wealthy lasses that often came into his shop looking for a gift. Too him Briar had the face of an angel, even though she could easily frighten the Devil with her temper. But one thing was certain, when the time come and she did take herself to him, he'd make sure that the angel faced girl was dressed far better than she was now. She deserved far better, and he'd be able to make sure she got it. As Briar approached Ben's shop, his smile began to fade and his body tensed, a look of concern ageing his young face instantly. She looked withdrawn, in fact she looked ill, and if he didn't know better he'd even say she was close to tears. Briar Rose took one last breath as the distance between her and Ben across the market place closed in. How proud he looked standing there outside his own shop doorway. How very clean and smart he looked in his dark corduroy trousers and grey linen shirt, and how very warm his brown eyes were, eyes that were watching her intently, but that held a sincere welcome. He stood so very firm his shoulders looking even broader than they were. From where she stood, and for those who did not know him, nobody would have even guessed that Ben had made an instep inside his boot that resembled a wooden clog making his crippled leg more in line with the other. "Oh Ben." Briar whispered his name. How good things could have been. How happy she would have been working here alongside him, living here as his wife. But that was fantasy, just a mere dream and she had to forget it, and fast. She had written her own destiny the day she had married Stan, Ben's brother, and that would have to be the way of things.

"Yo' looken like yo' need t' si' down lass." Not waiting for an answer Ben took the child from her, holding out his arm for support. When Briar actually took it to steady herself Ben's concern grew. When she spoke in a broken whisper that they needed to speak upstairs Ben's concern changed to fear, but when her slate grey eyes that could pierce through a soul and spark in pure defiance glazed over with pitiful tears, Ben felt something he had never known before. He had always loved Briar, from the day she'd first been found in the workhouse dressed as a boy and stealing bread. He had felt bitterness and jealousy towards his brother when he had taken Briar for himself. But in this instance, his love knew only a fierce protective bond towards her, so strong that he would have feared no one if it meant keeping her safe. In that moment he knew the time was right for her to stay with him and never return home, her home had to be with him, how it should have been to begin with. He was ready to take the child and be the father to it that he should have been naturally. Briar sat motionless in the easy chair Ben had placed her in, her child safely playing on the floor, as Ben gently told Briar that it was time for her to make her choice and the only place for her was with him. Every beat of her heart agreed with him, how her soul wanted to jump up and dance and tell him it was all she wanted too, but nothing could make her speak those words of truth. All she could do was splutter and sob into the hanky that Ben had given her. She knew that life would be good with Ben, but she had Danny, and he had to be considered above all of this. Danny had a right of his natural father, her husband, and she could not deny father and son just for the sake of herself. Her only reason for coming into town today was to finish with Ben, to tell him she could never see him again, and to pray that he would understand her reasons. Then, when that was done she would have to face her husband sooner or later and pray even harder that he would understand what it was she would have to tell him. "Here yo' go lass, yo' ge' tha' down yo' an' believe me nowt will seem as bad as mi mushed brew."

Briar spluttered as she tried to laugh, only to release a strangled choke. "Thankyo' Ben." Taking the tin mug offered Briar immediately sipped the scalding liquid, flinching as it burnt her lips.

"Steady on lass, tek yore time. Yo' si' theer an' relax while I play wi' mi nephew, an' then yo' can tell me wha's upse' yo' so much." Ben offered his warmest of smiles, but when all he was met with was a look of utter despair, and the promise of fresh tears he knelt down in front of her taking her hands gently in his own. "Wha' is it lass? Is it our Stan? Come on Briar wha's the matter lass?" Ben's questions spilled out one after the other, for he had known Briar for so long now, but never had he seen her so distressed, so very lost, not even after the beatings she had received back at the workhouse. She looked beaten now, well and truly, for no spark of life had yet entered her eyes, and her shoulders were hunched up as if in pain. Briar struggled, she knew what she had to say, but when she did, she knew it would also end something so very wonderful that she had with Ben. Never would she be able to sit here so close to him again accepting his terrible mushed tea. Even that she found hard to contemplate. The feeling of never being able to have his warm arms around her again, or hearing the sweetness of his words when she spent the market days in his bed was tearing apart. To have to do without him, the only true love she had ever found in a man who did not hurt her was breaking her heart in two. Ben waited apprehensively, he could sense her turmoil, and he feared she had come to him not to be with him as she normally did, but to bring him bad news. Only even Ben did not forsee what he was about to hear. Briar closed her eyes as tightly as she could to shut out the warmth of his soft brown eyes. She did not want to see the warmth fade against her, as it surely would. "I canna see yo' anymore Ben, nod now, nod ever." As Ben squeezed her hands tightly, Briar opened her eyes. "I'm sorry Ben, bu' I canna, I 'ave t' stay wi' Stan fur the sake o' Danny, an'...an'."

"An' fur who Briar? Yoresel'? Yo' know as well as I do yo' 'ave ne'er loved mi brother. I know yo' better than tha' lass, so somethin' 'as changed yore mind. Has mi brother found owt an' belted yo' one?" Ben waited not sure how she would answer his question, but the answer he got left him speechless.

"No Ben, no he 'anna. I 'ave to' stay fur Danny, an' the child I'm now carryin'."

Child! As if some unseen force had pushed hard against Ben he stumbled backwards as he tried to stand, and then fought to compose himself. "Child?" His answer a mere whisper. "Whose child?

"Tha' dunna matter, I've said wha' I 'ad t' say, it's bes' if I go...an' please Ben dunna come near me again." With an urgency to get out, Briar stood up and rudely pushed past Ben her tearful eyes refusing to hold any contact with him as she reached out and picked up her son. She had to go for she couldn't bear to see the expression she knew was haunting Ben's eyes, a look that would tell her she had just broken his heart.

"I asked whose child?" Ben was not finished just yet, his love for Briar would never cease whatever she did to him, but he had to know whose child she was carrying, even though she had repeatedly told him that she had never slept with her husband as man and wife. "If yo' wanna walk owt on me Briar tha's one thin', bu' I wan' t' know now is the child mine?" Ben firmly took hold of her upper arm, forcing Briar to face him as he did so, waiting as she tearfully raised her eyes to meet his. "Is the child mine?" Briar took a deep breath and shuddered before holding her son even tighter for comfort. She could not lie, and even if she had tried Ben already knew the answer for it echoed through her tearful slate grey eyes. "An' jus' liken tha' yo' wan' me t' walk away? Turn mi back!" Ben's voice began to raise with frustration, he had so many sudden questions, and needed the answers, and he couldn't let her go, not yet. "Does Stan know? Does he know yore carryin' mi child? Well lass 'ave yo' though' wha' he'll say when yo' do tell him?"

Had she thought? What a bloody daft question to ask, she had thought of nothing else. She remembered only too well what had happened the last time Stan had seen her pleading with Ben, speaking of her love for him. Stan had lost all reason and had brutally raped her, forcing her son upon her. But to have to tell him now that she was in fact with child from Ben, Stan's only brother just didn't bear thinking about. How she was going to tell him she just did not know, she hoped beyond all reason that he didn't skin her alive when she did, and then aim for Ben. "Aye Ben, I've though', I've though' o' nowt else, an' its mi problem. I'll face wha' ever I 'ave t' an' I'll beg Stan's forgiveness if I 'ave t', jus' fur Danny's sake."

"An' the child, an' yoresel'? Yo' dunna 'ave t' face wha'ever, as fur beggin', it's me yore talkin' too now Briar, an' we both know yo'd ne'er beg t' save yore skin." Ben's voice rose even more, the anger evident in his eyes, only the wild pounding of his heart echoed the hurt that was shaking his body and turning his world upside down. "Yo' dunna 'ave t' mek this work, I can go an' see Stan..."

"No, no Ben, please...yo' 'ave t' le' me go. Danny needs his own Da'. I canna break tha' up."

"An' mi child, wha' abou' tha' needin' its own Da' Briar?"

Briar shuddered; the trembling of her soul would cause her to collapse if she did not leave here right now. She could not answer these questions; she could not think ahead that far. Only time would tell her what to do, and what was right. For now, she had made a dreadful mistake by Danny and he was all that mattered in this terrible mess. Her heart had no place in life now, as Ben had once told her she had made her bed, and now they were the words she threw back at him. "I've made mi bed Ben, an' now, I 'ave t' lay on it." An eerie silence engulfed them, turning the room into a cold unfeeling atmosphere. As two lovers stood so silently facing each other their bodies rigid, filled with desperation by the whole affair, their hearts breaking, each young mind in turmoil for the other, it was Ben that found the strength to speak. "I'll gi' yo' time t' tell Stan lass, an' t' sor' owt wha' yo' are really goin' t' do. Bu' the child yore carryin' is mine, an' I'm its Da', nod Stan."

"Yo' 'ave t' le' me go Ben, please...le' me go." Pulling from Ben's grasp Briar pushed forward, she had to get out, away from here where she could hopefully find the air to breath, and most of all think.

"I'll gi' yo' so long Briar, an' then I'll mek mi claim, yo' 'ear me?"

No answer was given as Briar backed towards the door, the tears now falling pathetically. Ben tried to reach her, but this time Briar was too fast, she was out of the door and down the stairs before he had the time to even think. Long after Briar was gone, Ben sat alone in his shop, his wooden toys his only company, his hopes for the future ripped wide open. He hadn't even had the time to take her in his arms; she had not let him that near. He could only assume the baby she was carrying would be born somewhere in the Autumn, she hadn't even told him that. He had not had time to hold his young nephew Danny as he always did, or to give him the toy horse he had finished making him. Danny, how the child had grown on him, but it was his brother's son, Briar had made that only too plain. Ben smiled sorrowfully as he gazed down at the wooden horse, Danny had the same bright red hair and blue eyes of his brother. Yes it was true, he did miss Stan, but that was a relationship that could never be reconciled. As for Briar, Ben closed his eyes. Whatever road she took he would never stop loving her. But as he had told her, he would make his claim on his own child. Briar Rose fled the Shrewsbury Square, leaving Ben and the shop way behind her. Her whole life was in shreds; her heart would never feel the gift of love and warmth that a man could bestow on her again. There was nothing in this world she wanted more than to be a family with Ben Lawson. But her love for him had stopped her doing just that. For to leave her husband and take Danny away only to move in with her husband's brother some classed as a crime. To be expecting her husband's brother's child was an utter disgrace beyond any decency of most people to comprehend. She knew what was right for Danny...to be with his own father. She knew what was right for Ben; it was to continue with his own career and life without her, for he would be finished in this town otherwise. As far as she and her unborn child went, she did not know. What she did know was she'd have to beg her husband to forgive her, beg him to help her, and bloody hard.

chapter fourteen

"Now yo' tell tha' lass o' yores t' come an' speak wi' me, I'm always 'ere when a lass needs me, an' yo' know wha' I mean." Emily Bunting chuckled aloud as she past a hot mug of mushed tea into Stan Lawson's hands. "Eh she's a strange one yore lass, thinken she'd wan' t' tell us all, bu' no, nod Briar Rose, kept Danny a secre' till she couldna any longer. Now seems t' me she's doin' the same... a big mystery t' me tha' lass." Emily shook her head as she carried on talking whilst clearing the parlour table. She'd had many a young girl in her service over the years, but Briar had come into her care a mystery, and she was a girl that had remained one. Stan stood by the parlour door, not a murmur escaped his lips as he watched Emily Bunting busy herself, but he listened intently, not one chuckle passing him by. For what he was being told, or more so been given a suggestion off had filled his soul with a dread, turning his blood cold until even the hot mushed black tea held no warmth. He could feel his heart pounding so fiercely that he wondered himself if it would just pack up beating and leave him dead. But he still stood, forcing a smile as Emily Bunting rambled on and on. "Yo' tell yore lass t' come an' see me, an' mind yo' do, she dunna come up t' the house often enough, an' I 'anna go' the time t' go trapsin' over theer."

"Aye Mrs Buntin' I will, an' thankin' yo' fur yore kindness."

"Yo' mek sure she teks it easy now. If I'm righ' an' I've ne'er been wrong ye', so yo' mek sure she teks thin's easier now."

Stan never answered; he tipped his cap in a farewell gesture and left the parlour of the estate house behind him. He had work to do, orders to give the garden hands and he had to make sure they were done. He had to finish on time today, for he was desperate to head off home to see his wife, there were things he had to talk about, worries he needed to put right. But the day was going to be no easy task, for Stan not only feared what he had heard, he knew the very worst was upon him. Frowning heavily to himself he marched towards his garden hands. Oh how her mood had changed over Christmas, she had been almost sociable towards him she had been willing to talk more and sit by the open fire in his company without causing a full scale argument. He had been willing to just enjoy her company and not expect more, the thought that she may even want to share his bed was something he no longer perused, and he hadn't even been to the village pub in months. But then her mood had changed, her mystery illness had began and she was no longer amenable, causing a row almost every evening over nothing he could put his finger on. Then he noticed how her change of heart towards going into Shrewsbury Town every week had altered. She found every excuse to go before and after Christmas. Now, she bluntly refused, and what was more, over the last month her attitude towards him had once more softened. She was being surprisingly pleasant to him and seldom had these nights raised her voice in temper. "God damn it, this is all I need." Glaring at the sky above Stan sighed, it was early April and the threat of snow showers was upon them. "Come on lads ge' yore backs int' it, I wan' the rubbish removed an' the ground levelled before anyone goes home."

"Aye Mister lawson." Voices came as one, but each lad knew Stan meant business, snow or no snow. Briskly Stan picked up the shovel; they had a whole hedgerow to get rid off, for Mistress Blanche had stated the need for standard rose trees instead. Leaning momentarily on his shovel Stan gazed towards the direction of his cottage, he could see the steady stream of smoke from the chimney. There was so many ways he just could not fault Briar, she never missed putting a meal on the table, and never failed to have got water ready for him at the end of each day. He and his child wanted for nothing. The only thing she denied him was her love, or any physical contact, if fact he hadn't been near her since the night he had brutally forced her down, and he still hated himself for being so cruel. But as it had that night, the same burning enraged jealousy had been turning his stomach all morning, his whole body felt tense with a hidden dangerous rage, and he felt sick to the core. "God 'elp yo' lass if what' they all thinken is true, I'll tek yo' apart, God 'elp me I will." Curious glances brought his attention back to earth with a sharp thud. "Come on lads, no time t' waste, Smith clear the res' o' the earth, Evans tek the rubbish an' burn it, yo' two louts can level the earth...ge' on wi' it."

"Aye Mister Lawson."

"Come on now Danny, now yo' si' theer a while, yore mam canna 'old yo' all day an' besides yore Da' will be in any time now an' I 'anna laid the table ye'." Briar smiled lovingly as her small red headed son held out his chubby hand towards her, his bright eyes sparkled with laughter at the sound of his mother's gentle voice. "Eeh yore a good lad." Humming to herself, Briar took a clean table cloth from the dresser and placed it neatly on the table, soothing out any creases as she did so. Next she placed two tin plates, side plates, and mugs opposite each other. She was nearly ready, the bread she had baked that morning was already sliced and there was enough salted butter left for Stan with a small helping of cheese if he wanted it. "I thinken yore Da' will like it alrigh' Danny." Briar spoke merrily to her chuckling child as she stirred the fresh rabbit hotpot. She had gone out of her way that morning to shoot a rabbit, even though she had been reluctant to make the trek up towards the Lyth Hill. But she had been rewarded by managing to find a rabbit already ensnared, a large rabbit, and now with the carrots, onions and potatoes she had brought from a local farmer, she had made the best hotpot yet. Sighing she looked around her, her slate grey eyes searching the room. Yes everything was tidy, she had a cauldron of hot water ready for Stan's bath, and the meal was wafting its tempting aroma all over the parlour. Everything appeared very welcoming and homely. Things had to be right for tonight; for it was tonight Briar Rose had to speak with her husband over a very serious matter that up until now she had attempted to push aside. Taking off her pinny, she brushed the skirts of her frock straight; it was her blue frock of light jersey with a full skirt and three quarter length sleeves. Stan had always said he liked the frock best of all since she had made it. Reaching for her brush Briar groomed her waist length silvery blond hair until it shone with glory allowing it to flow freely down her back. Again she sighed, "Eeh Danny, I'm glad yore too young t' understand." Briar paused, her attention on the parlour door, had she just heard Stan? "Well it's an early nigh' fur yo' Danny, straigh' after yore tea." Swallowing heavily, Briar brushed her frock straight again, she'd have to look her very best. Everything had to be just right, that way she could guarantee Stan would be in good spirits. Then, maybe, just maybe, he would be more understanding. Sadly Briar would be proved frightfully wrong, by the very next morning her life would take a completely different road.

Stan took a series of deep breaths as he walked into the small garden of his cottage making his way towards the cottage door. Any other time the wonderful aroma of fresh rabbit hotpot would have made his mouth water, but tonight he had a job to swallow, in fact he felt he would choke. He had to speak with his wife, and the sooner his son was settled for bed, the better.

"Hello Stan."

"Hello Briar, Danny come an' gi' yore Da' a hug." Holding his small son close to him Stan winked at him as the child's arms reached out towards his father's neck. "Yo' been a good lad then?" A series of childish chuckles was his only answer. Carefully Stan placed the child in his highchair, and then sat down at the table, his eyes very carefully following Briar as she made her way towards the cauldron of hot water. "I'll 'ave mi bath after, fur now I jus' wan' mi tea." Still his eyes sought hers as she flustered over the cauldron, before immediately turning her attention to the hotpot. She was making no eye contact with him at all, she even looked panic stricken, and if the rumours he'd heard that day were true, she had every right to be. So carefully Briar placed a large bowl of hotpot on the table, handing Stan a ladle with which to help himself. How nervous she felt, she could sense his bright blue eyes piercing into her, holding her in deep questioning. He did this sometimes, and she guessed he took great pleasure in watching her stumble about. Only tonight she felt sick, his presence was frightening, she hoped...oh how she hoped. "Yo' goin' t' si' down lass? I inna startin' wi'owt yo'." Slowly Stan spoke, his eyes not leaving her for a second. She was wearing the blue frock, the one he favoured, and how pretty her silvery blond hair looked tonight. As her slate grey eyes met his, she feebly smiled, and he couldn't help but offer her a smile back. The sight of her had always stirred within him such a deep powerful emotion of fierce love, her cream soft skin always so clean, how tempting it looked to reach out and touch, but she never let him get that close. No...he never did... lowering his eyes over her he stared even harder, he couldn't be sure, for her frock was quite loose fitting, but it did look as if she'd put a little weight on. "Si' down Briar, 'elp yoresel' t' some bread." He waited as she slowly sat down and took the slice of bread he offered. "Tell me Briar, 'ow are yo' lass? Have yo' been feelin' sick jus' lately?"

"No Stan." Briar lied.

So, thought Stan, as he frowned, she's lowered her eyes. He saw the slight colour turn her pale face a delicate shade of pink. "So, yo' a lo' better then lass? Some type o' strange sickness wa' it then? Yo' 'anna los' no weight lass, in fac' I'd say yo' may 'ave pu' it on around the middle. Aye, yo' looken like yo' 'ave, too much bread eh?"

Briar's slate grey eyes flashed at him as she glared across the table. Was he deliberately trying to upset her? Did he know something? No he couldn't know, nobody did except for herself and Ben, and she had finished that almost six weeks ago. No, Stan was just being himself, infuriating and even though her stomach churned wildly by what she had to tell him, she was quick to snap. "Yore nowt bu' a rude pig, I dunna know why I bother wi' yo'."

"Bu' yo' dunna, do yo' lass? In fact yo' dunna come near me. Yo inna liken a normal wife Briar, theer's more t' mekin' a man happy than a bloody rabbit hotpot." Stan glared long and hard, his voice slightly rising. "Bu' yo' dunna know anythin' abou' keepin' a man happy do yo' lass?" Stan sat firm, his elbows on the table, his chin resting on his fists. She had stood up to him quickly enough, but now she had turned her back, in fact she looked like she may faint. "Si' down before yo' fall down lass, come on now le's 'ave a happy family meal shall we? Jus' yo' me an' Danny. Then we'll pu' Danny t' bed an' we can 'ave a chat. Shall we lass? Jus' yo' an' me, how cozy." Once more Stan watched the colour rise up her neck, her face turning crimson, and he noticed the hesitation in her grey eyes. Deliberately Stan ladled a large helping of hotpot and passed it to Briar. "Fur yo' lass, do yo' good eh? Yo' are lookin' good, good enough fur two."

Briar sat completely silent, it was all she could do was to hold her spoon steady under her husband's scrutinizing glare. How tight her throat felt, how hot she had become and how very nervous she felt. He knew, dear God above he knew, but how? Ben had been nowhere near Bayston Hill she knew that, and she had not undressed in front of Stan. How did he know? But know he did, she was sure of that. Stan ate the remainder of his meal in silence, not even his small son now managed to bring a smile to his face. He felt utterly sick with dread at what may shortly face him. He hoped against all odds that Briar had not wandered, for he genuinely loved her, and if it meant having her for his wife, but not being able to touch her, he would settle for that, as long as she was true to him. But if she had gone and then fallen by another, he did not know himself yet what he would do with her. What Stan did know was it was best for Danny to be taken up to his room tonight as soon as possible and then he'd force the issue into the open. He knew exactly how to do it, and he knew it would cause a mighty scene. If he was wrong, he himself would beg her to forgive him, but if he was right...he just hoped against all odds that he wasn't.

"Theer's some stale cake lef' if yo' wan' it."

"No lass, no thankin' yo'. Tek Danny upstairs an' settle 'im, I'll ge' the bath ready in the back, then come down eh?"

"Danny...upstairs?"

"Aye lass, he can sleep wi' 'is Da' tonigh'...go on...the water wunna keep warm fur long."

Briar pouted heavily. Danny had only ever slept by her side, downstairs, but without any fuss she took hold of her child and stormed upstairs, enraged by her husbands request. But still she said nothing for she knew it was probably best that Danny was out of the way tonight. Stan took the cauldron, crossed the room and drew the floral curtain back emptying the scalding contents into the tin bath. So carefully he had planned his next move, placing the carbolic soap next to the bath he took a clean towel and laid it on the chair next to him. Now he waited patiently, his heart on his sleeve, for his world would soon be put at ease, or be totally destroyed. Briar took an age getting her son to settle, she rocked him sang to him and finally sat and told him stories until finally his bright blue eyes fell into a deep sleep, his body tired of the fight to stay awake. Briar sat at the edge of the bed and watched him for several moments. How small he was, how very peaceful he looked, content in his innocent life. A life she had to somehow keep that way. Exhausted, she stared around the room yet saw nothing, her mind only on the task ahead. She had to get up now, take a deep breath and get it over and done with. Reluctantly Briar got up and slowly made her way down the stairs. There sat Stan, still unwashed, watching her so very closely, the towel in his hands.

"Yo' 'anna bathed ye' Stan?"

"No lass, the waters fur yo'."

"Me?"

"Aye, fur yo', 'ere tek yore towel, then ge' undressed an' in yo' go."

Briar glared at him, he always bathed before her, but just for tonight she'd do as he asked, and she needed him on side, not annoyed to begin with. Reaching out Briar went to take the towel from him. "Alrigh' then if tha's wha' yo' wan'."

"Aye lass it is, yo' can 'ave the towel when yo' tek yore frock off. Tek it off...please."

Immediately Briar stepped backwards and gasped, completely misreading Stan's meaning. Stan grinned, a smile that did not reach his eyes. "Dunna worry lass, I inna goin' t' tek yo' down, bu' I wan' yo' t' tek tha' frock off 'ere in fron' o' me."

Briar wet her lips and held her breath for a long moment to try and ease the panic churning in her stomach. To be asked to take her frock off meant only one thing, and if she did remove her frock he would see the slight swelling of her stomach. "No, gi' me the towel, I wunna undress in fron' o' yo', how dare yo' ask such a thing."

"Dare I will, now tek yore frock off Briar, righ' 'ere or I'll do it fur yo'. Tek it off." Stan watched as her arms folded around her own body, the fear evident in her face, he could plainly see her chest heaving as she breathed. Briefly he closed his eyes, at this moment she feared him as she had the night she had conceived his son. She feared he was going to rape her again. "I wunna touch yo' Briar, I dunna wan' t' nod against yore will, bu' I'm askin' yo' one las' time...tek the frock off lass, or God help me if I ge' up I'll rip it off yore back." A sob escaped Briar's throat as she realised she had no choice but to remove her frock there and then in the parlour. She would be leaving herself so very vulnerable, and he would see, she only hoped he would not ask her to remove anything else. Stan sat, not moving as she undid the tiny buttons on the front of her dress bodice, her slender fingers trembling with anxiety. "Tek the frock off yore shoulders Briar." So slowly she obeyed, not a sound escaped her lips, not a hint of a pout, just a pitiful expression of a girl, such a young girl who expected the very worse from him. Stan also said nothing as she lowered the frock revealing the creamy nakedness of her shoulders and collar bone, how very slender she looked, how very tempting. But he wasn't asking her to undress for that pleasure. "Drop the frock t' the floor lass." Briar clung to it so very tightly, and shivered. Standing there with just her cotton camisole and petticoats keeping her from being completely naked gave her no comfort at all, and now he was asking her, no telling her to let her frock fall.

"Please Stan."

"Jus' drop yore frock t' the floor." Again Stan briefly closed his eyes cutting her off dead. If she pleaded too much, he was scared he would hold back and leave her alone, but what good would that do? "Le' yore frock go Briar." Firmly he spoke, so very upright he sat, in full command, only the pounding of his own heart failing him, for he was just as terrified as what she was. Briar tearfully looked at her husband, still clinging to her frock, but he wasn't going to back down and she was more scared of the consequences when he firmly stated once more. "Drop yore frock." Briar did begin to cry pitifully, sobs fast to escape her throat, her slate grey eyes pleading with her husband as she muttered through tears. "I'm sorry, I am so sorry Stan." As Briar lowered her gaze, closing her eyes tightly, she let go of her frock and there she stood in just her camisole and cotton petticoats, not daring to open her eyes and look into those of her husband. Stan had also closed his eyes, but only to save his own pride, to stop his own tears from falling that were now choking his throat to be released. Smothering the sound of his own sobs Stan was hit with the cold realisation that left him in utter disbelief and despair. He would clearly see the slight swelling of her stomach, and when he so very gently reached out as if touching a fragile rose, his hand resting on his wife's abdomen, he could feel the hardness around her, nature's way of protecting an unborn child. What could he say? What could any husband say? Slowly Stan stood up, his shoulders hunched, his head bowed against his chest, as he crossed the parlour he didn't even look back at her. He had to get out of here, and there was only one place to go where a man could freely drown their sorrows, The Three Fishes Inn at the bottom of the Common. The hour of truth was upon them, all of them, the cruel awareness that had loudly declared itself to be real was only about to get far worse. For before Stan left the Inn, he would also know the father of his wife's unborn child.

"Aye, an' thankin' yo' Mr Jackson sir, it's been a real pleasure doin' business wi' yo'." Ben Lawson enthusiastically shook the stout gentleman's hand. He had just received an order for Christmas, and they were only in April.

"Two dolls houses, two wooden dolls, and a fine rocking horse if you please."

Ben had proudly walked the length of his workshop imitating the stout gentleman long after he had gone. His orders were coming in fast from folk as far away as Chester. In fact it had been discussed that very day with Jonathan Hampstead about taking on a young apprentice, a lad from Hampstead Mill at Bayston Hill. Ben had rubbed his hands together with delight at the idea, him train an apprentice? "Aye, I can do tha'." He had boldly told Jonathan. It wasn't all that had been discussed. Ben as always asked about how Briar was faring. Usually Jonathan gave little away, he had made it plain he was not interested in 'matters of the heart' he was interested only in work and profits. Anything else and the door was closed. But that very morning Jonathan had actually said that although there were seldom 'fights' at the Lawson cottage, and even though Stan worked as hard as he always had, and never faltered, he resembled no young man he had ever known. In fact Stan Lawson had aged. Ben had pushed as hard as he dare, but was met with nothing more than a shrug of the shoulders. "Maybe it's the friendship he misses. He is your brother, maybe it is time you both put behind you whatever it was that come between you. Make amends." Words of wisdom. As simple as that...if only. Jonathan Hampstead had left then, pleased with the profits young Ben was still making him. He himself had wondered at the brothers refusal to speak to each other, but if he had to lay a bet on anything he would confidently gamble that the girl Briar Rose was somewhere in the middle of all of it. Ben had thought long and hard that day. He did miss Stan's friendship, for he was his only brother, one that had done the best to look after him along the way. What the future held for them he himself had to wonder, for if Stan ever found out the true parentage of his wife's unborn child there would never be any chance of reconciliation. But even still, that would have to be the road he would have to venture down, for he loved his brother without a doubt, but he also loved Briar, and the child was his, a child that would one day need it's own father. As the afternoon drifted by, Ben found himself more and more concerned about Briar, his unborn child, and also his brother. If there was things he needed to know then he would have to find out for himself. The last cart left the town centre for Bayston Hill about four thirty. If he caught that he could wait at the Three Fishes Inn in the hope that Stan would turn up for a drink. Hopefully Stan would sit and speak with him, and then Ben would hopefully find out just how Briar Rose was.

"If it's the Hampstead's yo' wan' I can tek yo' up The Common, it's no problem lad."

"Aye thankin' yo' bu' I've other thin's t' do. The Three Fishes on the side o' the road will be jus' fine."

"Well it wunna be open ye', bu' old George wunna mind yo' tappin ' on the back door, he's been known t' le' folk in fur a ho' toddy." The cart man laughed heartily, his broad grin revealing the few teeth he had left.

"Aye, thankin' yo' fur the tip, I migh' jus' do tha', good evenin' t' yo'."

"Aye, an' t' yo' too lad."

On the long country road that lay in the heart of Bayston Hill, The Common just to the right hand side of him where Jonathan Hampstead's estate stood, Ben took a long deep breath. It was better he waited here, for The Three Fishes, would probably give him a far better welcome than if he had have knocked on his brother's door.

So many questions turned in Stan's head, utter despair had left his heart pounding heavily, his chest heaving as he stormed towards The Three Fishes. When had she found the time? It was either with one of the mill workers, or his own grounds men. But no, the rumours would have found their way back to his ears by now, and he would have surely seen somebody leaving his cottage. It had to be somebody she had met whilst Christmas shopping in Shrewsbury. Kicking out wildly at a stone, Stan swore loudly as his disturbed thoughts fiercely crashed around his head. She would have had their child with her as well. Clenching his fists tightly, Stan bit deep into his bottom lip, as if punishing himself for his wife's actions. There was one other possibility, and that would explain her change in behaviour, her mood swings, the pleasant times, then her refusal to go near the town so suddenly without any explanation. Somebody had taken her down, used her against her will. That would explain her shame and apologetic attitude when he'd made her undress. She would have found the whole ordeal very difficult. Yes, it was a possibility, a high one even. Well, when he went home later he would confront the issue and demand the full truth. If she'd been forced he could cope with that, but if she'd freely gone with another, he'd want a lot more questions answered, and then God help the man in question and come to that Briar herself.

"A tankard o' ale please man, a tankard o' ale." Slamming his money on the bar, Stan pulled up a stool, not looking the barman in the face or anybody else. He had one aim, to drown his sorrows, and to free himself of his problems.

"I'll pay fur tha', 'ere pu' yore money back Stan."

Grasping his money tightly in his fists Stan placed it back swiftly into his pocket and was just about to pick up his tankard when he stopped. So slowly he turned, his eyes rising to meet those of his young brother. A brother he had not seen in well over a year. "Bloody hell, looken wha' the cats dragged in. Come t' gloat 'ave yo' Ben, or come jus' t' buy yore brother a few ales?"

Ben never answered, he watched as Stan downed the liquid in one fair swoop, then banged the tankard on the bar counter. "Fill it up mate, an' our Ben 'ere will pay, righ' Ben?"

"Aye, I'll pay, fill it up please." Ben gave his answer to the barman who was already scowling at Stan's boisterous attitude. Again there was silence, Ben watched intently, leaning against the bar as Stan stared vacantly into his tankard, not drinking the liquid now or even muttering a sound. It was right what Jonathan Hampstead had told him that morning, Stan had in fact aged, he was not yet quite twenty three, but he resembled a man in his forties. Ben noticed he hadn't changed out of his garden work clothes, or come to that had even looked as if he had washed, ground in dirt discoloured his finger nails, and his bright shock of red hair had been left to grow around his ears. He looked a mess. He needed a bath, a haircut, but all he seemed interested in was staring vacantly into his tankard of ale.'

"Yo' wan' a bite t' eat our Stan? Theer's mea' and potato pie on offerin'."

"No." Stan sharply replied, but then raised his gaze once more to meet the warm brown eyes of his brother who he had cared so strongly about, and come to be honest still did. "No thankin' yo', I've eaten, an' thankin' y o' fur the ale."

"Aye." It was all Ben could softly say, for the look behind his brother's bright blue eyes spoke with disturbing echoes. Stan's eyes had always sparked with mischief, he had a ready smile for all who spoke to him. But here he was, just a vacant gaze of hurt and sorrow sketched over his face, making him older, taking any light he'd ever had from his eyes. Stan resembled a man beaten, a man that would maybe never find the path back. Sighing deeply Stan picked up his tankard and raised it high in the air.

"Cheers our Ben, 'ere's t' yo' an' all yo' 'ave achieved." For the first time Stan looked Ben straight in the face as if seeing him for the very first time. Just for a sheer moment the old look of pride shone in his blue eyes, but was quick to vanish as a forced smile turned back to a look of utter despair. Once more Stan stared into his tankard before downing the liquid and slamming it back on the bar. What could he talk to Ben about? There he stood in half decent cloth trousers, and a blue checked shirt. He was clean shaven, and his red hair though much lighter than his own was cut short and well kept. He had not seen Ben for an age, but he could clearly see how well Ben looked. So, he was obviously doing fine without him? Yet who needed him anyway? His wife certainly didn't. "Another ale mate… please." Quietly Stan spoke his words then bowed his head, resting it into his hands as he did so.

"Come on Stan, I've go' yore tankard, le's go an' si' over theer away from the bar. I wan' t' know how yore farin'." Ben affectionately placed a hand on his brother's shoulder; he could see Stan was not doing well at all.

"Nod as good as yo' lad, nod as good as yo'." With no argument Stan followed Ben across the Inn towards some well weathered seats. "It's been a while Ben, bu' God its good t' see yo' lad." Stan spoke the truth, he had been in a complete fury the night he'd told Ben he never wanted to see him again, the night he had brutally forced his wife down. How he had regretted it ever since, for Ben had always been his responsibility in a way. He had looked out for his back from the time he was hardly more than a toddling infant himself. He had never needed Ben, it had always been the other way around, and as the home brewed ale was beginning to have it's effect, Stan knew he would need the help of another in the stark reality of the months that lay ahead of him. One he would be able to trust, who would listen to his heart felt sorrows, and that person was Ben, his only brother. Ben listened patiently as the evening wore on, offering as much support as he could under the circumstances, for he dearly wanted to build a relationship back with his brother, but his mind drifted back continually to where his own heart longed to be, and that was with the girl with the silvery blond hair and the slate grey eyes – Briar Rose and his unborn child. Ben had to be very careful. He tried to advise Stan, but as the evening wore on he began to refuse to pay any comment where Briar was concerned except to tell Stan. "Yo' 'ave t' gi' the lass space, gi' 'er time."

But Stan never heard, on and on he rambled, his voice a steady slur as he told Ben openly how he had made Briar undress to find out if the rumours were true. Ben lowered his tankard to the table, the horror creeping over his face as Stan confessed, but it was more than that, Ben could feel the deep undercurrents that were tearing Stan apart tempting him further into another tankard of ale. But how would Ben have felt? Exactly the same he knew that, if Briar had been his wife, he too would have turned to the drink for comfort. But where Ben would never have harmed her, the cold glare that had glazed Stan's eyes over opened up a whole new fear for Ben, for he truly sensed that both Briar Rose and his unborn child were in immediate danger. "Yo' tek it easy our Stan, wha'ever 'as happened, she's wi' child, yore 'er husband, yo' 'ave t' stand by 'er wha' ever yore feelin's are righ' now." For a long moment that was almost swallowed up in time the brother's eyes locked in a sudden fierce, yet unsought battle. Each brother holding back on the other just a little, but with Ben's statement, the wave of goodwill that Stan had felt towards him had been lost in the smoky atmosphere that filtered out through the door. The turmoil of unanswered questions he still longed to ask Briar, that had appeared as muddled up pieces of jigsaw puzzle were now flying into place right in front of his eyes, conjuring up a picture, one he did not want to believe, but the knew when faced with it, it would be true. Slowly Stan took the last of his ale, and for the first time that night he felt in perfect control placing his arm on the table, his bright blue eyes sparking with fury as he spoke slowly, his fists now clenched as he growled his next words. "Aye Ben, she is mi wife, an' no man should ever 'ave come between us, bu' we know who 'as done dunna we Ben?" Stan waited with baited breath, oh yes, by the look on Ben's face he was definitely on the right track. "Yo' see Ben before I lef', I made 'er tell me who the father wa' because if she didna I'd 'ave teken the skin off 'er back, an' nod a soul would 'ave blamed me if I di'."

"Dunna yo' touch 'er Stan." Ben's voice slightly rose, his fists clenched tightly, he didn't like where this was going, his fear for Briar safety growing by the minute.

Stan smirked, and sat straight, the control now fully his. "I wunna touch a hair on 'er head Ben. For the truth is I love 'er too, an' still do fool tha' I am. Bu' as fur the child Ben, yore child, it'll find in me the hardes' Da' it could ever find. I'll be worse than the workhouse master ever wa' wi' us. I wunna spare the brat the rod, an' by the time it ge's on it's feet, it'll be down the mines wi' the other snivelling brats." Stan didn't have to wait for a moment longer for his answer for the table was upturned as Ben's fists met Stan's face in a fury he had never known Ben could possess. Sheer chaos echoed swiftly through the Inn as men stepped in grabbing the brothers back from destroying anything else in reach. Tankards of ale was tipped and the air turned black with colourful language as each brother attempted to half kill the other. As they were both turned out into the street to sort it out Ben fought as hard as he could, his heart set on keeping the girl safe, a girl he had loved since the day she had glared at him with those slate grey eyes of hers. But Ben had never fought anybody before, and though his limp was not so evident with his wooden clog, his leg was still crippled never the less, and when he stumbled badly Stan lost no time into laying into the brother he had once thought so highly off, his own hurt and frustrations released into a terrible fury. By the time the other men who had stood by decided it was time to step in once more, Ben lay motionless on the street, his nose broken, blood coming from his mouth, the last blow fierce against his temple rendering him helpless. Stan stood over his brother's crumpled form, his knuckles split open from the punches he had delivered, but fighting Ben had not left him feeling any better than he had before. Turning to a local man who he knew to have a cart he simply said. "I'll pay yo' mate, bu' do me a favour an' tek this piece o' filth tha's teken mi family life away, an' dump 'im back in Shrewsbury Town."

"Aye lad, wi' pleasure, an' pu' yore money back, this ones on me."

Stan stood back and watched as the three men eventually bundled Ben roughly into the back of the cart. It was clear what the men thought as well, for as the argument between the brothers had spilt over, disgust had passed around the Inn fast, for to lay with another man's wife was bad enough, but ten times worse when that man was your own brother. As Stan watched the cart go he wiped the blood from his hands over his trousers and took a deep breath. He no longer felt the hurt and distress he had felt earlier, what he felt now was an indescribable sickness. To think he had kept his distance from Briar with the hope that against all odds she would eventually forgive him for the night he had given her their child. If she had just looked at him differently without the glare that always echoed disgust if he stepped too closely. He had lived in hope, for he had held her so very dear, and he had honestly loved her, but now? He did not know, but one thing he did know was that by morning she'd regret what she had done. He would never forgive her this. To have been with another man was enough for most husbands to half beat her to death, but to have gone with his own brother, well she had eventually shown her true colours in his eyes. He had married a girl who had once belonged to the field gang masters, the type most knew to be sluts. Well now he had no room left in his life for her, and another thing he was more than sure off. She would not have Danny; the boy would stay with him. His son would not have a slut for a mother, one who was obviously unfit to raise him.

chapter fifteen

"Yo' can tek yore clothes lass, bu' nowt else is goin' owt this 'ouse. Now move it, I go' work t' come back too an' yo've wasted enough o' mi time."

"No, nod wi'owt mi son, wheer's mi son? I wan' mi child." Briar screamed out in distress, her whole being trembling with fear and complete exhaustion. Her eyes were swollen from the tears she had shed throughout the night, until she could hardly see straight. "Please...Stan... gi' me mi child."

"Ge' in the cart lass, yo' inna a fi' mother, yore nowt bu' a slut, a common little slut an' yore goin' nowheer near the child. He's mi son Briar, an' tha's the way it is, he dunna need yo', now ge' in the cart." Stan stood firm, his body rigid, his own heart pounding until he thought his chest would explode. To have thought that this time only yesterday he could not have imagined his life without her, but that now the very presence of her disgusted him. He had spent months regretting his attack on her; he had sobbed tears of remorse in the dark of night that he had raped her. But now, after last night, and what he had found out...well...what had occurred when he had got back, he felt no guilt whatsoever.

"Please Stan...he's jus' a babby, please gi' me mi son, he needs me... please."

Briar could take no more, for she had no fight left within her. As she stepped towards Stan she swayed, her legs would not hold her much longer, she ached so badly, the pain in her back had been crippling and she could feel the loss within her beginning to release from her soul, for the warm trickle of blood she felt drip between her legs terrified her. "Please Stan…mi son."

Stan glared hard at the girl in front of him, his wife, but a girl he no longer recognised as anything. "God looken at the state o' yo'. Wha' decen' man would wan' yo' now?" Sneering Stan took a breather, looked her up and down and then snarled. "Ge' in the cart, I canna keep it fur long, we've all go' work 'ere. I'm tekin' yo' t' Ben, he can 'ave yo' he's welcome t' yo'."

"Nod wi'owt mi son." Briar gasped, but she was losing the battle fast. The pain deep within her stomach was warning her, and as she wrapped her arms around her stomach leaning forward to try and stop it she cried out with the searing pain that took full grip. Stan faltered slightly, he knew she was in pain, and he knew why. He had to get her to Ben he would no longer take responsibility for her; they had brought all of this on themselves. When he saw her break out into a cold sweat, her face so pale and gaunt he didn't waste another moment. Stepping forward Stan picked her up, holding her close to him, almost lovingly, and then he walked outside the cottage and laid her down in the cart alongside her one bag of clothes, all he would allow her to take. Stan swiftly stepped up onto the front of the cart and took hold of the reins, the sooner he did this the better for him, for he needed to get back and pick up his son from the main coach house, he needed to start rebuilding his own life. Briar pleaded for her son and sobbed inconsolably, her tears pitiful and heartfelt, but by the time Stan had left Bayston Hill behind them and had turned down towards the tiny village of Meole, and onwards for Shrewsbury Town, Briar's sobs had turned into pathetic whimpers and moans. Briar shook uncontrollably, every bump from the cart left her in even more pain, her whole body lay twisted in agony as she struggled to breath more easily, she could feel the loss of more blood as she fought to win at least one battle. It was hardly seven in the morning when the cart Stan borrowed stopped by the market square of Shrewsbury. Casually Stan got down and tethered the horse, he was glad there was no market today for the Square was very quiet only the April sun threatened to shine upon them, letting them know she could see. Stan slung Briar's bag over his shoulder then as gently as he could took her in his arms, and carried her across the market square. So this is where she had come too regularly with their son. Hardly out of sight. When Stan saw the sign 'Ben Lawson Toy and Cabinet Maker' he felt his stomach churning, his heart pounding deeply with so much hate and bitterness. But after today he would not have to set sight on his brother or his wife again. Briar whimpered in her husband's arms, broken sobs escaping her dry lips every so often. She no longer had the strength to hold herself up, she could scarcely speak. But she was aware of where she was being taken, and she was very aware that her small son had been left behind.

"Ben...Ben...yo' better face me one las' time. I 'ave somethin' fur yo' 'ere...yore little slut." Stan's voice bellowed from the street below before he kicked the door with one almighty belt, the door opening as he did so. As he crossed the shop floor Stan shook with anger, but he carefully lay his wife on the floor by his feet. Briar made no attempt to get up, she could not, the pain that ripped through her had finally rendered her helpless, and when she peered downwards, she could see the bright crimson shade of blood seeping through her clothes. When Ben made his way downs the stairs and the brothers met face to face across the shop floor, each one held his own bitter hatred against the other that would never be resolved. A hatred that would eventually lead to the untimely death of one of them.

"Wha' the hell 'ave yo' done t' her?" Ben hobbled to where Briar laid, his nose swollen and distorted, his one eye almost closed from the beating he had suffered the night before. Throwing his old walking stick to one side Ben crouched on the floor over the girl he had always loved and then panic gripped him. He could see the pain she was in, her face damp from cold sweat. "Wha' 'ave yo' done?"

His voice raised but Stan simply turned and walked back towards the door. As he neared the door, he turned just once more and stared at his only brother and the crumpled figure of his wife. The beating he had given his brother had been well needed, he deserved everything he got, and Stan had noticed he had needed his stick again. As for his wife, when Stan looked down at her broken form, he did feel one regret. He wished he'd never met her, but his brother should never have gone near her to begin with.

"Yo' bes' go an' ge' her a doctor, she needs one." As Stan turned and touched the door handle he heard the soft voice of his wife plead one last time. "Mi son...please...mi son."

Stan turned, his bright blue eyes locking hard with her slate grey ones. "Yo' 'ave no son."

With that Stan turned and left, slamming the door behind him. There were no winners of the battle that day. Stan felt no jubilation as he left his wife behind. Arranging care for his son while he worked and raising him alone could and would cause him problems he knew that, but even still he would never allow his wife near the child again. She had chosen to live a life away from him; well she would have to learn to live it. But there was one thing left he would do for her, for deep down Stan was not the beast his wife thought him to be. He had been severally pushed to have done what he had the night before. He had only meant to give her a few sharp slaps to make her aware he would not stand for anymore of her attitude towards him. He had not really known that he was going to kick her out of his life then, not really. But Stan had been frightfully drunk, and his own emotions had been badly damaged. He should have known that Briar would fight him back whatever her condition, and she had, punching out, biting and kicking him until she had spat at him, her venom slicing into his face, her own hate scarring him for life. Stan had found in him a fury that had forced him to make the decision to rid himself of her, for he had felt he could have quite easily killed her. Before Stan headed home he made a call on a local doctor he knew to be in Alkmond Square. What the doctor found was a girl covered in fresh bruises under her clothes from the beating she had received from her estranged husband. It took almost two hours before he could stop her from bleeding, and he explained as kindly as he could to Ben that if she had any hope of carrying the child she would have to stay in bed for some weeks. Her inside injuries had not helped her, for she had also been so brutally raped that the doctor had even suggested that her attacker had tried his very best to guarantee her the loss of the child, and it would take a miracle for her to keep it.

chapter sixteen

"Here yo' go lass, now it dunna looken much bu' theer's a slice o' the bes' ham wi' tha' bread, an' the breads warm. Better than tha', theer's a mug o' warm goats milk, canna be bad eh?"

Briar offered a weak smile, her slate grey eyes never far from fresh tears, vacant to the wild spirit they had once held so fiercely. Carefully Ben lay the tray down on a small table next to the bed, and without a word puffed up the pillows behind her, before offering his hand for support. Briar pulled herself upright, then stared at the tin plate with the warm bread and ham, the same nauseous feeling creeping into the pits of her stomach.

"Come on lass, I know it's the las' thin' yo' wan', bu' yo' 'ave t' eat." Gently Ben coaxed her on, placing the tray safely on her lap. "Yo' need yore strength lass or yo' wunna be no good fur anybody, our child, or Danny." Ben watched sadly as Briar simply bowed her head, so very silent, she was just a mere shadow of the girl he'd grown to love. But who could blame her? She'd been through hell. Ben cringed, just to think of the condition she'd been left in almost four weeks ago, it was still so hard to believe whatever his brother's feelings were at the time that he could have been so cruelly brutal, and then to rob her of her infant son. Ben took a deep breath as he kissed the top of her head. "Come on lass, try...please." For what seemed an age Briar remained perfectly still and silent, then still without a word she picked up the slice of warm bread and slowly began to eat what Ben had so kindly given her. "Tha's the way lass, now I'll fetch some water up fur me t' mek mysel' a mushed tea. Then if theer's nowt else yo' wan' I'll ge' on wi' a cabinet I'm mekin'. Bu' remember lass yo' wan' me fur anythin' all yo' 'ave t' do is call."

"Aye."

"Then I'll go an' ge' tha' water." Ben turned for the door, at least she was willing to try, and it was more than she'd been prepared to do a week ago. That had proved a nightmare in itself for Ben had been at his wits end, and had even thought of having to force feed her, and he had no desires to force any issues upon her, none at all.

"Ben."

"Aye lass."

"Will...will I ge' mi son back...ever?"

Ben stopped his warm brown eyes full of compassion and slowly he hobbled back towards the bed. "Now listen t' me lass, an' listen hard." Sitting down on the edge of the bed he gently held her by the shoulders as he spoke softly. "The lad should be 'ere now, bu' 'e inna. One thin' is certain, an' tha' is Danny will be 'ere wi' his mam wheer 'e should be." Ben smiled trying to offer her the confidence she needed. "I wan' yo' t' ge' well lass, an yore fee' on the floor righ' owt o' danger. When the time is righ' an' yo' know when tha' will be, I've already said, I'll go an' ge' yore son mysel', an' ge' 'im I will."

Briar desperately tried to smile back, she so needed to believe it would be that easy, but the emptiness she felt inside for not having her child with her now was far worse than any attack any man had ever bestowed upon her. When her heartrending sobs began once more Ben moved the tray and pulled Briar safely into his arms gently stroking her silvery blond hair speaking words of comfort as he had done so many times over the last month. When her tears of sorrow subsided and she had worn herself out once more, the need for sleep still strong to want take her, Ben's gentle voice still whispered gently.

"It's bes' owt than in lass, now yo' res', I'll mek tha' brew, an' I thinken fur both o' us now, 'ere le' me puff those pillows again."

"I'm sorry Ben...so very sorry."

"Wha'ever fur lass?" Ben puzzled by her words sat back down tilting her bowed face upwards to look at him. "Sorry fur wha'?"

"Yore leg Ben...yore usin' tha' stick again an' limpin', it were mi fault, I know it."

"Tha' inna true, an' it's nowt t' worry abou'. When I fell tha' nigh' I twisted mi leg an' pu' a fracture on mi wooden clog. Yo' know me lass, I liken mi work perfect, an' I 'anna 'ad the time t' mek mysel' a new one, so stick it is...satisfied?" Ben grinned mischievously, and just for a fleeting moment thought he saw a glint of life in her slate grey eyes. A sparkle that in times gone by would have promised a mouthful of cheek, and a pouting lip. But now her lip merely quivered and then the tears began all over again.

"Well its mi fault yo' 'anna 'ad time to do it." Snivelling Briar wiped her tears on her sleeve only for fresh ones to emerge even more quickly.

"Eh lass, wha' will be yore fault is me drownin' in yore tears. Now I've ne'er shed a tear over mi leg, an' I dunna expec' yo' too, so come on now enough o' this. Dry yore eyes, ge' tha' ham down yo' an' pick up tha' warm milk. God almighty lass, now I need a brew." Briar stared in complete silence as Ben stood next to her and tutted loudly, winking as he did so. It was enough to force a single ray of sunshine into the thunder cloud that had hung so heavy over her. Briar spluttered as she tried to take a mouthful of warm goat's milk, spilling its contents over the sheet as a giggle escaped her lips.

"Well tha's gratitude I mus' say, firs' yo' drown me, now yo' throw mi own milk back at me. Eeh lass, I'll 'ave yo' downstairs scrubbin' over a dolly tub if yo' keep this up." Mockingly Ben put on the firmest voice he could possibly muster, and then had to quickly calm down the situation when Briar spilt the whole contents of her mug over the bed in her fits of sudden laughter. A good hour later Briar sat in a freshly made bed, against the far wall, her hands clasped tightly together as she watched Ben's every move. It was a large room above the shop and workshop, a room that was comfortable even though it still held the bare necessities. There was Ben's bed where she now slept, and a small table that Ben had made and put next to it as well as a small chest of drawers. In the centre of the room stood a table and two chairs that Ben had also made, an easy chair sat between the two windows that overlooked the Square below. By the far window lay a small hearth and a burner, with a large sink next to it. That was it, any water that needed boiling took a while, and the nearest pump was in Milk Street just before you reached the nun refuge. A refuge for fallen women to hide, or for those who were taken there for punishment for having dared to sin. Ben's living dwellings were simple, but even under the sad circumstances Briar preferred this naked room to the cottage she had shared with her husband. "Righ' then lass, I'll leave yo' a while, theer's enough logs t' keep yo' warm, bu' if yo' wan' me, yo' bang the floor wi' the stick I lef' yo'…understand?" Ben frowned, it was clear to see Briar was drifting back into her fretful world, pining for her child, her face so gaunt and weary. "Sleep fur a while lass…I'll check on yo' soon."

Sighing heavily Briar forced a smile, for she knew Ben was doing the best he could, and she was a burden to him, being bedridden like this. "Aye Ben I will, an' I am sorry abou' yore leg."

"Ssh, I dunna wan' t' hear tha' again." A slight edge crept into Ben's voice, but he was quick to smile, when he was met with a look so very forlorn, he winked. "And I mean wha' I said lass, I'll ge' yore son back, bu' fur now yo' 'ave go' t' ge' well." With that Ben turned and left, he really needed to get on with his work, he had an order to finish within a week, and he wanted Briar to rest. Lost in thought, his mind in a dozen places Ben set to work in his workshop, his fingers gently checking the cabinet over for any signs of roughness. "Good, perfect." Casting his eyes carefully over his work, he checked for any small imperfection that would damage his good craft name, but nothing. The cabinet was ready for the next stage, he could now plan his own unique mould to guarantee this cabinet to be one of its kind. Whistling loudly as he went Ben carefully chose the veneer he would need. If he started now he would have the edging moulded and finished by nightfall and he would be pleased with his days work. Glancing upwards at he ceiling, Ben sighed, for Briar was up there just above him, her presence so very close. He'd have to stop work before nightfall to make sure she was fine, he already had a broth gently on the boil so hopefully she would accept it and try to eat a little more without spilling everything. "Briar Rose, God lass." Just the thought of her brought a mutter to his lips. How hard the last few weeks had been, so very tiring and sad, and so worrying, for Ben had not been hopeful for his own child. But the doctor had told him that as long as she stayed in bed for a while longer, and continued after that to take it easy with no excitement, there was a good chance that the child she was carrying would be fine, and had gone on to declare that that was a small miracle in itself. Ben had proved to be as good as his word, for he had refused any help, and had tackled the problem himself. Briar was all he'd ever wanted, and his determination to keep her safe would win the day in the end. He had managed to keep his orders on track, as well as playing nurse maid. He had cooked for her, talked with her, and had mostly been there just to hold her, offering words of comfort the whole time, words that were so true. He would get her son back, one way or another, for what his brother had done to the girl under his roof sickened him every time he thought about it. Her bruises had been dark and heavy, as for the other...it was a miracle that she had not lost her baby as well. But as Ben had firmly, yet as kindly as he could have done told Briar, he would get her son back once their own baby had been born. That way Briar would be at her fittest to cope with whatever would occur, and their baby would be safe in a crib that Ben would make for it. His words had caused a torrent of tears that had made Ben choke up, but he had to think of Briar and with that he had refused to do anything yet, going on to tell Briar that when she did get on her feet properly, she would not be permitted to leave the shop unless he assisted her, and it would not be to Bayston Hill. It was very hard for her, Ben knew that, for Danny was hardly a year old, and their child wouldn't be born until October. She would have to wait, and be patient, and if he had to mop up an ocean of tears in-between time. Then so be it.

chapter seventeen

May and June moulded gently into each other, the promise of summer clear in the air as the bright elegant rays shone down onto the roof of Ben Lawson's shop, sparkling upon it a fresh gift of life that brought the busy market shoppers old and new into the shop to admire the work of a very young man. "Lightly lass...very lightly, keep tha' hand steady, le' yore fingers feel the shape an' go wi' it, nod agains' it...aye tha's better." Ben grinned as Briar Rose sat rigidly on a high backed chair, a small trinket box lid in her hands. "When yo' thinken yo've finished lass, run yore fingers smoothly over it, as soft as yo' can, then a bi' more firmly. Any splinter..."

"I'll ge' no supper, I know." Mischievously Briar smiled a glint of life lighting up her slate grey eyes, that hardly sparked with anything these days.

"Well, I'll stop it if yo' wan' me too." Ben chuckled, as he checked over his latest dolls house.

"I wunna work fur yo' if yo' do." Proudly Briar looked over the small lid, wincing as a splinter embedded itself the moment she ran her finger over it.

"Sand it over again lass, smoothly, an' go wi' the mould, yo' handle tha' roughly it will ruin, an' then I'll stop yore milk allowance."

Briar gasped then squealed with laughter. Often just lately when she helped Ben in the workshop, they fell into a joke over the workhouse rules they had once been so used too at Crosshouses. But it felt good to laugh, even if at times Briar felt guilty for feeling more like her old self in Ben's company. The last three months had been anything but easy. Briar had felt she had cried her entire past away, her hurt, her abuse, and the loss of her son. When the day came that she should have celebrated her sons first birthday, she felt she was mourning his death, for her heart had been so heavy that every time she saw a small child with it's mother gaze through the shop window hopeful for a wooden dolly or brightly coloured duck, Briar had fled upstairs and had thrown herself on Ben's bed sobbing pitifully until she could cry no more. How dry her throat had felt, how red and swollen her eyes had become. All she wanted was to see her son. Did he ever say Mam? Had he taken his first steps yet? Did he cry at nights cutting his teeth? All these things she should know. Would her son soon forget who she was? The very thought of that had ripped her heart to shreds and just when she thought there was no tears left, she sobbed even harder. Ben had given her all the support he could; he was always ready with a clean hanky and a shoulder. However busy he was, he found time to talk to her, to hold her safe and gently tell her he would get her son back. She just had to hold on. There was nothing that Ben would not do for her, he praised her efforts when she made new curtains for the top windows, and laughed when frilled pillowcases suddenly appeared. His living space over the shop had begun to look more homely, it certainly felt more homely. Briar had taken over the cooking and cleaning and had even begun to sweep up in the workshop at the end of each day. All Ben asked of her was two very simple things. One, she did not leave the premises unless he escorted her, and two, that she took a rest each afternoon. Briar had reluctantly agreed, for in her fifth month of pregnancy she felt as fit as she had done with Danny, but Ben was taking no chances.

"Fur once in yore life yo' can do as yore told Mrs Lawson an' dunna yo' pout at me."

Briar had pulled her face, and Ben had seen that spark of sudden defiance in those slate grey eyes of hers, which misted over at the sound of being called 'Mrs Lawson'. Again Briar had found great comfort as Ben had quickly gone on to say. "Yore t' keep bein' known as Mrs Lawson lass, it's bes' tha' way. People who dunna know will assume yore mi wife...an' 'as we both know yo' should 'ave been." When Ben winked, his warm brown eyes holding fast onto hers, Briar had warmly smiled.

"Aye...bu' only if yo' say Mrs Ben Lawson...I inna 'avin' it any other way." And so it was settled, Ben often called her just that, and Briar abided by his simple wishes.

Under the watchful eye of Ben, Briar grew emotionally stronger every day. Her hair shone, and she smiled much more often, her outlook on the future became far more positive. Ben felt the comforts of a woman in his life, one he had loved for so long. Never did he tire of her, and the aroma of fresh vegetable broth and warm bread often enticed him up the stairs long before he needed too. Ben shared details of his new ideas with her, and his pride was evident when she managed to finish her first trinket box that he had checked thoroughly for any faults before placing it in the front window for sale. "Aye lass, I knew I could teach yo' craft given the chance."

"So, am I finally industrious then?"

"Aye lass, I guess yo' are, as fur decorum an' virtue, well tha's another thin'."

Briar had burst into giggles as Ben had walked over enfolding his arms around her.

"An' I'll tell yo' this lass. When our babbys born it will too be taugh' industry. One day I'll 'ave a notice above the shop door, 'Lawson and Son.'"

"And if it's a girl?" Briar had pulled back slightly, her voice held a certain tone of annoyance.

"Especially if it's a lass, mi daughter will 'ave a place in life. I'll teach 'er t' craft as good as 'er Da'." Ben had gently cupped Briar's chin in the palm of his hand as he tilted her face towards him. "I'll teach mi trade t' any children we 'ave, boy or girl, fur one day I'll mek a business t' pass down, an' I'll teach Danny too."

"Yo' will?" Briar had smiled hopefully.

"Oh aye lass, when I ge' yore lad back, I'll star' him t' work as young as 'e is. I'll be fair Briar, a good teacher, an' a Da', bu' I'll teach a high standard, an' I'll expec' it."

For the first time since she had known him Briar gulped as she stepped back again taking a real hard look at Ben. Was she just seeing him for what he had become? Ben stood so proudly, so very sure of himself, speaking of his future and hers so very confidently. He no longer looked up to the brother he once had, or anybody come to that. He kept shop, his accounts, and saved every penny he could declaring that when the lease was up and he had served his time with Jonathan Hampstead, he would buy his own place. When Ben had smiled, his warm brown eyes locking tightly to hers his shoulders held back, his light red hair combed well back Briar returned his smile. Ben stood a few inches taller than her, and very firmly, for now he had made himself another clog for his boot, his limp once more not so evident. Yes, Briar had seen him in a new light. Ben Lawson was an established toy and cabinet maker, he was a man in his own rights who could take charge of his own life and future and gently guide and take charge of those he loved. In that very instance, Briar knew she had found her own life. The home and love she had always yearned for. No harm would ever come her way with Ben, for his love was a deep caring love, one that would protect her and their children. Briar also knew that he would indeed somehow get her son back. From that very day, things became much smoother. There were no more tears of despair. Ben concentrated on his business, his orders, and he showered Briar with as much love as she could take. Briar concentrated on one thing, her unborn child. She delighted Ben by keeping the place spotless, and amused him no end with her renewed interest to learn his trade. Briar gave no problems or cause for any concern. Each afternoon she rested as he had requested and she had no wish to leave the premises without him.

chapter eighteen

"Eeh lad, nobody's tryin' t' tek yore lad, bu' thinken on." Emily Bunting sighed deeply as she took the small boy from his father. "The Master said we can all 'elp as long as it dunna affect the work."

"Yo' said Danny were fine, an' the lasses didna mind helpin'."

"Aye, they dunna, an' the lad is a good little mite, bu' it inna a place fur a nipper sittin' in the parlour hangin' around the girls frocks. Eeh they're slow enough wi' their chores at the bes' o' times." Emily waved her arm as if in sudden frustration, but her tone softened as she saw a look of helplessness cloud Stan Lawson's face. "Wha'ever 'as gone on wi' yo' an' Briar Rose shouldna be allowed t' ruin good common sense. The lad needs 'is mam, an' I wouldna mind bu' say I be' Briar needs him."

"So will yo' manage a while longer? Until I ge' somethin' arranged." Stan spoke sharply, he was not going to discuss his affairs with anybody, even if they were all bending over backwards to help him.

"Aye, I will, now go on, or else we'll all ge' the sack." Emily waved her hand in dismissal, then tutted loudly as she hurried towards the child who had already toddled over to a large pail of water.

Stan turned on his heels and left not speaking another word or acknowledging his son. He had other things on his mind besides his ground duties and the lads in his service. Stan's mind was terribly troubled, and in total turmoil, his soul heavy with guilt chewing away at his conscience. Every night he took his son home, the child still cried regularly for want of his mother, and nothing Stan could do ever seemed to console him.

But there was more, his own tears were never far away when the cottage door closed behind him. In the first couple of weeks he had fiercely destroyed anything that reminded him of Briar Rose, any stray ribbon or handkerchief, her shawl he burnt. When he discovered the wooden toys that Ben his brother had obviously bestowed upon his son Danny on their 'visits' to Shrewsbury, Stan had been so incensed he had hurled them straight through the window. Last to follow had been the wooden trinket box and small pendant that Ben had given to Briar on his wedding day. God, what a fool he had been not to have seen the obsession between his wife and brother. But his anger had been spent, he had bullied his garden hands, and had even struck one of them, and now he had calmed down, enough to know that what he had done to his wife the night her pregnancy was revealed was an act that sickened him to the core and would leave him forever regretful. He had been so angry, and terribly drunk, his common sense had left him that night, good and proper. But now, as he approached his cottage very night, the emptiness was the harshest punishment he could have ever encountered. His home had become an empty sad place that lacked any warmth. There was never the tempting aroma of rabbit stew, or warm bread to greet him. There was never any boiling water for his bath or the sweet scent of field flowers decorating his table. Housework was just a fragment hidden in the imagination, and even though Briar had treated him with contempt at the best of times, he'd get down on his knees if he could just have his pouting wife back with her high spirited temper accusing him once more. But what could he do? Demand her to return home? No, Briar would never accept that, and what could he offer her? A lifetime of apologies could never undo the damage he had caused her that night, the unforgivable things he had said to her. He had thrown her out, left her on his brother's floor in great pain and bleeding badly. Had she managed to keep the child she was carrying? He sincerely hoped with every beat of his heart that she had kept the child, and that somehow, she was managing to live, and to smile, not just to hold a great fear in her heart, a fear he had helped to put there the night he had tried... oh yes, he had, he had tried so desperately to make her miscarry, just to hurt her and his brother the way that they had hurt him. Maybe Emily Bunting was right. Where Danny was concerned Stan held the trump card in his hands. Briar had been a good wife to him in many ways, and a very loving mother to their son. Just maybe, if Stan took the child to see her from time to time, she may just see there could be a life with him yet. He would take the child on she was carrying, and he would promise her he would be a good father to it, if it meant her returning home. Stan nodded to himself; yes he could do that if he tried hard enough, for she had far more to forgive him for at the end of the day. Stan took a deep breath, yes she had, he had forgiven her, but would she ever be able to put their past behind her and start again, as man and wife really should? As far as Ben, his brother was concerned, he understood perfectly why he loved Briar also, for nobody could love her as fiercely as he himself did, a love that he could so tenderly have shown her if she had just allowed it. A love that brought out a highly protective streak in him, one so strong and possessive it could burn with rage and destroy anybody that endangered his life with her, including her, herself! But if she came back to him, and he could just shut them away in the cottage for long enough without the outside world interfering, he was sure he would make her see just how much he loved her, and that he could offer her a good life. But where Ben was concerned in all of this, well, he could go to hell.

chapter nineteen

"I inna tekin' no fur an answer lass, now it's a choice fur yo' t' mek." Ben grinned, his eyes alight with mischief as Briar sat steady, her arms folded on her evergrowing stomach, a pout covering her rosebud lips. "Well, wha's it t' be lass? Yo' can either go an' rest as yo' know yo' should, or yo' can si' theer an' pout at me all day, bu' yo' inna workin' in this heat." Running his finger carefully over his latest creation, he smiled. "Perfect, fi' fur a Prince or a Princess."

Briar watched intently as Ben proudly admired his own work, her pout turning to a smile of satisfaction for him. He had amazed her yet again; she had watched him in the candlelight put his ideas onto paper, puzzling it all out until he eventually chose the right wood to bring his ideas to life. And now, he had done it again, only this time with a baby's crib, one that would indeed be fit for royalty. Every rung was finely engraved, the ends of the crib had small teddy bears carved deep into the oak, and when gently pushed the crib began to rock. "It's wonderful Ben, I'll be sad t' see it go, even though I know this will fetch yo' a pretty penny or two." The soft whisper behind him gave Ben cause to look up, and for a long moment he was lost for any words, as he saw her slate grey eyes mist over with tears. He'd spent painstaking hours making the crib between his orders, and even though he had firmly told Briar at times to get some sleep, he had turned to find her standing silently in the shadows watching over him as he had worked way into the night, her appreciation of his work always clear on her face, as her tears of pride were now. "Well then lass, tha's the other choice fur yo' t' mek. Theer is no gentry comin' fur this crib, an' it' ne'er wa' an order."

His own voice now so very soft as he spoke. "Yo' can go an' res' or yo' can go owt theer in the Square an' buy wha'ever it is yo' need t' mek the bes' beddin' yo' can. The cribs fur yo' Briar, fur our own child."

Briar gasped, she was speechless, it had never entered her mind, and then the tears did begin to fall, but out of sheer excitement at having the crib she had watched been made. With a squeal of delight she was across the shop floor almost taking Ben off balance as she threw herself into the arms that were always ready to hold her. "Steady on lass, or yo'll 'ave me on the floor, an' then I'll need mi stick t' ge' back up wi'."

"It's wonderful Ben, I ne'er though' fur a minute it were fur me, bu' I hoped I really di'. Eeh its fit fur royalty, mi babby's crib!" Taking a sharp breath Briar suddenly peered around her quickly, worry clouding her pretty face. "Ben it's time t' open the shop, tek it upstairs before somebody comes in t' buy it...nobody's 'avin' it Ben, hide it, an' I'll go an' buy a length o' fine cotton, aye I will."

Ben roared with laughter as Briar frantically pushed the crib towards him spluttering over his words as he spoke. "I'll tek it upstairs lass when yo' calm down. Tek yoresel' owt int' the marke' an' quietly, or if I 'ave t' brin' the doctor back yo'll spend the res' o' yore time upstairs. Now go, theer's money in the tin nex' t' the larder." Not another word was said, the smile that greeted him was worth more than any words, and the sparkle that shone from her slate grey eyes spoke for her. Ben watched as Briar made her way across the shop floor towards the workshop that would lead her upstairs. It was the first time he had witnessed the girl he once knew, the pouting, highly spirited girl he knew she could still be. More than that, for those few moments she was truly relaxed and genuinely happy as if she didn't have a care in the world. Ben took a deep breath; there was one thing that would make this all so perfect, something that had been playing on his mind for a while now. He had promised to get her son soon after the birth of their own child. It was a promise he intended to keep, yet how he would keep it, he had no idea.

"Thankyo' Ben, oh thankyo'…I wunna be long." Briar's cheerful entrance broke his stream of thought.

"Yo' tek yore time lass, I've customers t' see an' work t' do. Yo' enjoy yoresel', bu' be careful, an' dunna stray from the Square."

"Aye Ben." Briar feebly smiled back now, for it was the first time she had left the shop by herself, for Ben had done his work around her when things were needed and had always been by her side on these occasions. "Would yo' liken me t' brin' back some bacon Ben?"

"No lass, jus' keep t' The Square eh?" Any doubts about her leaving the shop at all vanished when Briar hugged him fiercely, and once more Ben was fast to hold her safely against him. "Go now, yore enough t' pu' a man off 'is work."

Waving as she left the shop Briar stepped straight into the heart of the Market Square. The bustle had begun, tables were already set up, horses had been safely tethered down Milk Street, just beyond The Square, and already housewives with their many off spring dragging behind them, were loudly bartering for the cheapest bag of flour. "Well 'ere we go then." Thinking aloud Briar made her way to the first table not far from the shop. Today she wanted as cheap as she could get, but the finest quality.

"It's fur the bes' lad. A babby needs 'is mam, an' yo' need t' keep yore job, or wha' will become o' the laddie then eh?" Emily Bunting nodded knowing, her arms folded tightly in front of her. "Well go on then, the cart wunna wai' furever, an' watch tha' laddie's head dunna burn."

"Aye Mrs Buntin', an' I'll thankyo' fur yore kindness."

Tutting loudly Emily waved her hand dismissively and returned to her parlour to check on her young maids. "Eeh tha' lad is jus' a bi' above himsel', a good kick up the pants is wha' he needs."

Stan had knowingly used the sarcastic tone, and without a hint of a smile on his face he had taken his son and had clambered onto the cart. "Bloody Shrewsbury Square, she shouldna be theer at all."

Over and over the same thoughts carried on plaguing Stan's troubled mind, but he knew full well it was by his own doing and cruel hands that Briar was not with him. Since she had gone he'd fought within himself to control his resentment, his bitterness and fearful hate. Then he had realised he had but one chance left, to try and win her back by using their son as bait. But it still didn't stop the sudden burst of anger he felt now. He would have to work very hard at it, hard to keep her at all that's if he got her back, when his own brother Ben had done nothing at all. Why then had his wife's affections then gone so freely to Ben and not him? He had not been a husband to fear every night he walked through the door, he never raged about his meal or raised his hand at her rudeness towards him. He's never kept her short of money, and he had never enquired what she had spent it on. But no, even Stan shook his head, for he had come to terms with his biggest downfall of all. Drink. Why? He did not know, only that when he had been drinking heavily he lost all reason, sense would drain from him and leave behind a frightening bitter, violent young man, a man he did not wish to be. But now, he would take advantage of that also. He would speak with Briar, and tell her he would never drink again if only she would return home. He would admit how wrong he had been, how unforgivable his behaviour had been and he would beg her forgiveness. Once she had heard all of that he would plead with her better side that her son still cried for her, and badly needed his mother's love. Once she had listened to him and had seen her son, the little boy she loved so much, then surely it would erase any doubt in her mind concerning him. Hopefully he would not have to work too hard in gaining his wife's return. If things went accordingly he would be bringing her back to Bayston Hill by nightfall.

"Yo've had a righ' bargain theer lass an' no denyin' it, bu' wha' abou' a little somethin' fur yoresel'? No, dunna turn yore back on ole Ma Smith, tek a look at this lass, now it's as fine a cotton as ever I saw, an' it's as blue as the bonniest bluebells in Spring."

Briar smiled, a spark of mischief lighting up her slate grey eyes, it was a beautiful shade, and would make a fine frock for next Spring. "Go on lass, mek yo' a fine frock fur when yo've dropped yore load. Who knows, yore ole man migh' well like it, by this time next year yo'll 'ave a belly load again."

Briar spluttered, and then had to suppress her own unladylike giggles that threatened to surface.

"Aye, ol Ma Smiths righ' inna she lass? So wha' do yo' say then?" The older woman waited in anticipation, she was doing real well with this young girl opposite her, and for once she hadn't been allowed to take her youth for granted. The silvery blond haired girl with the most striking of slate grey eyes had given a fair argument of words, and Ma Smith had cut a fair bargain. "I'll tell yo' wha' lass, two lengths o' this will mek yo' a fine frock. I'll pu' in a length of lace an' ribbon an' some hook and eyes, all o' tha' fur three farthins."

"I'll tek them buttons instead, a dozen o' them pearl shaped ones, an' yo' can keep the hook an' eyes."

"Yo' cheeky young bugger." A wide toothless grin covered the woman's plump red face. "Tekin' advantage o' mi good nature." The woman folded her arms and nodded, proud of her use of the word 'advantage'. "Bu' I liken a lass who knows wha' she wan's, so I'll pu' in them buttons an' when yo' wan' another frock, yo' know wheer t' come... Ma Smith."

Delighted with what she knew to be a bargain Briar Rose accepted graciously, and watched eagerly as Ma Smith carefully wrapped the white cotton and frilled lace for her baby's crib, and then cut the length of blue that Briar would use wisely for herself, hoping there would also be enough left over to dress her newborn. "Thankyo'," handing over the money Briar took the package, "it's been a pleasure, an' I will come back."

"Mi wife made a good choice theer, she always di' looken good in blue." Stan had been watching in the background for a while now, and decided it was time to make himself known. Briar grasped the package in front of her as if it would protect her, and slowly she looked up to meet the bright blue eyes of her husband, Stan Lawson. She would have fled with no word, the fear so evident in her slate grey eyes, her stomach churning as she felt the life inside her kick out.

"Dear God yo' go' mi babby wi' yo'." With a gasp of hope before her, hope beyond all her dreams that Stan was about to return her son to her, Briar dropped her package, the anxiety draining from her as she held out her arms and took her beloved son, holding him so close to her as he wept uncontrollably, raining kisses upon his unsuspecting face. "Eeh Danny, yo've grown so much, yore nod a babby now, looken at yo'." Briar so overjoyed at seeing her son forgot her fear of Stan, to her there was nobody else in this world right now as she stood under the radiant rays of the July sun. She paid no attention to Stan or Ma Smith who looked on most confused by the pregnant youngster who was now close to sobs of joy as she held what was obviously her own son anyway. Stan watched intently, so far so good, her reaction towards Danny was just as he suspected it would be. She looked well, in fact very well, her cheeks held a glow of rosiness and her slate grey eyes sparked with life. Looking her up and down Stan took a deep breath as he felt his chest tighten, the back of his neck beginning to prickle. She was still pregnant then? The doctor he had called for, the day he had left had saved her child. Briefly Stan closed his eyes, taking a long deep breath. No, he was not to feel angry, the bitterness that had almost destroyed her must never surface again. If she went home with him, he would have to take on the child she was carrying as his own, even if it would be an everlasting reminder. "Briar, we need t' find somewheer t' talk, come on lass. Yo' can pu' Danny down, he's a good little walker."

Walker! Just one simple word stopped her tears of utmost joy, her endless soft words of affection that she had poured onto her son now silenced. As Briar looked up at her husband her mouth twisted into a frightful pout, her slate grey eyes turned cold with hatred. Fear was no longer evident as she stood there in the Market Square so very still. Resentment stabbed her heart; sorrow filled her soul at not having her child to even know what a 'good little walker' he was. Her son had grown so much she in fact hardly recognised him as the child she had been so cruelly parted from five months ago. She had fretted for him way into the night when even Ben did not know; she had cried needlessly on his first birthday and had mourned over not hearing his first words. All the times her small son must have needed her, they had both been denied because of her husband. And now, out of the blue, here her husband stood, wanting her to talk with him. Had he forgotten his violent treatment towards her? Or the fact he had nearly killed the tiny life she now carried? Conscious of her unborn child Briar gently put Danny down, but held his tiny hand tightly in her own, her other hand resting on her stomach as if to protect it. "I'm goin' nowheer wi' yo' Stan, theer's nowt t' say, an' I'm nod t' leave The Square."

Not to leave The Square? Stan raised his eyebrows, since when had she done as she had obviously been told? "I thinken we 'ave a lo' t' talk abou' Briar, come 'ere son."

Just a simple quiet command and before she could think, Danny had slipped his tiny hand from hers and was now safely in his father's arms. Stifled sobs passed her lips, her absence from her son's life had lost her his childlike trust, and now it was too hard to bear and her tears had already began to fall silently. "Yo' bastard, yo' heartless bastard."

"Now now lass, tha's no way t' talk t' yore husband is it? Seems t' me yo've lost the few manners yo' ever had." To escape from the many curious shoppers that were now glancing their way, the stall holders that were watching with interest, Stan quickly took Briar firmly by her upper arm leading her away from The Square and the safety of his brother. Briar gasped aloud, and fretfully peered over her shoulder, her eyes searching for a glimpse of Ben, but it was all she could do was to keep her footing. "I inna goin' t' hurt yo' lass, I jus' wan' t' talk."

Blindly Briar felt herself pulled through the busy streets of Shrewsbury Town, but nobody took any notice, it was market day after all and there was so many other things to look at. "I canna walk too quickly Stan, please slow down, an' yore hurtin' mi arm."

"Nod fur now lass, an' yo' can keep up." Briar glared up at her husbands face, he was not angry, his tone towards her was almost warm, and when he suddenly smiled down at her, the smile reached his bright blue eyes. "Nearly theer lass." Pushing through the narrow cobbled lane of Fish Street, and the stink that fermented the air with it's lingering odours of over ripe kippers, Stan led them as fast as he could to a tiny tea shop, one tucked just back from the street, and almost out of sight. Briar took a deep breath as they entered the tea shop. She was glad to be able to sit down and take a breather; she so badly needed to collect her thoughts.

"Si' wi' yore mammy lad, I'll ge' us a drink."

Briar said nothing, the chance to hold her son once more, to feel him gently nestle against her body; his arms warm around her immediately calmed her. Yes, for once Stan was right, they did need to talk. She wanted her son back, and her son needed his mother permanently. For what seemed an age Briar sat just staring blankly as Stan had a large pot of tea placed on the small round table. "I'll pour lass, an' theer's some sugar too, yo' 'elp yoresel' t' tha'. As fur yo' Danny be careful wi' tha' milk, it's warm an' we dunna wan' it spillin' everywheer do we son?"

Briar watched as Danny smiled at his father eagerly taking the tin mug into his small chubby hands. How much like his father the child was. His hair the same shade of brilliant red and his eyes were also the same bright blue. Even at the tender age of just sixteen months, the small boy did not seem upset by the turn of affairs in his life or her sudden reappearance. He was content being with his father, she could see that. Taking the cup offered her Briar stared coldly into the eyes of the husband she hated with every beat of her heart. He was very neatly turned out in black cloth trousers and his shirt sleeves carefully rolled up to allow the air to his arms. He was a very tall man with a lean figure and the brightest crop of red hair. His face was attractive, and when he smiled, his eyes lit up with a certain mischief. There was many a girl that would be interested in him, for he held himself well and always had a certain air of authority over others, over making decisions and carrying them out. "Well then lass, is theer anythin' yo' wan' t' say? I dunna mean name throwin' though, or are yo' goin' t' si' and pout at me all day?" Stan watched as she sat back, her cheeks flushed with a warm rosy appeal to them. She looked angry, ready to battle with him, but here, in a tea shop! Would she dare? When she sighed heavily Stan grinned, she hadn't changed at all he could see that. Her silvery blond hair still shone with life, and flowed loose over her shoulders and down her back to gently nestle into her waist. Her slate grey eyes were as dashing as ever, eyes that could sparkle with pleasure then pierce with temper, striking into any man who looked her way. Suddenly Stan had no shadow of a doubt as he gazed into her angelic heart shaped face. Yes, he had forgiven her the affair with his brother. He would willingly take her home, and accept the unborn as his own. He could cope with it, he really could, if only she would enter his life and start living with him the way a wife should. If he could persuade her to return home to him and Danny, and to take her place beside him each night as she should have done to begin with, he would shower her with as much affection as she could take from him. He would never lay a hand to her again and he would allow no harm to come to her. As she sat so still, her face resembling that of an placid angel, Stan smiled warmly. She'd be acting like a wild cat now if they were anywhere else. But whatever faults lay deep within Briar Rose, Stan loved her, his love was as strong as ever as he sat there face to face with her now. If he got her home he'd willingly keep her locked up there if it meant keeping her away from the tempting charms of a man like his brother. He felt the strength inside him rumble in the pits of his stomach, and grow in his chest, he would be able to destroy anybody that did try and get too close, even if it took the last breath from his body. Nobody could love Briar as much as he did, not even his brother, for Stan would happily give life and limb for her.

"Why 'ave yo' come? I wan' mi son back. Is tha' why yo've come? Can I 'ave mi son back now?" So quietly the words spilt upon the table. She had tried to speak firmly, but had stumbled badly; a shake could clearly be heard in her voice.

"I've come t' tell yo' wha' an unforgiveable fool I wa'. To say I'm sorry, an' tha' I'm glad yo' an' yore babby are well." Stan looked fleetingly to where her hands rested on her stomach. "I dunna expec' yo' t' trust me lass, an' even come t' furge' all tha' has happened...no ssh le' me finish." Placing his fingers to her lips to stop her interrupting Stan carried on. "It wa' all a shock Briar, bu' I can accept tha' now, an' the babby. I love yo' lass, I always 'ave, sometimes wi' a madness tha' has sickened even me. Bu' I'll ne'er raise mi hand to yo' again or anythin' else. Come home Briar, come back wi' me an' Danny now an' le' me tek care o' yo' an' the babby when it comes...please Briar, Danny needs 'is mam, an' I need yo' too." Now he waited, he had said his piece. He had seen her tremble, her bottom lip had quivered, and her slate grey eyes had filled with tears.

"No...please Stan...I beg yo', if yo' really love me, please gi' me back mi son." Beseechingly Briar pleaded her voice soft but broken, she was trying so hard not to cry, and it wouldn't take much more. Stan briefly looked around him, the small tea shop was crowded and smoky, but nobody seemed to notice them, and for that he was thankful. Gently he reached out and took Briar's hands in his own.

"I love yo' Briar, an' I love mi son also. If yo' dunna come back I've los' a whole par' o' mi life, bu' if I lose mi son as well, I'll 'ave nowt lef' t' live fur. Yo' canna expec' me t' lose yo' both. I've broken yore heart lass by tekin' the boy I can see tha', bu, if yo' tek the boy from me yo'll tek mi whole life, an' I canna le' yo' do tha'... come home Briar, come now wi' me an' yore son, an' I'll mek yo' the husband yo' can be proud off." Clasping her hands tightly in his own he waited with baited breath. There was nothing left to say, would it prove enough? The sob that escaped Briar's lips attracted the attention of a nearby table, but only momentarily. As her tears did begin to fall Briar leant forward and brokenly whispered in her husbands ear. "I wan' mi son...I'll do anythin'...please...I jus' wan' mi son."

Stan smiled with a blessed relief, and he too choked on his words as he said "Then its settled lass, I'll pay the bill, then we'll go t'gether fur the car' an' back home eh?" Stan watched her simply nod her head before bowing it, and then he turned from the table to go and pay his bill. He would be true to his word; he would treat her like a princess and make sure their life ran well together. When they got back to Bayston Hill he would beg leave for a couple of days so he could spend it with her. He had only one interest left now, and that was to make sure that Briar settled with him, and then he would begin the task of helping her forget the last five months. As Stan cheerfully took his change, his heart filled with hope at starting over, he turned towards the table to face Briar and his world crumbled before him. His wife was gone, and so was his son.

chapter twenty

"Ben...oh Ben 'elp me...he's righ' behind me, he'll kill me...dunna le' him tek mi son...oh please."

"Tek the child upstairs now an' stay theer." As Briar fled through the shop out of breath and terribly distraught Ben slammed the door behind her, but not before he picked up a mallet. Grabbing his stick for support Ben made his way towards the shop door, and stood outside. If he needed help he would not hesitate but to use the mallet in his hand and then yell for assistance. Faced with the rage he knew his brother would be in Ben feared only for the safety of Briar and their unborn child. This conflict right now was just what he had not wanted. Stan would not hurt his own son Ben was sure of that, but he'd seen the damage he had done to Briar the day he had left her, and he too felt that Stan could be capable of killing her. Ben took a deep breath, for now Danny was with them, and he would not allow Stan to take the child off Briar again.

"Ben...Ben, I know she's in theer, yo' tell tha' little bitch t' hand the child back, or God 'elp me I'll finish 'er fur good." Stan's bellow boomed through the market square startling busy shoppers who swiftly moved their own children out of the way. "Yo' 'ear me? The pair o' yo' destroyed me, bu' yo' inna tekin' the lad, now 'and me back mi son, or I'll 'ave t' see t' yo' first. If I 'ave t' Ben I'll kill yo' an' then yo' can rest assured I'll do fur 'er an' yore child will ne'er be born."

Ben stood fully in the shop door not taking his eyes off his brother for a second. "Yo' wunna ge' pas' me Stan, nod now, nod ever. The lads wi' 'is mam an' tha's wheer he'll stay. Now if yo' go' any sense yo'll clear off before yore arrested an' thrown in a cell wheer yo' belong." Ben faced his older brother head on. Stan stood much taller, but now as close as he was Ben felt no fear of him. What Ben saw was a weak bully of a man destroyed by his own resentful jealousy, he believed to be love. As Ben glowered into his brother's bright blue eyes he saw the vision of a man who had so cruelly left his young wife brutally beaten and raped bleeding on the floor where he had dumped her. His brother had nearly caused the death of an unborn child, and also the mother, Ben would never forget. Gasps and wild whispers echoed around the busy market place as shoppers began to stand still and listen. Threats were being hurled wildly at a young crippled man in his own shop doorway, a man who not only had a mallet in his hand but a walking stick to lean on. It was Ma Smith, the plump woman that had served Briar who sensed the real danger and wailed loudly. "Ge' the police, wheer's the police when yo' need them? Yo' over theer, yo' go' better legs than me, go on ge' on up t' The Row, the police are always theer, go an' tell them t' move it, theer's going' t' be a murder tell them. RUN." On her final screech the young beggar that Ma Smith had yelled at ran as fast as he could, he'd be rewarded for this that was for sure, rewarded for stopping a murder!

"Calm yourself sir or you will be arrested and charged for a breach of the peace."

Angrily Stan faced the policeman. "Mi wife is up theer." Pointing to the top window Stan then turned accusingly towards Ben. "He stole mi wife, an' now mi son is up theer. Ge' them down 'ere both o' them, an' then I'll tek mi family home,"

Ben saw exactly where Stan was heading, and he could also see the policeman was becoming very agitated with Stan's loud behaviour. So rationally and politely Ben spoke. "The child is wi' 'is mother sir, they live here wi' me, they are nod 'ere against their will."

"Yo' lyin' bastard, the bitch is mi wife. Yo' tell 'im, then yo' go up theer an' ge' them down." Ordering the policeman, Stan now spat his next words. "Yo' tell tha' little bitch up theer t' come 'ome wheer she belongs, an' t' brin' the child down 'ere righ' now."

"I strongly suggest you calm down now." Turning towards Ben the policeman now spoke. "I'll go up and see the girl for myself, and then I will resolve the matter...quietly."

"Aye, yo' better, an' dunna come back down wi'owt 'er." Stan spoke sharply, but stood firmly, his shoulders well back, he was confident that the policeman would make Briar stop this silly nonsense, and he'd take her home. Taking a deep breath and now just staring up at the top window Stan sneered, she'd made a real fool of him to try this, well he'd no longer try the nice approach, when they did get back later he'd treat her the same as many wives were treated when they stepped over the line. He'd belt the living daylights out of her. Briar had listened to every word, crouching nervously on the floor next to Ben's bed trembling, holding her son close to her she sobbed quietly. She had gone against Ben's wishes, she should have screamed the place down and not left the Square, he had yelled at her when she had returned to go upstairs, would he be that angry with her after? As the policeman quietly walked into the large room what he saw was a very young slip of a girl hardly any older than his youngest daughter. There she cowered terrified on the floor, a small child in her arms and her stomach full with another one.

"Now then young lady, what is this all about?" Kindly the policeman knelt down beside her, his face concerned but his voice gentle. The girl was hardly more than a child herself.

"The boy is mine sir, I'm 'is mammy, an' we're livin' 'ere wi' Ben, we 'ave been fur five months now sir." As her last words trailed of on a sob and tears began to fall the policeman gently reached out and touched her shoulder.

"Now calm yourself, getting in this state will do you no good. Come on now at least sit on the bed or somewhere."

As she stood up the policeman guided her across the room

towards the easy chair. "Please sir, he wan's t' tek mi child...I fear 'im, if yo' mek me go back he'll..."

"Now now, wipe yore tears, I'm not here to force you to do anything. I just came up to check on you and the child, and I'm happy with what I see. Now go and make yourself a hot drink, and I don't expect to hear any more fuss."

"No sir...o' course nod."

Satisfied that the girl and the child were in fact fine, the policeman stepped back into the street below. Back in the Shrewsbury Square the shoppers had got far more than they had bargained for, for as realisation hit Stan full in the face that he had just lost his son to his wife, a fury so strong unleashed itself as bitter bellows and wild threats rang out for all to hear. Several blows were lashed out towards Ben and the policeman until Stan was fully restrained with the help of four trading farmers. Stan screamed out his revenge as he was led away handcuffed, threats that left many of the shoppers feeling cold inside. Support was fast coming Ben's way, for he was well respected among the traders that sold their wares in the market square weekly. All were shocked however by the turn of affairs, a little curious, and strangely excited. After all it was an odd affair. Two brothers fighting in the street over a slate grey eyed youngster, who was obviously married to one brother, yet living with the other, and who would have a child by both of them in a few months time. It was a sheer scandal if ever one was seen, and one that was likely to cause a lot more trouble yet. As Ben limped back into his shop, blood on his sleeves caused by a blow to his nose he very sharply addressed Briar who now stood by the workshop door. "Go upstairs an' tek the child wi' yo'. I'll call fur a doctor t' check yo' over, an' then if yo' dunna res' I'll skelp the hide o' yo' mesel'." Ben was concerned for Briar, but very very tired. She had put herself in immediate danger and was now trembling violently, but as she turned to leave the room falling into heartrending sobs Ben was fast as ever to make his way to her, holding her close in his arms speaking just words of comfort, showering her tearful face with kisses. Ben was fast to let her know he was not angry with her, just concerned and always would be.

"Eeh theer yo' are lass, now then I jus' heard yore young man theer wan's yo' restin' an' seein' a doctor, now le' me tell yo' this." Ben and Briar turned as one towards the voice that now stood in the shop doorway. Briar looked up into Ben's surprised face and began to splutter with a sudden burst of laughter as the voice carried on. "Now I'm the one yo' wan', delivered hundreds o' babbies I 'ave an' ne'er los' one ye'. Ge' off up them stairs lass before it's me tha' skelps yore backside an' no arguin'." Crossing the room the strange woman who was well over weight simply took Danny from his mother and handed him to Ben, who stood with his mouth open, wondering who on earth this woman was who had just barged into his shop. "Well dunna stand theer gawpin' at me lad, go an' mek a ho' mushed tea while I looken at the belly on this one. Eeh yo' may as well ge' used t' ole Ma Smith, fur when she's go' a belly load again nex' year, I'll be back." Ben stared down at the woman, his warm brown eyes wide with disbelief as he was offered a large toothless grin. What had he done to deserve this? Dear God in heaven. "Well go on lad, quick, quick, oh an' theer's a package o' material on yore counter. Pu' it safe, it's the lasses." Still Ben stood aghast by the woman's bluntness. But Briar was giggling, and she seemed happy to go with the woman, so he would trust her also.

Alone for now Ben sat the small boy on his shop counter, and ruffled his bright red hair. "Hello Danny boy." He was immediately answered with a smile. When Ben looked at the lad, he could see a mirror image of his brother, a man he had lost all respect for. But with this small boy, Ben felt a love towards the child he had once had for his older brother. Now they had Danny, Briar would be completely happy, and come to that so would he. Gazing up at the ceiling Ben could clearly hear the woman's voice echoing against his walls as the woman firmly reprimanded Briar for being such a 'naughty lass', and when he heard Briar's giggles getting right out of control he had to sit down. It had been a very strange day, and Briar had managed to do what she had since the day she had walked into his life. She had caused total chaos all around her turning his world upside down until his stomach churned, and it was her first time out without him.

"Wheer's tha' tea yo' promised me?" Ma Smith loudly walked back into the shop. "Well the lass 'as come t' no 'arm, an' the babby is as lively as its young mother. Eeh yore goin' t' 'ave yore hands full, aye yo' are." As Ma Smith loudly said her piece Ben bowed his head and began to splutter, and then the laughter began to shake his whole body until he could hardly breathe. When Ma Smith folded her arms on her over large stomach, Ben felt he would go hysterical with the laughter he could not stop even if he tried. "Well now I've seen it all. I've ne'er seen so much disturbance in all mi days, an' me a mother o' ten, an' theer yo' are, yo' canna even mek poor ole Ma Smith a cup o' tea wi'owt laughin'."

"Aye, I'll mek yo' a cup o' tea, an' if yo' mean t' be around mi lass Briar Rose, then yo' better ge' used t' disturbance, it wouldna be Briar wi'owt one." With that Ben cheerfully took Danny with him, his laughter ringing through the shop as he went.

chapter twenty-one

"I have never condoned the beating of any employee, and find it very hard to justify it this time."

"Wi' respec' sir, may I defend mesel'?" Stan Lawson stood firmly, his cap in his hand, but he had the sense to bow his head and wait for his master's answer.

Jonathan Hampstead frowned but sat back in the high backed leather seat. Stan had proved over and over in the last few years that he was a true and hard worker. He was very firm, but had been fair with the younger lads in his care. Never had he given any cause for concern that was until just lately. "I'm waiting." Jonathan nodded, his willingness to listen, he had to give Stan the benefit of the doubt.

"The new lad Benson wa' wi' me all las' week an' I gave 'im bu' one task sir." Stan locked eyes with his master. "The lawns around the new rockery 'ad been cu' down by Jacobs an' a border tha' the Mistress Blanche asked t' be dug…"

"Yes I know all of that Lawson, but why did you deliver the Benson boy the thrashing you gave him?"

"It were 'is job sir t' mek sure no stones were lef' on the lawn. He had bu' one side t' tek care off. I asked 'im more than once an' he told me he had cleared it well an' good."

"And?"

"The Mistress Blanche came t' see the work fur hersel', I wa' theer sir. She nearly fell over a large stone tha' 'ad been lef' on the side, the size o' a small rock. Nod good enough sir, the Mistress Blanche could 'ave hur' hersel' real bad."

"I see." Jonathan took a deep breath, where the job was concerned he could not argue that Stan was a perfectionist.

"I took the lad t' one side sir, an' gave 'im a real piece o' mi mind. I wouldna o' touched the lad sir, bu' he gave me a righ' mouthful o' cheek. Canna allow tha' sir."

"So you dragged him I believe to the nearby stables?"

"Aye sir an' I dealt mi belt across 'is back."

Jonathan fell deep into thought. He had heard Stan's voice a lot just lately bellow at the lads in his care, but this was the first beating he had ever rendered. He had feared at first it was Stan's way of relieving himself of his own anger, but now, after talking to him, he had given a very clear reason. For now he would assume that Stan had only had his Mistress Blanches safety at heart. Even still, long after Stan left the room Jonathan sat deep in thought. He'd keep a very close eye on Stan Lawson, and if he did suspect bullying of any kind, then he would not hesitate but to send him packing.

"Pu' yore backs int' it the lo' o' yo'. Jacobs, tek the far end o' the grounds, the hedges need cuttin' an' dunna leave a mess lad."

"I wunna do tha' Mr Lawson, ne'er do leave a stone owt o' place...sir."

Stan glowered, a crimson tide rising up his neck brushing warmly against his cheeks. Taking a deep breath Stan walked towards the young grounds man, his bright blue eyes sparked with a new anger, but for now he would have to hold back. "If I should fin' one stone owt o' place I wunna thinken twice t' thrashin' the hide off yo'. If yo' ever show yore sharp tongue to me, I'll knock yore head straigh' off yore stupid shoulders." Stan stood firm, his eyes not leaving the much smaller lad. "Ge' on wi' yore work lad, an' keep yore tongue fastened in yore daf' head." Stan stood alone as the young lads went about the tasks he had set before them. He knew that Jacobs had meant no harm, he was a good young worker, but even still, he was not about to let the episode of the thrashing he had given Benson make him lose face. Grumbling under his breath Stan put the remaining tools into the wheelbarrow. "Dunna know 'ow easy they 'ave it." Briefly Stan remembered the severe beatings he'd been dealt as a small child at the workhouse, but only briefly, for the past reminded him also of his only brother Ben, and then his wife, and that alone ran his blood hot and then fiercely cold until the palms of his hands became cold with sweat. The loneliness he felt now he had lost his own small son pierced through his heart as sharp as any knife. There was nobody Stan could really confide in, who would understand his despair, and the raging anger it left burning inside his soul as hot as any roaring fire that held within it a hidden danger that feared even him. Stan did not know how far his anger would take him if he did have the pleasure to be left alone with his brother, or worse still, his wife. If only he could forget her, rid himself of those striking eyes of hers, forget how soft her hair was and how silky her skin had felt under his brutal hands. Just to touch her! He'd have never forced her if she'd have just given him the chance to show how much he loved her. "God's sake, pull yoresel' owt o' it man." Mumbling wildly to himself Stan sneered at the sight of Benson, the young lad he had beaten to ease his own stress. Picking up the rake he set about his own task, his mind now more highly troubled than before. How could he get on with his life as Master Jonathan had told him too? And the Buntings come to that. In fact everybody had said the very same thing. Rubbish, the lot of it. He loved his wife Briar Rose with such intensifying heart pounding ferocity, that he would tread upon all around him if it meant he could get her back home, and his son. Nobody had the right to have taken them from him, and nobody should have had the nerve to tell him to forget them. Nobody had past judgement on Ben had they? Only him. Well those that laughed first would not laugh last, there would be remorseful regret, tears of sorrow, and he would personally make his wife beg, plead with him to spare her their child, and then he would take her for himself one last time. Twisted plans formed dangerously in Stan's mind, how he would get hold of her, he did not know, but he would, he would find a way and then both she and Ben would laugh no more. If Stan would have only spoken to any of the Hampstead workers, or even his master instead of displaying his disdain and unpredictable temper, he would have discovered just how much support and sympathy he really had. But nobody from the Hampstead Estate, or even his own brother Ben, never mind Briar Rose would have ever contemplated in their wildest of fears how desperate Stan would become over the following weeks. Nobody would know just how disturbed and dangerous his mind would become when the unborn child he had tried to destroy would enter the world, the world he had once tried to deny it. For if they had of known, Jonathan Hampstead himself would have found the power to have Stan institutionalised.

chapter twenty-two

"Yo' tell yore man t' pu' yo' down Danny boy. Yore a big lad tell 'er." Ben smiled as the small boy wriggled from his mother's arms and cheerfully crossed the workshop floor, his arms outstretched for his Uncle Ben to pick him up. "Tha's the way Danny, now tek this piece o' wood an' very carefully run yore fingers down the side o' it. If it's smooth, or feels soft on yore fingers, yo' tell me. Then it's ready." Briar Rose stood by silently, a genuine mother's pride shone from her slate grey eyes as she watched her small red haired son take a seat next to his uncle. Danny could have easily been Ben's son, and anybody who did not know any better would have believed he was. "Danny's alrigh' wi' me lass, why dunna yo' tek the weight off yore fee'?"

"Well...I'm fine really...it's..."

"I know lass, yo' dunna need t' explain. Pull yoresel' up a chair an' si' wi' us fur a while." Ben smiled warmly, his brown eyes always so full of concern and warmth for her. But he knew she had been without Danny for so long, and now even though he had been back for two months, she could not bear being parted from him not even for a moment.

"Aye, I will, at leas' before Ma Smith ge's 'ere." Briar answered with a note of mischief. Since the day she had snatched her son back and brought the material from the market square, Ma Smith the stall holder had been a regular visitor. She had proved to be not just a friend, but a woman who knew just what birthing was all about. Her advice to Briar was sometimes sharp, but caring, and she was fast to put Ben's mind at ease, though her colourful language and often vulgar sense of humour never failed to make Briar blush furiously.

"Yo' alrigh' lass?"

"Aye Ben, I am tha'." Briar smiled, the pout she had often wore seldom touched her lips these days. Carefully she sat down on the seat, she did feel very tired, but she did not want to take her eyes of the two people she loved so dearly, her son, and Ben. How perfect her life had become, she had a roof over her head, a workshop and a shop, she had a man who loved her and would do anything for her, and she had her son. She had learnt that a man's touch could prove always kind, and his presence was something to enjoy, to look forward too and not dread or fear. For the first time in her life Briar Rose was truly happy, she had enjoyed the last of the summer months, and had welcomed the heavy rains of September, and the warning of long dark nights. Now as October had opened it'd door to her, she felt a sense of excitement, a restlessness of endless energy. For in the next few days her unborn child would enter her life, and she could hardly wait to hold another child close to her breasts.

"Is anybody goin' t' answer the door, an' le' ole Ma' Smith in?" The loud banging coming from the shop door broke Briar's gentle thought of joy and brought a loud laugh from Ben.

"Well go on lass, tek 'er upstairs away from me an' the lad, an' dunna keep 'er 'ere till early mornin' eh?"

"No Ben, I wunna do tha'." On a giggle Briar made her way slowly from the workshop. Once out of sight she sighed, how heavy she felt today, and how very slow she was. She was glad it was Saturday evening for tomorrow she would take Ben's advice and sit down for longer periods. With the shop shut on a Sunday she would not have the need to keep running up and down to the shop with Danny, even though Ben had repeatedly told her sharply not to do it.

"Eeh abou' time too lass, the rains comin' down so hard nearly took me off mi feet." Looking around her Ma Smith 'oohed' at Ben's work as always and then marched straight through the workshop with Briar slowly trudging behind her. "Aah look at the little lad, an' yo' go' him workin' already! Yore a hard bugger!" Loudly Ma

Smith declared herself to Ben then carried on. "Eeh laddie yo' learn well, yo' 'elp tha' daf' bugger keep off 'is feet, he canna keep mekin' himsel' special shoe bits or limpin' abou', an' heaven knows yore mammy will be ready t' drop again nex' year."

Briar gasped in horror at the outrageous remarks over Ben's leg, but she needn't have bothered for Ben knew that it wasn't meant as an insult of any kind. In fact Ben himself had Briar blushing wildly and Ma Smith cackling with spluttered laughter as he answered simply. "Aye Ma Smith, we canna do wi'owt yo'. Yo' bes' tek mi lass upstairs an' tell 'er t' 'urry it along, fur I wunna settle until I 'ave a workshop full o' Lawson toymakers."

"Ben." Was all that Briar could mutter.

"Oh aye lass I told yo', now 'ave yo' finished tha' frock yo' started? Yo'll look a real bonny piece an' it wunna tek anytime at all until yore lookin' liken this again." The loud cackle rang out again, but it was only short lived, for a loud gasp brought both Ben and Ma Smith close to the girls side. A sharp pain had engulfed Briar Rose at the foot of the steps, and as she clung to Ben's hand for support she muttered to the older woman. "The babby's started, an' I dunna feel too good."

In the hours that followed, Ben would hear and witness a side of Briar Rose he had never encountered. He had seen great strengths in Briar and had witnessed her wild tempers. He had seen the girl despair when she had been robbed of her son, but her character had still shown itself to be strong and true, her will adamant to survive. But upstairs on that long Saturday night as he waited helplessly downstairs with a small boy to comfort Ben came to know what fear was all about. When fretful cries began Ben's sympathy flew upstairs on his echoed words of encouragement until Ma Smith yelled at him to. "Shu' up, yore enough t' send a woman mad." Even though she had patted Briar's hand behind the closed door and whispered. "He's a good man love; many would 'ave ran t' the pub by now." But when the hours slowly past, and the cries turned to screams and then pathetic pleas for it to end, Ben began to feel very uncomfortable. When he crept up the stairs and stood outside the door only to hear Ma Smith urge, "come on mi darlin', dunna gi' up on me now, try a bi' harder, come on lass push harder." Ben had held his young nephew close against his chest and had bowed his head, his eyes firmly closed as his heart pounded heavily. He was losing her, he knew it in his heart, the girl he'd always considered so strong was laying in the next room as weak as a kitten, life slowly ebbing its way from her as she continued to struggle to bring their child into the world. After all they had been through; Ben was going to lose her. As the chimes from the clock of Ben's workshop welcomed the early sacred hours of Sunday morning, the healthy shrill cry of a newborn sounded out into the room above Ben Lawson's workshop. But Ben felt no joy or hope for the future. He had long since settled Danny on his jacket to sleep on the workshop floor which he was glad off, for the small boy would learn of his great loss only too soon. As Ma Smith opened the door exhausted, but to congratulate the new father, her sudden shriek was enough to wake the dead, for there stood Ben, his candle in one hand, hardly offering a flicker of light, his walking stick helping him keep on his feet, his head bowed against his chest as he needlessly sobbed alone in the darkness of the small hall. "God above, wha' type o' welcome is tha'? Theer I am up t' mi neck in…well it 'anna been easy an; theer yo' are cryin', worse than the babby tha's jus' come into' the world." Ma Smith folded her arms indignantly, but as Ben raised his tear soaked face, she sensed his fear and understood his tears of sorrow. "I told yo' I ne'er los' no lass in birthin', an' I 'anna los' yores. It wunna easy, bu' she's a will o' her own, an' she wunna ready fur the tekin', she's jus' worn owt." When Ben choked, but swiftly dried his face on his sleeve he was met with a wide toothless grin. "Well yo' goin' t' stand theer all day? Or are yo' goin' t' ge' in this room an' le' me go 'ome t' mi bed?"

"Aye, bu' before yo' do…" Another mighty shriek echoed in the hallway as Ben tightly hugged the older woman in a rush of sheer relief and high emotion.

"Eeh ge' on in theer wi' yo', I'll be back in the mornin', lots o' res' lad...bu' I guess yo' know tha'." Affectionately Ma Smith touched Ben's arm as she turned to leave. How strange life could be. To think that a girl who was merely a customer had simply walked into her life and with it had engraved herself deep into Ma Smith's heart was a surprise in itself. Ma Smith had her own family, and a large one at that, but this young couple had unwittingly won her love, and Ma Smith enjoyed their company as much as she did her own brood. In the glow of oil lanterns and a few night candles Ben unashamedly felt the heaviness close up his throat as fresh tears began to burn his face. "Yo' looken beautiful lass, aye yo' do." So relieved to see her staring up at him, Ben sat down, suddenly very tired himself. But there she was, Briar Rose, her image one that would never leave him, for she lay so very fragile against a puff of pillows, her waist length silvery blond hair still shining with life as it fell over her shoulders. When she meekly smiled, her slate grey eyes shone with quiet joy, Ben winked his own smile warm to see. She resembled a silent angel, a young girl so very meek and mild, and a girl he would willingly give his life for. When Ben gazed down at the tiny babe swaddled in a shawl in her arms a chuckle escaped his lips, for as Briar gently pulled the shawl down for Ben to see, the newborn child's lips pulled into a natural pout as it whimpered. Ben touched the tiny hand that grasped his finger tightly, he could feel great strength in the child as it pulled its lips into a greater pout and threatened to cry. There was no shade of red in this child's slight show of hair, its nose was perfectly shaped, its face so very perfect for a child that had just been born.

"It's a girl Ben, yo' 'ave a little daughter."

"Aye lass, I can see, fur she's as beautiful as her mam." As Briar gently handed the child to her father, Ben looked deeply into the tiny face that screwed up relentlessly before still offering a heavy pout, and then his eyes rested on the girl he had loved for so long. "I'd liken t' name 'er if yo' dunna mind?"

Briar smiled and nodded, she was happy for him to do so. "I can see yo' Briar in this child, an' I'd liken t' tek par' o' yore name…" With the little bit of strength she had left, Briar touched Ben's arm and made a feeble protest, for she after all had been born along the road side, and had been named because of being born beside a wild hawthorn bush. She had no wish for her child to inherit such a name. Ben smiled warmly, but placed his finger gently against her lips. "Theer will only ever be one Briar Rose in mi life, bu' I'd liken the child t' be named after yo' bu' after a flower as pure as the snow." Briar smiled wearily, whatever name he chose, she would be happy to abide by. "Lily, I wan' the child t' be named Lily Rose." Just for a moment Ben's eyes lingered over his tiny newborn daughter, and when he looked back at Briar, he was met with another silent nod of satisfaction, her slate grey eyes now so heavy with the much needed sleep that she wanted. "Yo' res' Briar, I'll place the crib righ' nex' t' yo'. Danny's fas' asleep downstairs, I'll carry him up an' then in the…" his words trailed off into the sacred bliss of the rich October Sunday morning as Briar closed her eyes, sleep taking it's toll, a sleep of such peace. Ben gently laid his daughter down in the crib he had made then turned to fetch Danny upstairs, how perfect his life had become. Briar sighed heavily in her sleep as Ben quietly left the room; with him she had always been safe.

chapter twenty-three

"Eeh lass, it's as pretty a frock as ole Ma Smith 'as ever seen, bu' no lace?"

"No Ma Smith," Briar smiled warmly, "it's practical, I dunna need no fancy frock t' serve the customers." Turning around to show off the frock fully she asked once more. "Well do yo' thinken Ben will like it?"

Ma Smith cackled loudly, her toothless grin wide as she bluntly declared. "He wouldna be a man if he didna. Eeh lass, yore a bonny piece, bu' if I were yo' I'd keep yore drawers on or yore legs closed if yo' 'anna go' any, because lookin' the way yo' do, yo'll 'ave a belly full in no time, an' yo' can still ge' caugh' even if the babby is still on the titty."

Briar spluttered, the colour rising in her face as she glanced towards the door. Thank goodness Ben was out of the room. Briar had a soft spot for Ma Smith and would always be grateful for her being there at her greatest hour of need, but even still, Briar would never get used to the loose way Ma Smith expressed herself, and Ben also found it highly embarrassing at the best of times. "Dunna tek no notic o' me lass, I'm jus' an old woman wi' a dirty mind. Yo' look grand, eeh yo' wouldna even know yo' 'ad such a young un." Briar smiled once more; yes she was pleased with herself. Her figure was almost back to normal and Lily Rose was hardly six weeks old. "Oh looken 'ere's the man himsel', now yo' looken after tha' lass an' keep yore pants on. I'll drop in jus' before Christmas, go' mi own brood t' feel now an' mi own man t' keep happy."

"Yo' tek car now Ma Smith, an' dunna worry abou' us, I'll tek good care o' the nippers, an' Briar Rose."

"Aye, tha's wha' I'm afraid o', as I said keep yore pants on."

Ben closed his eyes briefly as Ma Smith loudly left his shop. "Dear God above, 'ow 'er old man managed nod t' strangle 'er in all these years I'll ne'er know."

Briar giggled as she crossed the shop floor, her tiny daughter in her arms, Danny close beside her. "Yo' dunna 'ave t' do this Briar, yo' know I can manage." Ben grinned mischievously as Briar placed the baby down in the crib he had carried downstairs, placing it safely behind the counter. Briar had pleaded with him for almost two weeks to allow her to serve in the shop part of the day. Ben had rebuked the idea to begin with, his only concern was for Briar to take it steady, to sit back and simply enjoy the children. But he should have guessed that Briar would not sit back for too long, she had always been far too inquisitive for her own good. So thinking that it could be best to allow her to work, but on a part time basis Ben hoped that this way she would see for herself she would be happier to let him do the work for both of them. "Alrigh' lass, bu' I'll be keepin' a close eye on thin's. If I dunna thinken it's workin' owt yo' bein' 'ere in the shop wi' young Lily, I wunna mince mi words, yo'll be upstairs before yo' know it." Ben saw the slight shade of pink creep up her neck towards her cheeks, and when he witnessed just the slightest of a pout resting on her lips he burst out laughing. "I mean it lass, an' yo' needn't pout at me."

Embarrassed by her own childlike actions, something she had never been able to help, Briar smiled sheepishly. "Are yo' tekin' Danny?"

"Aye lass, I am, the lad can 'elp me. An' when Lily can up an' walk, well I'll teach 'er too, as I promised yo' Briar some time ago. Any child in mi 'ouse will learn mi trade, be it lad or lass." Ben spoke softly for he meant every word. Briar herself had taught him long ago that girls could pull their weight in the working world of men, and make a good job of it. As Ben was met with a smile so warm, as he often saw now, his eyes began to roam longingly over what was still a very young girl. How slender her figure still was, her skin always so soft to the touch, her long silvery blond hair shone with life, and was never tied back. The blue frock she had made herself certainly brought out the slate grey of her eyes, and her heart shaped face that resembled that of an angel was alight with the life she now led. No longer did Ben witness the wild stubborn streak she once had, and seldom did her grey eyes pierce through a soul with fury. Now, the young woman glowed with an air of sheer promise. Her natural beauty had been allowed to settle and shine through. More than that Ben had come to know the happy go lucky, loving lass, a girl whose manners were that of a well brought up girl, whose temperament was as gentle as a lambs. She was a loving mother to the children, and though she could never be his wife by law, in his heart she was the wife he had dreamt off. "Well lass, I'm on mi way in the back now wi' Danny. Ma Smith is righ' though, yo' do looken pretty in tha' frock. Bes' keep mi pants on eh?"

"Ben." Briar spluttered with laughter, and then quickly raised her hand to her mouth. For Ben to even hint at such a thing and so loudly was so unlike him. "I thinken it's a good thin' Ma Smith inna comin' until Christmas, I canna cope wi' loose tongues from both o' yo', an' in front o' the children." Briar mockingly frowned, but smiled immediately when Ben approached her and took her tightly in his arms, his kisses teasing her lips.

"Then worry no more lass, mi lips are sealed, bu' now I really am goin' int' the back t' ge' on wi' orders, or I may jus' furge' mesel'." Briar gently kissed him back, the sound of her heart beating with his, and then she stepped back and looked towards the workshop. "Until later lass."

Briar watched as Ben made his way into the back, Danny's hand safely in his own, and she sighed. Things with young Danny had worked out far better than she could have ever anticipated. Ben had a real liking for the boy, as he'd told her, Danny was of his own blood, and it would be easy to forget that Danny was not his own son. Whether it was this unique bond, Briar was not too sure, only Danny never muttered 'Da' anymore and pointed to the door. When he did mutter the word, his arms went straight up to Ben, and neither Ben nor Briar had corrected him. Briar seldom thought of Stan these days, for she knew he must have had enough pride not to come back to the shop, and was hopefully getting on with his own life. When she needed to shop herself however on market days she still did not take her son, he was left behind with Ben. She had never forgot that Stan had ventured into the market the day she had snatched her son back, and that was her only fear that given the opportunity Stan would take Danny back again, and if he did, she knew she would never see her son again. "Well then Lily, le's open the shop."

Talking to her sleeping infant, Briar set about work.

"Wheer's tha' bloody young skit?" Stan roared at the young lads under him.

"Dunna know Mr Lawson."

An echo that fell short of a whisper. Grumbling under his breath Stan stormed towards the cobbled yard that fell to the back of the main house. He'd seen young Benson come from Mrs Bunting's parlour several times just lately, but today he had left work unfinished, and what he had done was plain shoddy. More infuriating, he had gone without seeking permission to do so. Stan had just seen his twenty third birthday, but had the appearance of a man much older. He was sharp and unforgiving, and where he had once held the respect of the younger lads under his care, they now feared him, and greater than that, they hated him. Stan had once been fair but firm, only now he was downright unreasonable and seemed to look for any cause to raise his hand. None of the lads had complained since the beating of Benson, but how much longer they'd keep silent, well time would only tell. "BENSON." The bellow caught the attention of the lad in question.

"Aye Mr Lawson?"

"Wha' the hell do' yo' mean by 'aye mr Lawson'?" Stan glared at the boy in front of him, a lad of just fifteen and of very slight build, a lad that was slightly backward for his age and had trouble with picking up what was needed of him in his line of work. "I'm waitin' lad, wheer 'ave yo' been?" Sneering Stan waited for an answer.

"I 'ad t' tek a pee Mr Lawson, an' then I came righ' 'ere t' ge' a drink, an' wash mi hands like."

"Wha' are yo'? A bloody fussy wench? Wash yore 'ands jus' so yo' can ge' them dirty again?" Stan could see the lad felt uneasy by the way he stepped from foot to foot and then nervously glanced towards the parlour of Mrs Bunting. "Yo' 'anna been cryin' like a girl again 'ave yo'? Or 'ave yo' been fillin' yore face while yore workmates are lef' t' do yore work?"

"I do mi work an' I only spen' a minute over at the 'ouse, I di', ask Mrs Buntin'."

Stan took a deep breath, the fury in him growing. He had no liking for this boy, none whatsoever, in fact he took up a lot of Stan's time. Looking the lad up and down Stan shook his head, the boy had the lightest of blond hair and the softness of blue eyes, he could have easily passed for a girl, his face was almost pretty not like any boy Stan had ever known, and come to that he even moaned like a girl. "Yore work lad, 'as nod been finished, in fac' it's hardly been started, wha' yo've done is a pile of shit." Stan watched the colour rise in the lads face. "Yo'll do the whole lo' again an' when tha's done the fron' o' the house needs weedin' wheer the carriages stop."

"I do mi work, I canna do the fron' o' the house, it's abou' t' rain, it inna fair."

"Nod fair? Wha' the hell in this life is fair? Yore nowt bu' a lazy skit tha' needs t' toughen up. Yore nowt like a girl, yore worse than any bloody lass." Making a grab Stan reached for the lads collar to give him a sharp kick up the arse as he sent him back to work, but Stan was right about one thing. The lad Benson was backward or he would have known better when Stan did have a firm grip to actually squeal out loud.

"I'll go t' the master, I will, it inna mi faul' yore wife up an' lef'" then took the babby. Yo' ne'er looked after the babby he were always stuck wi' Mrs Buntin', all the lads say so."

For what seemed an age the world stood still, lost in an echo of time when Stan could hardly breathe. But as the hands of time ticked slowly by, so the cloud that hovered over Stan's head darkened his day, stealing from him any reason he had left in his body. What happened next sent the whole of the Hampstead Estate into disarray, pulling the mill workers together, bringing both shock and sympathy from the housemaids, right up to the Master and Mistress themselves.

"Eeh, wha's the fuss? Bangin' on the door liken tha', mi Joseph will skin..."

"Please missus fetch 'im, theer's trouble an' we canna find the Master."

"Slow down, wha' trouble?" But as Emily Bunting spoke she could hear the irruptions and sickening cries sounding across the courtyard from behind the stable doors. "Joseph...Joseph." Emily had to call no more for Joseph Bunting had already been alerted by one of the maids that had been cleaning the windows who had hysterically screamed for his help frightening the Mistress Blanche in the process. It was a scandal, a serving wench screaming like that, he'd make sure that maid got a true piece of his mind later. As fast as Joseph could he crossed the yard, his wife behind him, and the maids behind her. Outside the stables stood the other young grounds men and the stable hands.

"He wunna le' us in sir, I go' this when I tried." The stable hand revealed a bright red weal that ran the length of his arm, his shirt ripped. "He's gone mad sir."

"Stand back all o' yo'." Taking full charge Joseph bellowed his orders for everybody to stand aside where they were safe, then turned and yelled at the closed stable door. "I'm comin' in, an' God 'elp yo' if yo' raise a hand t' me."

Silence. Not a sound, only the heartrending sobs of the young lad from inside as he pleaded. "Help me…Help me please…"

What Joseph Bunting faced as he opened the stable door was something never before seen on this estate, by him or any of the other workers there. Something that would cause the Mistress to faint when she did hear what had happened. The colour drained from Joseph's elderly face as she saw the wretched bloody form of the young lad Benson writhing on the ground, his face soaked with tears of fear and pain, his hand reaching out towards the elderly man to help him. There just to the side of the boy stood Stan Lawson, not a glimmer of remorse on his face, his hand still grasping the riding crop that he had used to rip through the boys skin. Benson's back was lost to a sea of blood and torn flesh, his shirt no longer visible except for shreds that had been left behind and lay soaked on the ground. "Stand back boy, well back. Yo' lo' 'elp me carry the lad int' the parlour. Yo' lasses clear the parlour table we'll need it." Joseph's own pleas for help shook as his own fears for this boy grew by the second. "Run now lasses fetch clean linen, towels, an' lint, boil some water, hurry. Jacob's run t' the main 'ouse an' dunna come back wi'owt the master."

Left alone Stan stood in the stable glaring down at the blood covered riding crop still in his hands. The lad had deserved it, he'd know better next time. But Stan had only seen one other in his mind as he'd stared down into the eyes of the terrified lad. He'd seen the face of his own wife Briar Rose and he had spent his built up frustration as he thought of her and had laid that frustration deep into Benson's back. Closing his eyes Stan bowed his head and dropped the riding crop to the ground. "Dear God in heaven, wha' the hell 'av I done?"

When Jonathan Hampstead was eventually found and made his way towards the stable he found a shivering, sobbing wreck of a man crouching on the ground his hands covering his face as he muttered over and over again.

"I loved yo' Briar, why di' yo' do it lass? I loved yo'."

chapter twenty-four

Briar shivered as she placed the broom up the far corner of the workshop. It had rained relentlessly for the last week now, and with it the cold gales that only winter could offer crept into every crack possible. It was almost the end of November and the rain looked as if it would never ease. Looking all around her she nodded to herself, yes she was satisfied that the shop was just how Ben expected to see it. She had served her last customer over an hour ago, and now that the door was locked, she had made sure that every wooden doll, every brightly painted duck and trinket box held no dust. She had gone over the large rocking horse that stood proudly in the corner and had checked for dust on every cabinet Ben had made. The floor was spotless, she had emptied the till and had bagged it as Ben had instructed and now she stood for a moment behind the locked shop door and sighed.

"Cold lass?"

"Aye." Briar smiled as Ben walked in from the workshop, she hadn't noticed until then she had been visibly shivering.

"Well come on then, le's go upstairs, the stoves heatin' up the room an' Lily needs 'er mam."

"Is it tha' time already?"

"Aye lass, it is." Ben spoke softly as he led Briar upstairs towards the large room they all shared, he would need to speak with her over supper, she was looking increasingly tired. Briar sighed again as she stepped into the warm room, the smell of vegetable broth welcoming her, and her small son was washed and ready for bed, a tin mug of warm milk in his hands.

"Hello Danny, yo' been a good boy?"

"Aye." The child muttered, and then raised his mug to his lips once more. Quietly Briar picked up her baby daughter from the crib, settling down on the one easy chair. Without a word she undid her frock buttons and held the child to her breast. Ben watched intently as his daughter lay safe in her mother's arms, then set about laying the table for them both.

"Yo' dunna need t…"

"Ssh, yo' looken worn owt Briar, when the children are settled we'll eat." For once Briar did not argue the point, in all honesty she had not expected to feel this tired, and she was glad that Ben had taken over what she should have done herself. "So then lass, yo' goin' t' wear yoresel' owt? Or are yo' goin' t' listen t' sense?" Briar took the plate offered her and just for a moment the pout she'd once worn so often hinted at teasing her lips. But when she saw the smile creep over Ben's face, lighting up his warm brown eyes she too smiled. "I canna leave yo' t' do everythin'."

"Now looken 'ere Briar…no listen." Ben placed his finger to his lips and waited until he could see that Briar was not about to interrupt him. "I know 'ow yo' feel lass an' more than tha' I understand. Bu' I canna le' a babby even if it is mi daughter wail in the shop when she needs attention." Ben saw the colour creep into her face and he immediately felt sorry he had embarrassed her. "Briar I canna run in the shop at the drop o' a hat when I've go' Danny wi' me. If he go' 'old o' one o' mi tools…" Pausing just for a moment, Ben carried on. "Now if I run it all the way tha' I 'ave been, I'll know wha' I'm about, an' I can teach Danny in the early evenin', wi'owt havin' t' leave 'im."

"So yore tellin' me, I'm nod allowed t' work wi' yo'?"

"Nod exactly." Ben reached out and held her hand for he knew she had meant well. "I know you've always been a nosy lass, aye I do, an' if yo' ge' bored, well I'd hate t' thinken o' the trouble yo' would ge' int'." Ben grinned as Briar gasped in disbelief. "I'd liken yo' t' looken after the children up 'ere as any other wife wi' a young family, bu' I'd liken yo' t' sor' owt the daily tekin's, baggin' the money, an' when I've done and closed the shop, I'd liken yo' t' dust it, sweep it, and mek sure every toy and cabine' is dust free." Ben could see his idea settling in her mind, this way she could work for him, but she would be from under his feet in the daytime. "After tha', late in the evenin' if I 'ave a big order, would yo' consider maybe sandin' down a piece o' work fur me?" Ben grinned as he saw a heavy pout settle on her lips, a frown marking her forehead as she thought long and hard about it. It had to be for the best for the last few days had proved chaos when Lily had wailed loudly. Customers who had been waiting to be served had actually asked to speak with him personally, and had then complained about the wait. After a few moments Briar gave her answer. "Aye Ben, I can live wi' tha'."

"Good, bu' theer's one more thin'."

"Oh." Briar placed her fork down, he really hadn't been impressed by her last few days in the shop.

"Briar this set up wa' grand when I wa' alone, bu' four o' us sharin' one large room! I 'ave somethin' t' pu' t' yo', I've already spoken wi' Jonathan Hampstead concernin' it." Ben paused; he could see the look of trepidation turning Briar's pretty face suddenly very pale. "Now I inna tryin' t' ge' owt o' mine an' Jonathan's agreement concernin' sales, bu' I've saved enough over the las' two years t' pu' a reasonable sum down on a property. I've made enquiries abou' a small cottage wi' a large workshop at the side o' it, at a place called Much Wenlock."

"Yo' 'ave?" Briar could only mutter her words. When it came to business not only did Ben know exactly what he wanted, but he made all decisions himself and guided those around him. Just for a fleeting moment Briar saw a large resemblance in his character that reminded her of Stan's. Both of them could lead, and well when it came to their work life.

"Oh aye lass, I dunna believe in lettin' the grass grow under mi fee'." There it was again, the resemblance. "It'll be a new star' lass, a larger workshop than this one, an' a proper home fur all o' us. The cottage 'as two bedrooms, an' a back garden, thinken o' tha' lass. It's nod a town, bu' it is a growin' village an' a pretty one at tha'."

"We can afford this?"

"Aye lass, I wouldna thinken o' it if we couldna. So wha' do yo' thinken then?" He watched closely as the realisation of what he was offering began to sink in. A smile covered his face as first she frowned, and then muttered and without any warning squealed with a sudden excitement upsetting her plate of broth as she did so.

"I tek it tha' means yes then?"

"Oh Ben, aye it does, when can we move? Will if be after Christmas? Can we go an' see it sometime? Wheer is Much Wenlock? Is it far?"

Now Ben did laugh, "I inna tellin' yo' nowt until yo' clear tha' mess up, an' then if yo' wan', we'll talk all night."

Briar clapped her hands with delight. Oh yes, she did want to talk all night. A new start for her and Ben, Danny and Lily. Nobody would know she wasn't in fact Ben's wife for she carried the name Lawson. It was far better than she could have ever hoped for. How very lucky she was.

chapter twenty-five

"One hour Lawson, and if I see you near this property after that I'll take you to the police myself."

Stan had stood still, dumbfounded by his own turn of affairs, his master's final words still ringing in his ears. As he gazed around the cottage one last time he found no answer, no comfort to help his heartbreak, just a cold chill that had frosted over his home sometime ago and had nestled deep within his heart. Picking up his rucksack of few belongings Stan took a deep breath, his hand patting the side of the bag, a slight grin turning the corner of his mouth as he felt the hard black case. The present his master had sent down to him on his wedding day, a gun. Well, he'd take it and sell it in the nearest town, and with what he would get for it including the last of his wages and what he had saved, well he would leave this place right behind him, and look for pastures new. As memories of his past clouded his mind, and hope for the future battled within him, Stan decided to do what he thought best, what most men would do to help themselves think more clearly. Slamming the door of the cottage behind him Stan pulled himself as straight as he could and keeping his head well up he left the Hampstead Estate behind him and headed straight for The Three Fishes, the Inn on the dirt track that led into Bayston Hill.

"Eeh Ben, I wish this rain would stop."

"Aye well lass wha'ever, canna expec' a sunny November."

"I know, bu' the frost is better than this." Briar stood in the shop doorway, a pout heavy on her face. "Eeh theer's nowt as forlorn as a dead town, it's so quiet when theer's no marke' Ben."

"Aye lass I know, gi' me more time t' sor' owt the orders I need an' then we'll si' an' talk properly eh?"

"Hhhm." Was all that Briar could answer her mind preoccupied. She wanted to take the children into the park for a walk, but it didn't look like she would get the chance. She had thought of leaving Danny with Ben and just taking Lily in her pram through the streets to look at the Christmas displays that already were beginning to take place. Christmas, it was only a few weeks away.

"Listen lass if Lily's sleepin' why dunna yo' mek a 'ot mushed tea an' come in the workshop wi' me an' Danny fur a while. If yo' keep yore hand steady, well I jus' migh le' yo' sand down one o' the dolls I've made." Ben smiled as he saw the spark of interest light up her eyes. He had no complaints with Briar at all, she was everything he had ever known she would be and far more. But since he had told her about the new cottage at Much Wenlock she had become restless, impatient to get going. With her impatience Ben saw once more the wild spirit beginning to surface, the spirit that had always got her into so much trouble and had often ended with her being beaten at the workhouse, and then by Joseph Bunting. Ben had wondered if he would ever witness it again, but here it was though not as sharp as it had once been. Ben had remembered how he had tried to keep her busy and occupied back at the workhouse, and now he was feeling he needed to do the same thing. Ben grinned to himself as he watched her still gaze out of the shop door waiting for the rain to stop. She was safe with him, where he was concerned she was in no threat of being dealt any belt or cane, or even his hand. He had never felt like laying a finger on her, and he still felt sick to the core when he thought of what his brother Stan had done to her. "Do yo' know Ben? I jus' migh' do tha'. Theer's bread ready fur later, an' a parsnip an' carrot bake. I could be of better use t' yo'."

"Aye lass, well go an' mek tha' mushed tea then, an' brin' down a plate o' tha' bread. Danny wouldna turn down a crust an' jam."

"An' neither would yo'." Briar giggled as she picked up the hem of her frock and skipped across the shop floor and out through the workshop, her waist length silvery blond hair hanging loosely down her back. Ben shook his head and chuckled to himself.

"Yore mam Danny boy, she'll ne'er be nowt bu' a lass."

"Babby."

Ben laughed as the small boy pointed after his mother. "Aye lad at times yore very righ'."

Throughout the afternoon, Briar sat in the workshop alongside Ben and her son, Lily in her crib beside her. Together her and Ben drank tea and ate bread and jam. She watched quietly as Ben gently guided Danny's fingers along a newly made toy truck. "Smooth enough?"

"Aye Da'."

Instantaneous Ben's eyes met with the slate grey eyes of Briar Rose, a warm yet somehow sad smile passed between them, yet neither of them said a word. As the afternoon slowly gave way to the darkness of a winter's night Briar softly sang to herself as she helped Ben to close the shop. It had been a very quiet day, but one that had given the four of them time to spend as a family, to work together and simply talk and enjoy each others company. Ben had also enjoyed the rare peace from the customers and he had discussed in full his forthcoming plans for the New Year with Briar. "We can be ready t' move by the first weekend in January. Master Hampstead wa' more than happy t' hear me owt, an' 'as supported mi choice." Briar had displayed her excitement once more that evening over the meal table and told Ben quite abruptly. "I'm glad yo' 'ave Ben. I've 'ad enough o' this town an' Much Wenlock by wha' yo' tell me is the place fur us."

"I dunna thinken yo' will be disappointed lass." Ben smiled warmly, for he didn't care where he moved too as long as Briar was by his side, and now with Danny already there, there had been no point in hanging on.

"I dunna regre' anythin' tha' 'as happened Ben. I've ne'er been as happy as wha' I've been wi' yo'. I only hope yo' dunna regre' mi nod comin' t' yo' when I firs' should 'ave?" Briar's comments clearly took Ben by surprise. Placing his knife and fork down he faced her squarely, he could see a sudden sadness cloud over her slate grey eyes and he was fast to put her mind at ease. "I regre' nowt lass, an' as fur yo' bein' mine t' begin wi', well I know yo' would 'ave been if it wunna fur me gettin' so damn tongue tied." Reaching out across the table he clasped her hands tightly in his own. "I love yo' Briar, I always 'ave, an' nowt yo' could ever do lass would mek me regre' anythin'. I 'ave wha' I always wanted, yo', an' two beautiful children." Briar bit down hard on her bottom lip, her words stuck tight within her throat. Why on earth did she feel like crying? Ben was fast to see the signs and before the tears did begin, he had made his way around the table pulling her to her feet. "It's been a strange few months lass, wha' wi' Danny comin' back, the babby, and Christmas jus' around the corner, an' 'ere we are, talkin' abou' movin'. Bu' dunna worry abou' nowt, we'll be as happy as the bes' o' them.

"Aye Ben I know, its jus' tha' nowt good 'as ever happened t' me, an' now it's all come at once. I'm jus' scared tha' if I close mi eyes I'll lose it all."

"Well then stop worryin' lass. As long as theer's breath in mi soul yo' wunna lose anythin', nod ever." For an age Ben stood, his arms tight around her, her face nestled against his shoulder. His words were heartfelt; he would not allow anything to be taken from her again, by anybody.

Stan sat amidst a small group of quarry miners, jokes being loudly shared, moans of hardship and nagging wives escalated between them as tankards of ale were drunk, and then quickly refilled. They appeared to be good friends, but they were just a group of local men, on their way home for the night they would not have recognised each other without the soiled faces they were so used too. Dust thick and heavy scratched their eyes leaving a swollen redness that even the ale could not claim to be the cause off.

"Come of lad drink up, yore probably late gettin' home so may as well le' the missus nag fur somethin' eh?" Loud laughter rang out and willingly Stan knocked back the ale.

"Aye, may as well 'ave another, go' nowt else t' lose."

"Eh yore too young t' thinken liken tha'." The miner sitting opposite sat up and nodded his head in Stan's direction.

"I've los' everythin' mate, everythin'." Stan bowed his head, but only momentarily, for with a mighty roar he suddenly loudly declared. "Ale all around this 'ere table, go' nowt else t' spend mi money on."

"An' wha' will yore missus thinken o' tha' then?" Stan glared at the miner, his bright blue eyes lost to any laughter that may have once given them life. "I go' no wife mate. She ran off wi' mi brother, took mi child, an' now I've los' mi cottage an' mi job. So yo' see, I 'ave nowt else t' lose, it's all gone." Silence fell among them, each man hidden in silent thought of his own.

"Well then, yo' keep yore money, we'll chip in the nex' round. I guess yo' need yore money even more than we do."

Stan said nothing.

"More ale over 'ere an' fas'. We go' drinkin' to do, eh lads?"

"Aye." A chorus of voices and a clink of tankards loudly placed on the table now waited to be filled. For a while now Stan would forget his troubles, he too had drinking to do. On and on the evening went, hot pies and more ale passed around as the jokes became even cruder and far merrier. Christmas was but a few weeks away. Stan sat and listened to how monotonous other men's wives were becoming at home as they tried to feed their ever growing brood of children. Stan sat back taking the ale that was finding it's place in front of him, becoming more drunk by the minute. All he could think about now was his own grief and how badly his wife had tricked him. She should be at home with his son, and he should still have a home and a job to go too. But where was she? Planning a Christmas without him, making her sweetness know to his brother, a sweetness she had bluntly refused him. In fact it was this time last year she'd been cheating on him and had been going to his brother behind his back anyway. Stan had often wondered how long she'd have lived a lie. For if she hadn't have been caught out with the swelling of her stomach, would she have ever come clean? The very thought incensed him, she had acted no better than a street whore, and he had been willing to forgive even that. But what had she done? Pulled the wool over his eyes the day he had tried to win her back. She had taken the opportunity and then she had stolen their son. Now she had everything and he was left with nothing except one ragged rucksack. Drinking the last of his ale Stan stood up abruptly and staggered towards the doorway, not a word of 'goodbye' to the miners he had been drinking with. But Stan was lost in his troubled mind, his soul bitter and twisted. It was late, very late, but he had a certain call to make before he left this town.

chapter twenty-six

Ben lay awake, tired but relaxed, Briar Rose asleep in his arms. He hadn't bothered to blow out the candle by their bed, he had been content just to lay, his eyes heavy as they roamed over the slender naked figure of the girl who shared his life. In the glow of the candle she looked like an angel, her waist length silvery blond hair as soft as silk to his fingertips. As he gently pushed her hair to the side of her face she slightly pouted in her sleep bringing a smile to his face. As Ben ran his fingers over her shoulders and down towards her small supple breasts Briar began to stir moving even closer to him, her slim legs entwining with his. Sleep no longer threatened Ben; his heart was on fire, warm for the touch of her soft creamy skin. As Ben rolled over, gently laying across her, Briar's sleepy slate grey eyes gazed deeply into his, a tired smile lighting up her heart shaped face. As she reached out, her arms warm around Ben's neck, she willingly pulled him closer still, her lips meeting his as she quietly gave herself once more to the young man she had loved for so long.

The cold air cut Stan like a sharp knife and he shivered violently. What he wouldn't give to have his own bed to lay in, his own home and roaring fire. But what did he have instead? Nothing, just the chill of late November to remind him he was nothing more than a tramp, a homeless unwanted piece of trash. "Well tha's wha' they thinken. I'll show them, aye, I will." Muttering to himself Stan pushed onwards against the rain that stung his face. He'd not let this get the best of him, he'd start his life again and to hell with his wife, and his brother, and come to that everybody else. But Stan was under the heavy influence of drink and that had only ever stolen his sense from him, or he would have known better than to come anywhere near the town square where his wife and brother lived together. Exactly what time it was, Ben would never know, but when the mighty hammering echoed from the shop door, followed by loud shouts of abuse outside, Ben was fast to get up and search frantically for his clothes.

"Wha' is it Ben? Wha's goin' on?" Briar woke sharply from Ben's sudden movement, and scrambled to the nearby table for more candles, lighting them as fast as she could before grabbing her nightgown.

"No lass, yo' stay up 'ere."

"Wha' is it Ben?" Panic welled up fast, fear evident in her slate grey eyes. As the shattering sound of glass smashed down below them, Briar squealed and clung to Ben.

"Stay 'ere, lass, dunna come down, it's Stan an' by the sounds o' him he's drunk owt o' his mind."

"Ben, no, yo' need…"

"I mean it Briar; stay up 'ere wi' the children."

Briar's eyes were wide with fear for all of them, she wanted to argue her point, but Ben had grabbed his stick for extra support and was already on his way down the stairs towards the workshop. Briar would have followed but her baby daughter began to wail and Danny was also up, his tiny hands clinging to his mother's nightgown, terror in his bright blue eyes. Briar held both her children close to her, but the shouting that was going on now had Danny fretful as he cried loudly for his 'Da'. "Ssh Danny, ssh." Briar held her son closer to comfort the terrified child, but nothing she did would console him. As the argument raged in the street below Briar shivered herself. She remembered the severe beating Ben had received from Stan the night he'd found out about them, Ben had needed his stick every so often because of it. She knew only too well just how violent Stan was when he'd been drinking, and Ben had clearly told her he was drunk. "Dear God." Whispering aloud Briar sat her small son on the bed. "Listen Danny, I wan' yo' t' be a big boy. Mammy needs t' go an' 'elp Ben. I wan' yo' t' stay up 'ere wi' Lily, understand?" Danny nodded and cowered swiftly in the corner of the bed. "I wunna be long darlin', then yo' can sleep 'ere wi' mammy tonigh'." Pausing only to gently swing the crib Lily lay wailing in, Briar quickly made her way from the room, her fear now for Ben. No sooner had Briar left the room before Danny had clambered down from the bed and as carefully as the small boy could he picked up his tiny sister and struggled across the room with her. Danny had just one simple thought; he had to get down the stairs to where the horrible sounds were coming from. He had to help his daddy Ben and his mammy, and he could not leave his sister behind.

"Stop, please Stan stop it an' leave us alone." Briar screamed as she approached the outside of the shop. Glass had shattered everywhere and much of Ben's handicraft had been littered in the Square, ruined by Stan's jealous hands.

"Briar ge' back int' the house wi' the children." Ben turned and yelled, but could see Briar was not about to move. "NOW." His bellow startled her, but when Briar saw blood on his face, the swelling closing his one eye rapidly, and his stick broken in half on the ground she would not be deterred.

"Stan go away, yo' 'ave no righ' 'ere, I'm nod comin' wi' yo' ever, an' neither is Danny." Briar's voice rang out clear and strong, only the slight tremor that trailed on her last words told a different story. "If yo' dunna go now, I'll run an' find the town police misel'."

Stan glowered at his wife then spat on the ground, his own lip bleeding, his eye also closing, but he had heard every word she had said and her coldness towards him angered him further. "Aye yo' would yo' little bitch, yo've teken all I had, an' now I've los' everythin' I ever worked fur thanks t' yo'."

"Clear off an' sober up Stan, yo' inna wanted 'ere." Ben spoke now, brushing his arm dismissively for his brother to go.

"Aye tha' would mek yore life better wouldn't it? Mi own brother shacked up wi' mi wife an' son."

"Go away Stan."

"Ge' inside Briar...NOW." Once more Ben turned and bellowed, pointing his finger towards the door, but then he stood rigid, a new fear flooding through his veins. There, right behind Briar making his way across the broken glass in his bare feet came Danny, onto the cobbled street, a small boy of hardly two years old, and his baby sister in his arms. "Briar fur God's sake lass turn around." His frantic whisper not only got her full attention, but captured Stan's as well.

"Da', Da'."

Stan smiled instantly at the sound of his son calling him, a sound he had missed dearly, and now he found himself fighting against his own tears of joy at hearing and seeing his son. But Danny had not noticed his natural father, for he had set eyes on Ben first and before Briar could grab him, Danny was at Ben's side. The choke that escaped Stan's throat was that of sheer sorrow, a stark realisation that he had truly lost everything including the love of his own son who he loved so deeply. As the final tidal wave of grief flooded him Stan would never come to know why he should then frantically reach into his rucksack for the gun he'd been given as a wedding gift, or why he should ever want to point it towards his own son. What followed was a deafening wave of screams, pleas and shouts. Ben and Briar united as one to save their children from this horrifying danger, neither of them fearful for their own life's. Stan let out a mighty roar as he pulled the trigger, the earth shattering explosion piercing the air, followed by a deathly more frightening silence. But only momentarily, for the moan of human sorrow had began to grind into the darkness of the night, but by the time the second explosion sounded the moan had died with it and the high pitched wail that carried long and hard found no comfort as hands of strangers gently tried to ease the pain of the breaking heart. In the bitter winds of the rainy November night Stan had taken his revenge. Town dwellers had stood in the cobbled street horrified at the sight of such pain and tragedy, as one lay dying on the ground in the arms of a loved one, while the man who had take a gun to the young family had then turned the gun on himself, killing himself instantly.

epilogue

"I di' nod do tha'...it wa' yo' our Danny, yo' big liar, yo' didna measure it righ'." Lily Rose Lawson stamped her foot defiantly, a heavy pout clouding her pretty angelic face.

"I inna tekin' the blame fur some daf' lass. Go an' play wi' yore dolls 'ouse yo' big babby." Danny loudly retorted, his arms folded, his bright blue eyes flashing angrily at his young sister. He was ready for her this time, if she did go for him how she always did, and he'd belt her one. Lily clenched her fists in a wild fury and ran across the workshop punching out at her older brother, who as always never did attempt to hit out in his defence, not once.

"Wha's all this then? Have yo' finished yore work? If yo' two wanna go t' the park yo' better behave, an' as fur yo' Lily, if I catch yo' fightin' Danny again, I'll tan yore arse well an' hard."

The small girl of just seven years old tearfully gazed up into her father's warm brown eyes. She hated to make him angry, and was fast to regret her spiteful actions towards her brother. "Sorry Da', I really am."

"Do yo' mean tha' Lily?"

"Oh aye Da', I do."

Ben stared down into his young daughters slate grey eyes and smiled. "Then I dunna wan' t' 'ear it again. So ge' yore outdoor shoes on an' we'll go t' the park as promised." Squeals of delight filled his cottage as Ben took his walking stick to help him over the unsteady ground of the nearby park that lay at the edge of Much Wenlock. Life had proved very hard for Ben since the night Briar Rose had so fretfully died in his arms after his brother had shot her and then turned the gun on himself. But Ben had had to pull through for the sake of his children, and had later gone on to buy the cottage he had promised Briar Rose, at Much Wenlock. Now his name was becoming widely known, not only in Shropshire but towns much further a field that had come to know the quality of his work. Now, seven years on Ben had managed to push his sorrow behind him, he remembered only the pleasant times he'd had with Briar and no longer dwelt on the horror that had twisted her pretty face, as the pain from the blast to her stomach proved just too much for her to bear. He could also think of his brother without the bitterness that had filled his soul when he thought of Stan's dreadful revenge that had left him wracked in inconsolable sobs. Briar's destiny had been laid out the day two brothers had hopelessly fallen in love with her. Ben knew without doubt that Stan had killed her, not through hatred, but from the love that he too had felt for her, a love so very possessive that its danger had never been far away from her, until it had reclaimed her. Many had asked over the years if he hated his brother, did he? The answer to that was no. How could he? Stan had left him a son, a boy who was almost nine years of age with the brightest of blue eyes and a shock of red hair, with a look of mischief that shone from his young face. The boy could be depended upon for good work and he had the ability to one day take over from him. When Ben looked at Danny he saw the brother he had known so many years ago, a brother who had always looked out for him when he had been a small boy himself, and for that reason alone, he could never hold hatred for his brother. As for Lily, his own natural daughter, she was a constant reminder of the girl he'd loved so whole heartedly and always would. Lily had spirit, a wild streak of temper that he would have to calm down, but also shared the want to learn from him just as her mother had so long ago. Lily had the blondest of hair which always flowed wildly over her shoulders, and when she looked up at him, he was met with striking slate grey eyes, that melted him with love for her. Ben had no desires to meet another woman. If there was another out there meant for him, then time would surely capture their meeting. But now, his immediate future, well Ben had a business to run and two children to rear alone, that would both be able to one day in the future run his business just as he had promised Briar Rose. "Any lad or lass tha' lives under mi roof will learn from me, theer will be no difference, a girl can learn industry too." Ben grinned now as he watched Danny just ahead of him grab Lily firmly by the hand, to stop her running too far ahead of him, the boy certainly had a protective streak where his sister was concerned. Ben nodded to himself, a contentment warming his heart as he cast his eyes to the skies above. He'd never be lonely, not with Danny and Lily, for the presence of Briar Rose and Stan had never left him, he could see and hear them whenever he watched their children.